dead brilliant

dead Brilliant

Christopher Ward

DUNDURN
TORONTO

Copyright © Christopher Ward, 2013

All rights reserved. No part of this publication may be reproduced, stored in a retrieval system, or transmitted in any form or by any means, electronic, mechanical, photocopying, recording, or otherwise (except for brief passages for purposes of review) without the prior permission of Dundurn Press. Permission to photocopy should be requested from Access Copyright.

All characters in this work are fictitious. Any resemblance to real persons, living or dead, is purely coincidental.

Editor: Allister Thompson
Design: Courtney Horner
Printer: Webcom

Library and Archives Canada Cataloguing in Publication

Ward, Christopher, author
 Dead brilliant / by Christopher Ward.

Issued in print and electronic formats.
ISBN 978-1-4597-0617-0 (pbk.)

 I. Title.

PS8645.A71D42 2014   C813'.6   C2013-902953-2
                                        C2013-902954-0

1   2   3   4   5   17   16   15   14   13

We acknowledge the support of the **Canada Council for the Arts** and the **Ontario Arts Council** for our publishing program. We also acknowledge the financial support of the **Government of Canada** through the **Canada Book Fund** and **Livres Canada Books**, and the **Government of Ontario** through the **Ontario Book Publishing Tax Credit** and the **Ontario Media Development Corporation**.

Care has been taken to trace the ownership of copyright material used in this book. The author and the publisher welcome any information enabling them to rectify any references or credits in subsequent editions.

J. Kirk Howard, President

The publisher is not responsible for websites or their content unless they are owned by the publisher.

Printed and bound in Canada.

Visit us at
Dundurn.com
@dundurnpress
Facebook.com/dundurnpress
Pinterest.com/dundurnpress

Dundurn	Gazelle Book Services Limited	Dundurn
3 Church Street, Suite 500	White Cross Mills	2250 Military Road
Toronto, Ontario, Canada	High Town, Lancaster, England	Tonawanda, NY
M5E 1M2	LA1 4XS	U.S.A. 14150

To Rachel

PART I

I remember everything I meant to say

One

Roc Molotov compared the face in the bathroom mirror to the one on the bottle of Midnight Velvet shampoo. He pouffed his hair to match the famous vinyl-black nest but couldn't manage the cool, enigmatic smile that stared back from his younger self. Dimming the lights, he tried sucking in his cheeks before tossing the container away in disgust. He lit a pair of Mission fig candles, lifted his guitar from the empty bathtub, climbed in, and checked the tuning. Some of his very best vocals had been recorded in bathrooms, and the echo always seemed to make the lyrics sound deeper. Closing his eyes, he let the magic of a handful of major sevenths wash over him, banishing his dark mood.

Minutes later, he was jolted from his musing by the phone and lunged over the tub to answer it. Before he could even say hello, he heard the silky voice of his manager, Uncle Strange. "Have you got MTV on? You're gonna want to see this."

"I'm in the tub ... with my guitar." Roc tucked the phone under his ear and produced a long, melodious strum.

"Nice reverb. Listen, come down to my room — we should experience this Cocktails interview together."

Roc had been trying unsuccessfully to ignore the upcoming release of his old bandmates' new disc. "Yeah, I guess. Order me a

Tuborg and a tumbler of Nembutals, will you?" He let the phone dangle over the edge of the tub and eased out, putting the guitar back in and blowing out the candles.

He padded barefoot down the hall of the Sunset Lagoon, the West Hollywood boutique hotel that he and Uncle had called home since their full-on touring days. He found the door to Uncle's suite propped open and took in the usual aromas of incense and pretence. Uncle had made modifications over the years to suit his carefully crafted identity, with the décor running to early Zen pimp. The hotel's faux O'Keefe nature prints had given way to Uncle's personal collection of Klimt's erotic drawings. Bamboo blinds, little stone stacks, and a bonsai garden underneath the glass-topped coffee table rounded out the feng shui.

Roc was greeted by the cawing and burbling of Uncle's current favourite nature CD. The lone connection to their mutual past, the beaded curtain that had been rescued from Uncle's first apartment of a couple of decades ago in Duluth, was now the gateway to satori in the Buddhoir. Above it hung his treasured photo of native rock 'n roll sons from the Gopher State, featuring Prince, Paul Westerberg, and a distracted-looking Bob Dylan flanking Uncle, whose head was unfortunately halved by the top of the frame. Gone mercifully from the room was the bento box that had held Uncle's stash in the old days.

On the carpet in front of the TV, seated on an embroidered pillow in the lotus position, Uncle Strange stared at a glowing laptop. "You sound stressed, my son. You want a traditional tea service, reflexology? Maybe Sandra's around to do some Reiki."

"No thanks, Uncle. A beer should take care of it." Roc picked up the remote and hit 'mute' as the theme from MTV's *Rocktalk* played.

When he unmuted, he heard the host intoning, "Now, everyone knows that Roc Molotov was the lead singer, songwriter, and founder of the band. How do you feel his departure will affect your sound?" The host, with whom Roc had done countless interviews over the years, turned up the sincerity and leaned toward the three ill-at-ease members of The Cocktails, peering dimly at each other through the fringe over their shades. Some clearing of throats and shifting on the studio couch followed.

"Uh … well … you know."

"I mean … it's like …"

Finally, drummer Danny "Double" Cocktail asserted himself. "Not at all, really."

Rhythm guitarist Frankie "Flaming" Cocktail found his confidence too.

"Yeah, rock and roll as usual, right?"

The third member of the group, the terminally shy and somewhat overweight bassist, Barry "Shaker" Cocktail, giggled. "We don't miss him much, do we?"

"So, the Y2K concert turned out to be the final show for Roc Molotov and the Cocktails?"

"Yeah," said Danny wistfully, "the time just felt right, you know."

"Sure," said Roc, fuming. "After I told them before the show."

"And there were some creative differences," said Barry.

"Oh right," said Roc, disgustedly, "like the difference between being utterly devoid of creativity and …"

The host nodded, changing topics. "And how did you prepare for this big event?"

"Well," said Frankie, brows furrowed, "I bought a really big generator, in case …"

"And I filled the garage with bottled water," said Barry.

"Oh my God, someone stop the madness." Roc covered his eyes with his hands.

Mercifully, the host wrapped up the interview. "Well, whatever you're doing now, it's working. Congrats on your first #1 record. Now let's take a look at the video, our sneak preview of 'Stop Before I Start' by The Cocktails. Thanks, guys."

"Wankers!"

The screen went blank as the remote bounced across the room, coming to rest under the window, which overlooked a tranquil southern California garden.

"Total wankers, the lot of them." Roc got up off the couch and began to pace.

Uncle spoke serenely. "Calm down, Roc, you know how it'll go. They'll have their moment of glory, and poof, it'll be over before you can say 'where are they now.'"

"'Calm down?' Easy for you to say, genius. Whose idea was it to fire them and go solo? And how come you didn't know they had a record in the can ready for release a week before mine?"

Uncle continued working his computer while picking up the remote with one foot and using the other to turn the TV back on. "Roc, relax, you'll leave them in your dust. Musically, you already did years ago. Trust me." He gestured at the television. "I mean, look at this nonsense."

On the screen, the members of The Cocktails, dressed as cops, were awkwardly arresting a gaggle of ten-storey-tall nymphets as the chorus of "Stop Before I Start" kicked in. Uncle looked up and appeared to be silently mouthing the words as he nodded along with the song.

> **"Stop before I start**
> **Look before I leap**
> **Listen to me**
> **Baby can't you see you gotta ..."**

Here Frankie held his guitar like a chainsaw and played his big lick — "wawawawa" — as the other band members froze in a tableau.

> **"Stop before I start."**

Uncle shrugged. "Catchy."

"So's herpes," mumbled Roc. He crossed and recrossed the room, his wiry frame practically twitching, all the while stealing glances at the television. "Uncle Strange, I've trusted you since the fifth grade, but right now I'm nervous. The last two albums have tanked, the hair product deal is toast, and now those morons have a #1 record riding on my reputation. Did you remember to check with the lawyers about the rights to the name?"

Uncle assumed his customary guru pose and opened his palms. "Remember? Roc, this is me. I always remember. We've got bigger fish to fry, my brother."

Roc tensed. For one thing, he hated being called "my brother," and he was convinced that Uncle had been polishing his bald head lately, so that in certain lights it would create a creepy halo effect. As it was now. "What fish, exactly?"

Uncle, still focused on the laptop, replied distractedly. "Like getting *Higher than Heaven* off the ground." He turned his attention to his number one client and oldest friend. "This is the best record of your career, Roc, and I want the world to hear it. There are no free passes out there at radio, and there's been major turnover at the label since your last release."

Roc didn't want to think about what this would mean. He ran his hands through his spongy hair then noticed the black stains on his hands. "Shit." He retreated to the bathroom to wash it off and muttered to himself, "No wonder no one's buying this crap."

Uncle called out from the other room, effortlessly slipping into stroke-and-placate mode. "Hey, top ten phones on the advance single at WSFT, and you just entered their 'soft parade' at 98 with a chub."

"Never heard of them. Major market?" Roc re-entered the room and leaned over Uncle's shoulder to look at the screen, a maze of call letters, radio station wattage, and colour-coded cities laid out in Uncle's own peculiar format.

"Flagship station on the gay network out of Miami." Taking in Roc's pained expression, Uncle continued, "Consumers, my good sir, using the same currency, last time I checked."

"Yeah, well, just don't take any three-dollar bills, *my* good sir."

He was praying that Uncle wouldn't remind him of last year's Pride parade in Toronto that had chanted the lyrics to his song "Damn Straight" as they marched on city hall.

Uncle shut down the laptop and unfolded his six-foot-five frame, a bit creakily, from his cross-legged position. "Let's go down and have a little recreational beverage poolside, what do you say? Check out the local talent. Unless you're hitting for the other side now."

Roc wanted to be mad but just laughed and grabbed his shades as the unlikely duo headed for the door.

Two

"Bless your heart, punkin', you are just rarin' to go, aren't you? Well, I've been pinin' for you, my little moon pie."

Bobbie Burnette eased her silver Toyota into the passing lane on San Vicente and smiled sweetly at her reflection in the rear view mirror. She abruptly slammed on the brakes to avoid hitting a rollerblader who was waving at a friend across the street. "Hey, dipshit, you're lucky to be alive!" she shouted, throwing up her hands.

"Oh, no, not you baby, you know I would never want anything bad to happen to you," she purred into the cellphone. She paused and her expression changed at the reply. "Oh, you like that, why, you bad boy, I didn't know that about you."

Noticing that her cappuccino had spilled on her new white jeans, Bobbie picked the cup up from between her legs. "Oh, damnation, I've got foam all over my muffin!" she growled in frustration.

"Oh, sweetheart, I am sorry, excuse me, but ..." She put her best southern belle tones into effect. A startled look came over her face at the sound of moaning on the line. "Are you all right?" she asked, concerned, as she pulled into the line-up for the parking lot of Earth's Bounty. "You just put your head between your legs or whatever you do and breathe deeply, I'll be right back, you hunky monkey."

Bobbie switched to call waiting, and a soft expression came over her face. "Roc, honey, I was just thinking about you. Hang on, let me get off this call." She hit call waiting once more. "Okay, time's up. Same card as always?" She paused. "Can't wait." She made kissing sounds before changing lines again while being suctioned into a minuscule parking place. "I was going to pick up some Sierra salad for us and come by the hotel, if that's all right, sugar."

Poolside at the Sunset Laguna, Roc and Uncle sat at a prime table with a couple of beers and a fruit plate in front of them. Around them, every link of the rock 'n roll food chain was in evidence. A big league easy-listening king was taking his t-shirt off for the hundredth time that afternoon and oiling his hairy chest. A Cuban diva with a major web of halo hair was strutting by and flashing her gleaming smile to all who'd notice, while an ex-prime-time comedian who was now hustling jewellery on late night TV passed unnoticed. Publicists, bodyguards, songwriters, and masseurs elbowed each other aside for access. At the next table, a trio of gauzy blondes was pretending not to notice Roc.

"Bobbie, I was just thinking of you too. I'm kind of right in the middle of a strategy session with Uncle right now. Maybe we could hook up a little later."

Roc noticed Uncle, in his usual lotus pose, making prayer motions at a mostly naked brunette emerging from the pool right in front of him. As Roc peered over his shades and the brunette adjusted her bikini top, Uncle bowed solemnly and said, "We have been blessed, my brother."

Bobbie sat in her parking space and saw a number she recognized well on the call display. "Okay, Roc, I'll be at home, or in the car, call me." She pushed her seat back and reclined as she took the call. "Why, Snagglepuss, I've been waiting to hear from you." She closed her eyes, rubbing her temples with fatigue. "I'm in the garden and my back is getting a bit of a burn, can you do something to help little old me?"

Roc put the phone back on the table and finished his beer. By the time he got back from the washroom, the blondes had evaporated, the sun had dropped behind the cabanas, and some kids were screaming in the crocodile-shaped pool. Uncle had relocated under the brunette's umbrella and was sitting cross-legged with his palms facing up, being fascinating.

Roc went back to the room for the advance CD of his new album and decided to go for a drive.

Three

Roc slipped the Lexus into cruise control now that he was clear of the tacky beach bum part of Malibu and into the stretch of Highway #1 that he loved. Driving was meditation, especially with nowhere to go; it always seemed to suspend the tough stuff — the problems, decisions, frustrations that were always waiting when you got back. Once he was through the light at Zuma, he hit "play," and the opening chords of the title track of *Higher than Heaven* filled the car. The long orchestral intro was a bit risky in the thrills-per-minute climate of today's pop world, but he knew it was good and set up the ethereal quality of the song. Besides, they could always edit for a single if necessary. Roc quickly wiped those thoughts before they spoiled the moment and breathed deeply as he rolled past Leo Carillo beach, a favourite haunt in the Tabatha days. Another thought that needed editing.

The album was coming out next week, and Roc was as worried as he had ever been in his career. *My god, has it been twenty years?* No, not quite, but still. He could blame video, but it had helped him considerably in the early days; computer games, piracy, the economy, executive changes at the label with bloody kids making the big calls — scapegoats for days, but he knew it was just the turn of the wheel.

Uncle had been diversifying lately, although he'd been mysterious about what was occupying his time, but Roc knew that even his manager's legendary ability to affect pop history was all smoke at this point. If anyone could see through Uncle Strange's bullshit, it was Roc. Uncle had made the swift journey from childhood friend and roadie to spiritual advisor and personal manager greased by the universal lube, money. His reputation as a financial whiz was based on managing a major cash cow, Roc Molotov. Being seriously math-challenged, Uncle had accountants to do the real work.

The visionary image was always hilarious to Roc, but it seemed to work wonders on A&R guys, concert promoters, and especially the young women who would do anything to be "in the biz." Roc wasn't looking forward to tomorrow's strategy session at the label, but Uncle had said that this time Roc had to be there to use whatever charisma he had in reserve to motivate the weasels.

Roc pulled off the highway into the parking lot at Matador Beach as he listened to the solo at the end of "Underwater Smile" and felt good. He locked the car and walked to the edge of the cliff overlooking the beautiful rock formations below. Another perfect sunset — California seemed to have an endless supply of them. He smiled as a pair of dolphins rose from the water in tandem then dove joyously back in. It had to be joy — why else would they do it? He realized he was getting hungry and decided to call Bobbie to see if the Sierra salad was still on offer.

By the time he ran into some traffic in the commercial stretch of Malibu, the last chords of the new album were fading into the roar of the ocean sound effects, and Roc smiled again at the appropriateness of the moment. *It'll be fine,* he thought as he grabbed the phone and hit Bobbie's number on speed-dial.

"Oh, hi baby," she said somewhat breathlessly, "I'd just about given up on you. I'm on my way back from spinning class. Hang on while I ditch this call."

The spinning was definitely working, thought Roc as he waited at the Cross Creek traffic light, picturing Bobbie in her pink danskin and matching warm-ups. Maybe he'd stop and grab a bottle of Phelps; just because she wasn't drinking wine didn't mean he couldn't. The phone let out a little squawk, and Roc heard what sounded like Bobbie in the throes of wild passion.

"Oh, yes, you randy panda, yes, that's it, you know what to do." Her voice was rising, and little squeals punctuated her speech.

Roc was stunned and could barely get the words out. "Bobbie, is that you?"

The squealing stopped abruptly and was followed by a silence, then, "Roc?"

"What the fuck are you doing, if I may be so bold?" Roc tried to keep his voice cool, but it shook, even as he barely whispered.

"Oh, Roc, I didn't think it was you ... I mean ... I wish it was, but ..."

"Bobbie, are you in your car?"

"Yes, Roc, and I'm almost home. Meet me there, I can explain."

"No explanation required. Later," he said coldly and smashed the phone against the dash.

At the last second, he pulled into the left turn lane for Sunset. He wasn't going to Santa Monica tonight, or to Bobbie's place ever again, he thought bitterly. As he followed the curves of Sunset toward Hollywood, he knew he had no right to feel so angry. He had no claim on her; he had blown her off countless times before, for totally whimsical reasons, once when he'd thought Tabatha was actually coming to see him romantically instead of with her lawyer. But this was beyond the pale. And totally unexpected.

When he'd met Bobbie, she had just arrived in California, having won the Miss Alabama Millennium Farm Implement Queen contest. She was so innocent, and almost ridiculously sweet.

Something about that sweetness had appealed to his jaded rock star heart, and they had been on again/off again ever since. *I guess L.A. gets to them all,* he thought, passing through the strip as the nightly spectacle was getting underway. Still, in her bloody car, for God's sake. He pulled into the leafy overhang that led to guest parking at the Sunset Laguna and was grateful for room service and a private entrance.

Four

In spite of the three-drink buzz that was cruising comfortably at 32,000 feet just behind his eyes, Delray Jackson was crystal clear about what he had to do. He'd left Farcry, Alabama, for the first time in his life to claim what was rightfully his. He looked away from the window at the bluehair in the next seat snoring over the plane's engines. He was having trouble averting his eyes from the ghastly sight of her pantyhose riding up as her mint green slacks headed south.

He drained the last of the glass, ice and all, swallowed the little slice of lime, and looked for the flight attendant. He'd never had a gin and tonic before, but on his way to California he figured it would be one way to work on his cool factor early, so he could hit his stride by the time he reached L.A. He'd had a couple of brown pops in the airport lounge and was wavering between cowboy swagger and a hayseed fear of the big city.

But what the hell, she was his, and Delray Jackson wasn't going to go back to Alabama without Bobbie Jean Burnette. Once back in Farcry, they'd start from scratch and get it right this time — kids, house, gun rack and all.

He leaned across the grand canyon of senior butt and tried to charm the attendant with a big old country grin, but this time she just wheeled the cart right past him. He was a little embarrassed to speak up, since she'd told him he was shouting earlier when he had the headphones on, listening to *Cloud Corral of Country Classics*.

Delray settled back, scratching one foot with the big toenail of the other. He was considering how he was going to handle Bobbie Jean and the whole situation, something he hadn't put a whole heckuva lot of thought into before getting on the plane. It would take some persuasion, so he'd brought a fresh shirt in his carry-on to replace the white t-shirt that was getting tighter around the neck and armpits by the minute. He'd change in the airport men's room, brush his teeth for sure, maybe buy a little packet of Old Spice if they had a machine like the one in the bus terminal at home. He pulled the little triangle of paper with Bobbie's address in Santa Monica out of his jeans pocket again, the one from the envelope of the Christmas card she'd sent his folks. He didn't have the phone number but figured a little element of surprise wouldn't hurt.

A little over an hour later, Delray was strolling down Bobbie's street in a quiet residential section of Santa Monica, with a six-pack of Lone Star under his arm. How cool was it that a liquor store out here would have his brand? So what if a couple of Mexican-looking guys seemed to be laughing at him in the parking lot.

He watched with some excitement from under the shrubbery bordering the property, about five and a half brewskis later, as Bobbie pulled her silver Toyota into the tenants' parking underneath the low-rise apartment building. Delray had been enjoying the cool ocean breeze and the smell of eucalyptus that he thought must come from the plant they make cough drops out of. He got up a little unsteadily, realizing that he needed to piss bad enough he could taste it, but hell, there she was. He didn't recognize the car, but you couldn't miss the headlights on the driver.

He squeezed back the beer buildup and watched as she turned on the lights in her unit. Sucking in his belly and trying out his best hometown grin, Delray rolled up to the front door and rang the bell. The porch light came on, and he heard Bobbie's voice for the first time in almost two years.

"Who is it?" She sounded kind of angry already. Not a good start, thought Delray, but he figured what the hey, might just as well go for it.

"It's me, hunny bunny, your big old boy come to take you home where you belong," he half shouted in his singsong southern voice.

This was followed by a too-long pause, but eventually the inner door opened. Bobbie stood there in a pink workout getup that was designed to break Delray's heart all over again. She stared in disbelief through the screen door, which remained locked.

"Delray Jackson, what on God's green earth are you doing here?" She leaned close to the screen to be sure he wasn't a hallucination, clutching a Kleenex in her hand. "And what have you done to your hair ... did you go as Sting for Hallowe'en?"

"Bobbie Jean Burnette, I love you. I always have. Ever since I saw you on that a-wards show with that weird singer guy, I knew I had to come out here and rescue you." She didn't reply, so Delray took a deep, beery breath and kept on going, "I've been saving my money till I could afford the fare; I just got into town a couple of hours ago, and here I am, baby. Lord, but don't you look sweet. Better than I remember, and I remember everything, sugarplum. Come on home!"

It all came back — the 4X4, the spit cup, the Hank Jr. tapes, and yes, a few hours of deep-fried southern passion that had gone from unforgettable to regrettable in a Mobile minute. Bobbie recovered quickly from her reverie. "Oh, God love ya, Delray, you're as thick as you always were, and you smell about the same. Get on outta here and get yourself back to that airport before I call the cops on you." Her accent got twangier as she went on, and she stopped to sniffle as she wiped the kleenex under her eye.

"Bobbie Jean, I swear you've been crying."

"No, no, Delray, I'm allergic to palm trees is all. Now, it was real nice of you to come by, but scat."

"Has that guy been mistreating you? 'Cause if he has, Bobbie Jean, you know you can count on me."

Bobbie didn't like where this was heading, so she blurted out, "No, Roc and I are through. Go on home, Delray."

"I'll kill him," Delray said, righting himself in mid-stumble off the porch before adding, "Listen, Bobbie Jean, can I come in? I gotta whiz something fierce."

As Bobbie closed her eyes and shook her head, she unlocked the screen door, and Delray eased on in. "Thank you much, baby."

Bobbie Jean listened as Delray unleashed a raging torrent punctuated with his trademark "oh yeahs" and grunts of satisfaction. She remembered why he'd been the first and last of the goat ropers to catch her fancy. He emerged from the bathroom, zipping and grinning. "Nice can, honey bunch; that little box with the shells on it over the bum wad is cool. Listen, do you mind if I crash on your couch, just for tonight? I spent all my money on the plane." He smiled lasciviously. "I won't make a peep, promise."

Bobbie stood with her arms crossed, holding the door open. "I don't think so, Delray. It's been a slice seeing y'all, but I've got plans." As soon as he had stepped on the porch, she slammed the door shut. "Say hi to your mama for me." She switched off the light and watched as Delray picked up a Lone Star he'd left hidden in the shrubbery and slunk off into the Santa Monica night, blowing kisses.

Five

It was in the blackest of moods that Roc picked up the phone in his hotel room on about the tenth ring. The odour of last night's room service sitting at the bottom of the bed rolled up to his nose. The TV was, of course, still on.

"Show time, superstar." Uncle began humming "I Don't Like Mondays." "Meeting's in forty-five minutes. I sent up some breakfast for you. Listen, I've got someone here who'd love to meet you. Won't take a minute."

Roc cleared his throat to try to object, but Uncle had already hung up. The doorbell sounded, and the room service waiter rolled in a tray carrying an urn of coffee, a few silver lids over breakfast, and an orchid in a tiny vase, the latter probably being the most edible item, thought Roc.

"Take this for you, Mr. Molotov?" the man smiled, indicating the disaster at the end of the bed.

"Yeah, sure, gracias." Roc yanked the blanket up so he could reach for his wallet beside the bed, causing the tray to cascade to the floor, launching remnants of last night's poached sea bass, vegetable medley, and crème caramel onto the carpet. "Oh, sorry, man."

"No problem, Mr. Molotov." As the waiter cleaned up, Roc doubled the tip and headed for the shower with a cup of coffee.

Glancing at the TV, he saw The Cocktails video playing with the sound off as he accidentally stepped on the remote, causing the room to suddenly fill with "Stop Before I Start." "Oh, God spare me," he grunted.

Eyes closed with the shower beating mercilessly on his shoulders, Roc told himself, *Focus, focus.* He had to put the image of Bobbie having it off with someone in her car while she was talking to him out of his mind. He tried to recall one of Uncle's meditations, but none would come to him.

He was putting on his trademark eyeliner while wearing his Sunset Laguna bathrobe when Uncle rang, then let himself in with his latest conquest in tow. Roc thought she looked vaguely familiar then remembered that it was the girl from the pool that Uncle had been chatting up yesterday. Uncle was dressed in one of his flowing white outfits, and his head glowed as he extended his palms outward and grinned a little lustily for this hour of the day.

"Introduction ... Marie ... Roc Molotov." Uncle sounded like he was rolling a spitball when he pronounced the "r" in Marie.

"Hi, nice to meet you, Marie." Roc adjusted the belt of his robe to make sure he was decent.

"*Enchanté*, Mr. Molotov, I'm such a huge fan of mine." She left the "h" off "huge," and her smile filled the room. Over her shoulder, Uncle was making melon shapes with his hands, which Roc tried to ignore.

"Excuse us, Marie, we've got to get ready for a meeting. Uncle, give me a minute, and I'll meet you out front."

"*Absolument, mon ami,*" Uncle replied in a hideous accent as he escorted Marie from the room, winking before closing the door behind him.

Uncle was in the back seat of the dark blue Lincoln Town Car with his laptop open when Roc slid in beside him. "What do you think of the mademoiselle, my brother? She's French, you know."

"Really?" said Roc in the most disinterested tone possible.

"Uh-huh, her dad's some big Parisian film director in town working on a sequel to *Madame Bovary*, I think she said. Marie's a singer."

"As Flaubert no doubt would have wanted it. Can she sing?" Roc wasn't looking at Uncle.

"Probably not. But did you get a load of the rack on her? *Mon Dieu!* You could serve a ten-course gourmet meal on those babies."

"Could we get to work here, Uncle?" Roc tried to ignore his manager's puerile obsessions. "What's the agenda today? Any new action on the single to talk about?"

Uncle ignored the question. "So, d'you end up seeing Miss Alfalfa Sprout last night? Anything organic happen?" he snickered. Roc just stared out the window at the passing cars on the freeway as Uncle's tone became serious. "Look, it's over to them today. We delivered a brilliant record. Now it's up to the suits to do what they do and shift some units. I'm not going to lie to you, the single is starting slowly, but sometimes that's the best way to go if you want long life at radio. Slow and steady, right? Remember 'She's Gone' by Hall and Oates. From *Abandoned Luncheonette*? Two years later it was a smash, right? Let's just listen to their plan and stay positive."

Roc closed his eyes again and tried to clear his mind as the car pulled into the record company's visitor parking.

Six

"Mr. Savage says he'll be right out. Can I get you something while you wait?" A narrow brunette with oversized glasses looked across her desk. They could tell she'd rather continue with her paperwork.

So it's last names for the executives now, is it, thought Roc. *It's all changed.* This was the first time he'd been asked who he was when he arrived, but it had been a long time between visits. He looked around at the décor, unrecognizable to anyone who'd spent serious time here in the bad old days. Gone were the posters, photos of groups of employees backstage at gigs, and the Polaroids of dogs and kids taped to the walls behind their desks. Okay, so everything changes, but there was something particularly odd about the place now. Then Roc realized no one was playing music. All he could hear was the hum of machines, broken by the soft purr of distant phone lines, all accompanied by the whoosh of air conditioning. It used to be you couldn't hear yourself think around here, never mind talk. Everyone had something they were crazy about, and they played it at full volume until someone else would come into their office and ask "What's that?" That's how the buzz would start, and that's how bands were broken. He'd be surprised if wind was broken in this mausoleum.

"Heyyy, Justin." Uncle unfolded himself gingerly from his chair and got up to shake hands with a handsome twenty-something man with slicked back hair and a coral-coloured Armani suit.

"Yo, Uncle." Justin smiled confidently, imitating Uncle's hands-open pose, then turned to Roc. "Roc, I'm Justin Savage, VP A&R, and it's a pleasure to meet you finally."

"Likewise, Justin." Roc extended a hand and the trio started down a long hall lined with platinum records.

"It's an honour to be able to work with you on this project. You're a legend in this place, even if it has changed," Justin said, indicating one of Roc's albums on the wall as they passed. "I want you to know that this is our priority for the third quarter, and we won't sleep till it's a hit."

"Justin, my man, now I recognize you. Ditched the piercings, did you?" Uncle grinned with a touch of condescension. "Seems like just last week you were bouncing around the copy room."

"As a matter of fact, it almost *was* last week, Uncle. You know the record biz." He turned to Roc and added, "Jerry asked me to say hey when I saw you."

"Cool. How is he? I haven't seen him since we broke up the band. It's been kind of bugging me, wondering if that had anything to do with his exit from the label."

Jerry "JJ" Jankowitz had signed Roc and the band to the label almost two decades before and had seen them through all the ups and downs of a dozen albums and almost as many label chairmen. He'd stood by Roc through every change of sound and style and look, and Roc wished he were around for this latest incarnation, which he sensed was going to be the most challenging yet.

"Oh, no tears for JJ. He got a sweet package from the label. He just let drop that he was thinking of forming his own little boutique thing, and they re-upped his exit deal to include a non-competition clause. I think he's using some of the extra cash to fix up his cliffside place in Mendocino. I'll give you his number up there; I know he'd love to hear from you. Right this way, gentlemen."

Justin did exhibit some charm, signs of intelligent life, and a modicum of respect, thought Roc. Could be worse.

"Jenna, get me Jerry Jankowitz's number for Roc. It's a full court press today, but I think we can find chairs for you," Justin added, smiling as he ushered Uncle and Roc into a large boardroom.

It was indeed full on. The new record played quietly in the background as they entered an ice-cool boardroom papered with posters for the upcoming release. The room was full of label types, some of whom Roc recognized, all chatting and laughing in small groups and holding cappuccinos or Evians. All heads swung their way, and an impromptu receiving line formed, with the veterans introducing the younger members of the team. Compliments on the new album were plentiful, each person having a favourite track they wanted to mention. The loudest greeting came from Stan Smiley, head of national promo, the same post he'd had, some said, since Rudy Vallee was on the label.

Stan, go figure, thought Roc. Of all the people to survive the Friday night massacre, as it was known in the business, when the heads of three majors, along with most of their support staff, had been jettisoned in one brutal weekend. The labels had claimed it was a coincidence, but no one believed it. Roc had heard that severance packages of over a hundred mill had been agreed on before the bell rang on Monday morning. Needless to say, in the following months, artists in droves were on the street looking for new deals. Managers were claiming it gave their clients a new lease on their artistic lives. Some signed with small labels, where they said they'd get the special attention that had been missing with the big guns. Some even had a second act, but most faded into pop history, waiting for their moment on "Where Are They Now?" shows. When the dust settled, it was still the giant media conglomerates that had the resources and the muscle to make records happen, like it or not.

In his heart Roc believed, despite Uncle's dismissals, that owning the rights to his catalogue for repackaging and re-release was the sole reason for today's upcoming dog and pony show. The label people couldn't hide their desire to acquire the rights to that treasure trove. *Oh well,* he thought, *might as well sit back and see what they've got up their corporate sleeves.* And it should be amusing if Stan was up to his old tricks.

As the staff eased into their assigned seats, Roc noticed that there were chairs designated for himself and Uncle. He couldn't help smiling when he saw the silk Chinese cushion on Uncle's chair. Then he noticed the large Strawberry Mango Delight at his place. They were good.

Justin Savage clearly commanded respect from all corners as he brought the meeting to order. He ran over general strategy, the usual litany of point-of-purchase promotions, network exclusive concerts, chat shows and so on. He soon got to the heart of the matter. "I think we're all adults here, and we need to come to grips with the fact that the lead single is not performing up to our hopes and expectations. We led with the ballad, thinking it would grab as broad a demo as possible for this new phase in Roc's career."

No one looked at Roc, but he could feel their thoughts on him as one. It certainly hadn't been his idea to release the most mellow love song he'd ever written as the introduction to his new record. His instinct had been the title track, edited for radio, of course. It was laid back but still had an edge that wouldn't blow it with the old fans as he felt this new approach had. But he was coming off of two weak albums with The Cocktails and had taken two years to write and record *Higher than Heaven*, so he wasn't in the best position to make the call. His mind drifted till he saw Stan getting up to address the gathering.

"I've known Roc Molotov longer than anybody in this room, Uncle excepted, and I think this is a fucking masterpiece!" Stan thundered. Obligatory applause followed, but bemused expressions were seen around the table as he carried on. "I'd roll over Mother Teresa, if she was still alive, to break this record, and I'm just getting started. I don't give a shit if the ballad hasn't been lighting up the phones. So what? We should be staying up all night making the calls ourselves if need be."

Stan was old school. He still believed hits could be bought with "booze, broads, and bullshit," and who could argue with history. Stan had all but invented the term "tour support," the euphemism for payoffs disguised as promotion. He liked nothing better than doing shooters and beers at Barney's Beanery and slipping an envelope full of fifties into the jacket pocket of a fallen comrade from a major FM station. Stan was starting to turn his usual shade of mottled red as he banged the table in front of him. Roc pictured Khrushchev with a goatee. "Time to put away the bloody café au laits and sissy water, folks. Let's bust some butt and go get this thing."

It was an embarrassing rant, and Roc could imagine the under-thirties recalling it in the cafeteria later, but for now he had to admit that he still admired Stan Smiley's commitment to the music. As if on cue, Stan leaned his gut into the table and grabbed all gazes. "You ever notice that no one listens to music in this joint? Why do I hear 'you've got mail' more often than I hear 'this is a hit'? You all know I'm outta here at the end of this year, and you won't have to listen to my bullshit anymore, but I intend to go out with a smash. Are you with me or not?"

General agreement filled the room, and Stan grinned as his nose pulsed on and off like the "Recording" light in a studio. Bluff or bluster, he had gotten the room going. Ideas for various local promotions and station giveaways were tossed around, along with ways to get precious front rack positions at retail, until the energy in the room seemed to be waning. Finally, a nerdy-looking junior in publicity cleared his throat nervously and spoke so quietly that everyone had to stop and listen.

"Hey, like, you know that guy who hosts *Beach Blast* on MTV, Chad Sparx?" Everyone did, seeing as how it was suddenly the highest rated show on the network, with its combination of surfing events, nearly naked extreme volleyball, and cool groups that would just happen to drop by. "Well, he's a bud, right, we used to be in a band called Underpuppy for a minute just before he got the show. I was thinking, you know with the record being called *Higher than Heaven* and everything, that wouldn't it be, like, so cool if Mr. Molotov, I mean Roc, were to fly by then parachute into, like, the interview set totally unexpectedly, but not really, you know what I mean?"

A deep silence followed this suggestion, and it was just a matter of who got their blade out first. Roc lowered his head and took a drink of Strawberry Mango Delight till the idea could pass quietly into oblivion. The nerd, whose name was Trey, immediately starting backpedaling and stuttered an apology. "Oh man, that is so lame ... I'm really sorry like ... I just started working here this week, you know...."

"Brilliant. Totally brilliant!" Stan Smiley clapped his hands and went over to slap Trey on the back with a little too much gusto. No one noticed Trey bounce off the table as Stan enthused loudly, "Now, that's exactly what I mean. Perfect! Who knows a pilot? Do you need lessons to be able to guide those things?"

Roc felt panic welling up. He looked helplessly at Uncle, who had his hands out in his traditional open palm gesture. The knives went back into their sheaths and the room came to life. Roc felt ill; once Stan got an idea in his head, there was no turning back. Uncle was nodding sagely and getting into the conversation. "I think our engineer's brother is a pilot at the Santa Monica airport.

Roc, you ever parachuted before?"

Roc shook his head numbly, trying to look confident, unable to speak as he saw his fate being decided. As the excitement in the room grew, Uncle turned and whispered to him, "Solution ... I smell a hit. Relax. I've never tried it myself, but I hear it's quite exhilarating."

Nausea crept over Roc, but at least he wasn't thinking about Bobbie.

Seven

Leaving the label's shiny Burbank offices, Roc reflected on the general ugliness of the San Fernando Valley, knowing he was not the first to entertain these thoughts. As the endless copy shops, taco joints, and manicure emporia blurred by, it struck him that the entire Valley seemed to have been designed one afternoon in 1956 by someone whose pinnacle achievement was the Bowl-a-Thon in Van Nuys. Uncle was staring at his laptop and ohmmming to himself till he turned to Roc.

"That wasn't too painful, was it?" Greeted by a sullen silence, he went on, "Oh, don't worry, I'll get you out of that beach stunt; we just had to play along. You ever try to deflate one of Stan's thought balloons while it's airborne?"

"Let's not talk about anything airborne for the moment, Uncle, if you don't mind." In reality, Roc was seriously trying on the idea of doing the stunt, realizing that it would be the only way he'd be on *Beach Blast* in this lifetime. Under the hype of the meeting, Roc saw it for what it was: a show for himself and his manager, and he knew from years of playing along that it would take a lot more than a few key interviews and some good reviews, if he dared hope for those, to break this record. Radio was tighter than it had ever been, and he wasn't up for a big tour; no one was convinced that touring was anything more than preaching to the choir anyway. Sure, he could do a couple hundred thousand copies out of the box, but that would barely pay for the catering at the video shoot, mention of which had been noticeably absent from today's strategy session.

"Hey, seems like Justin's got his shit together," said Uncle.

"Yeah, smart kid." Roc winced at his own description of the young exec in charge of his future.

"Recognize the last name?"

Roc paused before replying, "Savage wasn't it? Oh right, let me guess, Doc Savage's kid?" He laughed, thinking about the legendary concert promoter who filled arenas and federal courtrooms with equal ease in the eighties. "I'd almost forgotten about Doc. Did they ever put him away?"

"Nope. All the flunkies took the fall as usual. Doc owns one of the Netherland Antilles or somewhere like that. He just can't leave."

At that precise moment, Justin Savage was sitting at the computer in his office firing up his email. He clicked Warren Blade's address from the company directory and typed in "Roc Molotov" under subject. Just then, something on the MSNBC ticker caught his attention, and he accidentally entered Roc's name under cc. He turned back to the screen.

W - update me on the rm ctalaogue deal we ahd the mtg this am cool till some pimplein nikes came up witht areal idae fuvckhaed i don't know how much hang timw i canm give this turkey - J

In his office on the third floor, Blade was proofing the liner notes of the newest preteen divas compilation. The Stan Getz/Chet Baker Sessions was playing in the background and seemed right at home with the redwood walls that hadn't changed since that record was made. He looked at the e-mail and replied,

J - I'm on it - W

Curious, Warren thought when he noticed the cc to Roc Molotov. *Not like the old days,* he mused, *when lying to the artist was the way to go.*

Uncle snapped a handkerchief across his dome till it glowed. "I'm going to drop you at the hotel. I've got a little snog-and-bonk lunch with Marie. We can go over the new radio reports later. You wanna invite Nature Girl, and we can all check out The Cocktails at the Whiskey tonight? Should be amusing."

"No, thanks. I'd have to talk to them. And for the record, Bobbie and I are not happening anymore," Roc replied flatly.

Uncle arched a brow and a small smile showed through. "Marie's got a sweet little friend, you want me to fix you up? Remember her from the pool the other day? Stunning."

"Stunned?" Roc grunted.

"You gotta lower your standards, brother. What is it with you and these wholesome types? You're missing a world-class ledge on this one. You could hold the next G8 meeting up there."

Roc shook his head in disgust at Uncle's lasciviousness, but he couldn't help laughing as well. It was true, he liked down-to-earth women, and he slept alone most of the time, unlike Uncle, who pursued the rock 'n roll life with vigour and amazing success for a bald faux guru with the sensitivity of a vulture. Contrary to the image of his profession and the unwritten law that any man who makes his living with a guitar is expected to copulate until his member falls off from exhaustion, Roc sought relationships. Not always deftly, or with the right women, but he actually liked to know the middle name of the person in his bathroom.

"Later, Roc," said Uncle, patting his friend on the back as the doorman held open the car door. "Grab a little sleep, put a 'do not disturb' on the phone, and you'll feel better."

Once Roc was walking into the lobby of the Sunset Lagoon, Uncle leaned over to the driver. "Take Coldwater. We have to go back to the valley. I'll direct you."

He pulled his vibrating cellphone from underneath the white caftan and looked at the caller's number. "Hey, Danny, how's it going? I can't hear a thing. Tell those goofballs to stop playing for a minute.... Uh-huh ... it's going to be great, man, celebs for days, lots of press, everyone from the label.... No, Roc can't make it, I think his mother's in town or something.... I'm on my way, and we can go over the set list then. Later." Uncle then hit his newest speed dial entry. "Hey my little *bonbon* ... *oui* ... me too, listen I've gotta do something and then I'll pick you up. Don't overdress. *À bientôt*." He hung up, smiling. Inviting Roc to the Whiskey had been a calculated risk, but it had to be done, and if there was one client that Uncle knew well enough to take that chance with, it was Roc Molotov.

Eight

Roc sat distractedly strumming his guitar without realizing he was playing the chords to "Swan Dive," the current single from the new album. The TV was on the nature channel with the sound off, and an untouched room service tray sat on the coffee table. Having lived at the Sunset Lagoon for the last three years or so, Roc knew the menu a little too well. Sure, they'd make whatever he asked for, but he couldn't think of anything and had told them to surprise him. They had, and the julienne of jicima and mung beans with a pomegranate drizzle languished untouched.

> "Standing at the edge I leaned into the sky
> Held on to the air and closed my eyes
> This is my swan dive into you
> And freefall is all I can do
> This is my swan dive."

Roc sang so softly, the words barely took shape. Suddenly he realized what he was singing, and snapping out of his trance, he put the guitar down on the bed and went over to the window. He looked out on a grove of acacias and a flowering magnolia tree surrounded by birds of paradise, with a little waterfall bubbling in the centre. The sounds coming from the hotel pool on the other side of the building were indistinguishable, floating in and out on the breeze.

His thoughts drifted back to the first time he met Bobbie. He'd been waiting to turn into Backpages Bookstore on San Vicente, and she'd driven that ridiculous bubble-gum-purple rent-a-car, the one that looked like a sneaker, into the back of his Lexus. He'd been more surprised than anything, certainly not injured, but he recalled taking a couple of breaths before climbing out of the car, ready for the inevitable exchange of interpretations, unpleasantries, and ultimately insurance agent numbers. When he'd helped her emerge from the crumpled driver's side door, she'd been clutching a cellphone and wearing a peach-coloured sweat suit, along with most of a mocha frappuccino. She had long, tied-back chestnut hair and soft brown eyes. When she'd started her apology so quickly in that accent, which was at its most languid in those days, saying that she "reckoned" it was all her fault, and she hoped he wasn't too "tore up" about it, then thanked him for helping her out 'cause the door was all "cattywampus," he'd started laughing.

She looked shocked at his reaction, but then he straightened up enough to get the cars off to one side of the road and suggest they discuss the situation over lunch at Staccato across the street. It came out, over grilled vegetable salad for her and penne arrabiata for him, that she'd arrived recently from a small town in Alabama, had found a little apartment in Santa Monica, was doing whatever she could to make the rent, didn't want to be an actress or a model, liked jogging and old movies, and having been raised on a diet of singers named Merle, Buck, and Lefty, had no idea who Roc Molotov was. He went from charmed to smitten by dessert, and she agreed to let him drive her up the coast the next day. He called the car rental company and dropped her at her apartment.

That was the past, he reflected darkly, sitting down to open his email. The "I love you" message he deleted without reading, missing Bobbie's pained explanation for the previous day's misunderstanding. There was one from Danny, The Cocktails drummer.

Hey Molo: Long time. How's it hanging? Everything's good with the guys. Gwen's got a bun in the ov, thought you'd like to know. Can you imagine me covered in pee and pureed carrots? (Roc could not)

Hope you can make it to the Whiskey. Have you seen our vid? Love to jam some time.

Double

With some surprise and a little hesitation, he opened an e-mail from miaoumiaou@hotmail.com. Tabatha, the one that got away, and mother to the daughter who refused to recognize his existence.

Roc,

I'm going to Italy with the museum and may stay on and meet James in Geneva. Would you have your accountant direct deposit to Emma's account? She's old enough to handle her own finances now anyway. Did she thank you for her birthday present? I took it with me when I drove up to Vassar for the party. Hope you're well.

best, Tabbie

Roc sighed and closed his eyes before opening the next one from huskiefan254@minniemail.com.

Hi dear,

It's your mother, remember me? How are you? Have you finished your new record? You know they built the pyramids in less time than it takes you to write a song these days. Ha ha! There's lots going on around Duluth as usual. Your Aunt Denise and I went to the Mountie Art Exhibition at the Tweed Museum and there were some lovely paintings, although we did wish for a few less Mounties. Did you know there was a Mountie Barbie and Ken? You remember Douggie Grimsrud, well he was charged with operating a canoe intoxicated. I didn't know you could get nailed for that, they must be down on their quota. At least they dropped the charge of waving a paddle in a threatening manner. He was just upset about his old lab drowning in Rice Lake last month I think. Well I've got to go, the Huskies are playing tonight. Could you hurry up and send those posters for the rec center fundraiser?

I love you,

your mother, Winnie

Roc smiled and made a note to have Uncle send the posters. He was about to delete one from someone he didn't recognize, along with the usual virus warnings, offers for a cheap mortgage and penile enlargement, when he realized it was from Justin Savage. Roc's reaction went quickly from quizzical to stunned anger as he took in the meaning of the almost incomprehensible email. He sat back in his chair with a feeling of revulsion at the business he was in before forwarding the email to Uncle and shutting down the computer. Fucker couldn't even spell.

Nine

Bobbie checked her computer for what seemed like the millionth time. Roc wasn't picking up her calls, her messages went unanswered, and she was convinced he hadn't read the email that she'd composed so carefully, confessing the details of her thriving phone sex-on-wheels business. She'd explained how it had started by accident one day with a wrong number, a misunderstanding, and a proposal from the caller. She'd also been two months behind on the rent.

She picked up the remote, shutting off the player and the advance CD of Roc's new record. She had "Swan Dive" on repeat, and many tears had fallen as it played and replayed. Bobbie was sure, even though he'd never said so, that he'd written it for her. It had been that day a few months ago at El Matador Beach watching the dolphins that had seemed to mark a real change in their relationship. The usually reticent Roc, who could express himself so well musically, had, until then, been affectionate but silent about his feelings. Then, as they watched the sailboats sparkling on the horizon and the surfers bobbing in and out of the waves, they'd spotted a school of dolphins flashing in the late afternoon sun, dipping and diving in the Pacific, just yards from the shore. He'd taken her hand and said, "So graceful, they're so free. The only time I feel like that is with you." And he'd smiled so sweetly; she'd wished that he would take his shades off, but it didn't spoil the moment. They'd stopped at the Heavenly Blessings Center on the way back and fed the swans, and the glow from the day had lasted into her bedroom that night. The next day, he'd shyly played "Swan Dive" on his acoustic guitar for her, and she'd been speechless.

Bobbie's thoughts turned to the nasty client back-up that must be growing on her voice mail, given that she hadn't gotten in her car, much less left the apartment all day. She shut down her computer after checking one last time for a response from Roc, grabbed a cold lemonade, and headed for her car with her phone and an extra battery. She had pulled up the ramp and stopped at the curb to check for oncoming traffic when a figure came out of nowhere and jumped onto the hood of the Toyota with a demented grin and a can of Lone Star foaming over onto his hand. Bobbie stood on the brake, and Delray Jackson slid off the hood and out of sight. In horror, Bobbie threw off her seatbelt and leapt from the car. Delray rolled out from underneath like he'd been checking the transmission, something she'd seen him do on more than one occasion.

"Howdy, Junebug. Your trannie's not quite right, and you might want to air-up the left front sometime soon."

"Delray Jackson, I'm fixin' to flatten you."

"Ahh, Bobbie Jean, you'd never hurt your big old boy, and I know it."

She glared at Delray as he hauled himself up from under the car and swirled the contents of his beer around, checking for any losses. "What do you want, Delray?"

"You. With me. Makin' babies in Farcry in a little house with a baba-que, a clothesline, and a mess of dogs in the yard." He grinned stupidly as she stood, hands on hips, slowly shaking her head in disbelief. "They re-opened the drive-in this year. I'll bet you didn't hear about that," he added hopefully.

No, she allowed as she hadn't heard the good news about the drive-in before taking a deep breath to calm herself. "Delray, I don't want any of that. I'm happy here, hard as that may be for y'all to believe. It's real pretty, it don't rain but two or three times a year, and I can see the ocean any old time I like." His puppydog expression still had its goofy charm, and Delray did look good in his Levis, but Bobbie had to toughen her tone. "I like the food, the folks here are real nice, and I especially like being a good long way from Farcry and the likes of peckerwood like you."

"Whatever blows your dress up, Junebug, but I ain't leavin' without you."

"Oh, Delray," she said, exasperated, getting back into her car. She lowered the window and looked him in the eye. "You'll get bored of this place in no time. They're a bunch of phonies here. You'll run out of money and patience soon enough waiting for me to change my mind, which is not about to happen." As she put the car in gear and eased into the street, she heard Delray start to curse and yell.

"I know where his management office is, Bobbie Jean. I looked up the address on the back of one of his CDs in Red Barn Records 'fore I came here. And I brought a little Alabama toothpick with me in case he needs convincing."

Bobbie knew that an Alabama toothpick was big enough and sharp enough to gut possum, and she felt a bit sick. In the rearview mirror she saw Delray standing in the middle of her street, bowing formally and toasting her with backwash from his Lone Star as the cars navigated around him. She was grateful he didn't have wheels as she headed down to a favourite vista overlooking the ocean in sleepy Palos Verdes to catch up on a little work. She parked away from the only other car in sight, opened her lemonade, and pulled out a bottle of Very Cherry nail polish. She lowered the seat to full recline, propped her feet on the dash and picked up her cellphone.

"He-llo, my little throbbing cockatiel. You wanna show me your plumage today?"

With the phone under her ear, she painted a toe with one hand, and as she reached for the lemonade with the other, it tipped onto her bare leg. "Oooooohhh," she squealed. At the reply from the other end of the phone, she continued, "You wanna sing for mama, do you?" She'd have to get one of those hands-free thingies someday.

Ten

Roc pulled off Sunset into the parking area of Heavenly Blessings Gardens and Meditation Center. As always, the sounds of L.A. receded, and things got a little more peaceful for however long he was there. Roc had discovered this place soon after he'd moved to California, and he'd turned Uncle on to it. Uncle had more or less claimed it for his own, and it was about the only time that he dropped the rock 'n roll guru act and paused to consider life. Roc waved to Uncle's driver, Eddie Dyck, who was smoking a cigarette at the wheel, strictly forbidden at the center, as he pulled in.

"Eddie, what's shaking?" As well as being Uncle's sometime chauffeur, Dyck ran a little studio in the valley where Roc and The Cocktails had cut a lot of their early records. He was still the keeper of the band's archives, the future of which was being hotly contested these days.

"Rocco, how the hell are you? Long time. I'm just great. Busy with the studio when I'm not driving Mr. Clean. My son, you remember Rich, well he's in a band called Maureen's Ankle, acting like they just invented the minor chord. You? How's Bobbie?"

Roc winced to himself but gave a generic, "Everything's cool, Ed. Tell Rich I said hi."

"You bet. He'll be happy to get a hello from you. Calls himself Stick Neff now. Don't ask. Good luck with the new record, man. Uncle played me a couple of cuts, sounds great. I can't believe he'd manage The Cocktails when he's still got you, but there's no explaining the big man, is there?"

Roc covered his shock with a forced smile until he passed through the gates of Heavenly Blessings. He stopped and closed his eyes, taking a few breaths to gain focus for the upcoming conversation with Uncle. Here was something new to deal with. He shouldn't have been surprised, but he was.

Listening to the wind chimes, he made his way around the beautiful man-made lake, with its perfectly arranged bamboo plants, maples, and silk trees, the latter aglow with deep pink and white flowers. Even the rocks were harmoniously placed, he thought as a couple of swans glided up to the water's edge. Was everything designed to remind him of his career or his love life, both of which were in sad shape? Uncle had more or less summoned him here, and he was glad to escape the odour of raw ambition that hovered by the pool of the Sunset Lagoon these days. Maybe it always did. Maybe it was time to find a new place to hang his twenty-seven pairs of black jeans, he mused bitterly as he came in sight of the pink pagoda tucked in the trees, where he would undoubtedly find Uncle Strange contemplating his navel or his cellphone. Roc crossed the little zigzag bridge and recalled Uncle explaining that it was shaped that way so the Devil would fall off as you kept running. He'd probably made that up, but it seemed particularly apt as Roc approached Uncle and sat on the little stone bench across from him without speaking.

After a pause that was unnaturally long, Roc broke the silence. "So, when were you going to tell me you're managing The Cocktails?"

"Today," Uncle replied with a small smile. "I figured you wouldn't yell at me if we were here when I did."

Roc realized he was probably hearing the truth, but it didn't make it any more palatable. He also knew that for Uncle to keep his empire afloat, he was going to have to take on new clients, and why not The Cocktails? After all, it made perfect sense. He'd brought them this far. If only he hadn't led Roc to believe that The Cocktails were going with Two Penguins, the Canadian hard rock managers who were smoking hot these days.

As if to answer Roc's unspoken question, Uncle continued, "Two Penguins dropped them when they heard the final mixes. Called the record nose whistling for fags. Doesn't leave you much wiggle room, does it? Those pricks must be crying in their maple syrup now, beaver brains. And just so you know, your record was scheduled to come out before theirs, before the delays."

Roc was feeling uncomfortable with all this invective in such a peaceful place. "Forget about it, Uncle. It doesn't matter anyway.... I know I took too long to make the record, but ..." he changed the subject somewhat, "Hey, nice email from the Savage kid."

"Now I'm going to tell *you* to forget about it, Roc. We'll make it happen without them. I can still call some favours at radio. Speaking of which, we got the Milky Way network across the board. If you get some phones, it'll chart next week for sure. They're up to thirty-four stations, you know."

Roc knew that Milky Way was a group of stations in the northeast with common programming out of Harrisburg. He knew it was the softest of soft rock with an emphasis on "heritage artists" and that it meant airplay, not sales. He also remembered that they could be bought for little more than grocery store coupons from the local label promo rep.

"Uncle, listen to me. I'm done with this. My heart's not in it."

Uncle interrupted him and reached out to put his hands on Roc's shoulders. "I already told you, you don't have to do the parachute thing."

"I don't mean the stunt, it's much more than that.... What JJ's doing, the cabin in Mendocino, that sounds like living to me. I want to escape, pretend all the crap doesn't exist, just disappear. Can you understand that?"

"Sure, I have those feelings too, but listen to me. Every promoter in the country is all over me to sign The Cocktails and commit to a tour. The boys are nervous, with good reason, I might add. Why don't you go out with them, it would be amazing!"

"You *are* joking, I hope. Let me picture life as the opening act for my old band, who didn't know a drumstick from an asparagus stalk when I met them. Gosh, do you think they would let me use their spotlight?"

"Roc. Please." Uncle held his hands out palms up and tilted his head in his characteristic patronizing manner. "I'm talking co-headliners, of course. It's perfect. They'd probably back you on the old songs ... for a bigger cut."

"Forget it, Uncle. It's time for me to cash out. Let's make this catalogue deal while we still have some cards to play. We've had a great run together. Your plate's full, and honestly, I bear you no animosity over The Cocktails thing. They'll have a better shot with you pulling the strings anyway. How was the show last night?"

"Fabulous. Every label weasel that walks was there. A celeb gang bang — Cher, both of the Osbourne kids, Lisa Marie. Tonya Harding came with the guy from Skid Row, go figure. Marie swears she saw Johnny Hallyday, but that's unconfirmed. Three encores, they did a smoking version of 'Jukebox Hero,' the old Foreigner tune, and Cher got up. It was amazing."

Roc realized he had inadvertently hit Uncle's "hype" button, so he waited for the tape to run out before continuing. "Uncle, you're not hearing me. I'm done. 'Swan Dive' is my swan song."

"Oh, I hear you Roc, it's just ..." Uncle paused. He was having trouble getting the words out, and he went on in just above a whisper. "I believe in you, Roc, always have, as a musician and a man. And honestly, there's not many in the world, never mind the music business, I can say that about."

Roc was smiling as he saw the years between them tumble away. "Remember the gig at the rec center in Duluth? There were more people on stage than in the audience. And you went to the sound board and played back the crowd noise from *The Who Live at Leeds* album between songs?" Now it was Roc's turn to hesitate. "It's all right, brother," he said quietly with a slight grin, "it doesn't last forever."

The sound of the wind chimes echoing across the Heavenly Blessings Lake filled the space in the conversation. Roc looked away and watched the swans etching their curving patterns on the water. When he looked up, Uncle was wearing a very odd expression. "Maybe it does, brother. Maybe it does last forever."

Roc had seen similar moments of inspiration in Uncle Strange before, and he was more than a little leery of this one. He waited while Uncle formulated his idea.

"What's the hottest record right now?"

"I don't know. That daredevil soundtrack thing?"

"No, the new Nirvana record, with one new song."

"So what, Uncle?"

"And next month, the big hype is going to be the Doors demos, recorded in somebody's kitchen, with the lyrics half written and half improvised. It'll go platinum before you can exhale." Roc waited for the point of all this to make itself known. "Yoko could release an album of Lennon talking in his sleep and it would be a smash. Hmm, not a bad idea." Uncle scribbled a note.

"Yeah, Uncle, I get it, they're all dead. What are you going to do, kill me?"

"Not exactly." Uncle paused dramatically. "But what if, during your *Beach Blast* appearance, you just disappear? In front of Chad

Sparx, a bevy of babes playing extreme volleyball, and millions of awestruck MTV fans?"

Not wanting to wait to see where this was headed, Roc got up to leave the pink pagoda and the madman who was practically glowing with the aura of his own genius. "Call me when you're feeling better, will you."

But Uncle was not to be so easily dissuaded. He stood up suddenly and leaned toward Roc, unnerving him somewhat. "You never actually touch down. They see the parachute, enough to know it's you and then, poof, you float away to your destiny." Uncle grabbed Roc's shoulders again, this time clutching them ferociously. "Higher than Heaven, Roc. Where your destiny will include the smash that you deserve with this record." Uncle knew this would appeal to the artist's vanity, and Roc paused as he was about to leave. "And then, we do the dead guys one better. You begin your new career, making posthumous records ... in your own time ... in your own way ... with no interference, no label geeks, no tours ... just you and your music, the way you want it."

"I don't know, Uncle." Roc attempted weak resistance, but Uncle was on a roll.

"You want to cut vocals suspended from the ceiling like Peter Gabriel on his first solo album ... cool. Play drums with spatulas, rent a seventeenth century Greek lyre, have fifteen verses and no chorus ... do it, who cares!" As his voice rose to an uncomfortable intensity, Uncle was sporting a maniacal expression that alternately repulsed and terrified Roc. "You make the music, and I'll deal with the greed machine. Create and leave the rest to me ... me and your mighty label and your grieving fans."

Roc looked away to defuse the intense weirdness of the moment. But Uncle had hit a vein. They both knew Roc had lost his taste for the road. The thrill of the Denny's menu at four a.m. just wasn't what it used to be. The boys in the band were frozen in adolescence; the fans wanted the same-old. Planes, tour buses, mindless interviews, label toads — he was sick of it all. Roc had almost unconsciously been moving toward a new life with Bobbie, a kind of belated adulthood with a garden, tennis, maybe a kid. But now all that was gone. What was holding him? Nothing.

Still, he couldn't quite give in that easily. "It feels kinda creepy to me, Uncle. It is ingenious, but I would expect nothing less from you." Roc felt overwhelmed by the whole concept, this grand wild deception, but when he thought about playing out the string as a has-been rock star and life at the Sunset Lagoon and Bobbie ...something made it logical, even appealing.

Uncle knew Roc well enough to stop talking and let the moment be. He didn't know why, but he knew that things were funky in Roc's love life, very funky. He'd never seen him like this before, not even after the episode with that bitch Tabatha. After staring at the lake for a few minutes, Roc turned to look at Uncle with a smile, and Uncle knew it was a done deal.

"Dead brilliant, if I do say so myself."

Eleven

After saying goodbye to Uncle in the parking lot of Heavenly Blessings, Roc got in his car and started to drive unconsciously in the direction of Hollywood. Before he was aware of how he got there, he was in his hotel room at the Sunset Lagoon foraging through the fruit basket and kicking off his Pumas. He left the computer off and didn't check his messages. His mind leaped from an exhilarating sense of possibility to the terror of the actual skydiving stunt. From the promise of musical freedom to the fear of never going back to the life he had created and never knowing Emma. *This is ridiculous,* he thought, *I'm going to call Uncle and tell him to forget about it.* He picked up the phone then just as quickly put it down and walked over to the mirror above the bureau. He leaned in and looked at his face more closely than he had for years. The bone structure was good, skin pretty taut, not too many lines, no serious bags unless he drank too much wine, but it would all go south soon enough. It would certainly be nice to lose the weekly Midnight Velvet hair treatment and the eighties rocker eyeliner that he felt was part of his look, even now. As they had parted, he'd told Uncle that he really needed to think seriously about this for a day or so. But deep inside, his mind was all but made up.

At that moment, Uncle was in his office on Wilshire Boulevard, on the phone with Eddie Dyck's brother, Nick, who was at the Santa Monica Airport. "Yeah, you know, one of those rescue hoists for hauling someone out of the water. Okay, so there's one installed in the chopper already? Great. And you figure you can sit just above the cloud cover and reel someone in no problem? Even if they've got a parachute on? Cool.... Freefall velocity, what's that? Uh-huh. Yeah, I guess the depth changes as you get further from shore, doesn't it? No, not a swimmer really.... Oh, don't worry, we'll make it worth your while, you can ask Eddie."

At that moment the door opened, and The Cocktails came bouncing in unannounced, looking like they hadn't slept since the show at the Whiskey two nights ago. They hadn't. Uncle waved them in, hiding his annoyance at the intrusion, and shifted uncomfortably on his meditation cushion. "Okay, Nick, let me get back to you. But, basically, we're on for next Thursday ... no, thank *you*."

Uncle held out his palms and grinned at the dishevelled trio collapsed on the couch in his office, passing a bottle of warm Veuve Cliquot back and forth. "Incredible ... you guys were devastating the other night. I'm sorry I didn't hang for the afterparty, but I'm sure you held up our end of the celebration nobly."

They all started talking at once. "Whatta scene, man!" Danny spun his sticks like a wasted majorette while Frankie nodded bobblehead-style, unable to focus,

"Did you check out Cher singing 'Jukebox Hero'?"

"Was her mike even on?" Barry asked softly, sounding concerned.

"Stan Smiley brought a box of champagne." Frankie raised the spoils proudly. "This is the last bottle."

Danny drummed frantically in the air before stopping to look at Barry. "Was that Johnny Hallyday, the French Elvis?"

Barry shivered in memory of his own celebrity sighting. "I passed Tonya Harding going to the can. She looked more than a little scary."

Still nodding to the song in his head, Frankie said, "That Savage guy from the label is cool. He gave us our #1 awards and then this chick came out of a giant cocktail glass wearing nothing but a few olives. Owwwoooo."

Uncle let them spin for a while, intoxicated on champagne, lack of sleep, and their first hit record without Roc, before settling into business. "Okay, first, the tour. The double bill with Roc isn't going to fly. The promoter thinks it'll tie you guys too much to the past, and I agree. You could open the east coast leg of that reality show winner, Wendy whatshername's tour, but you'd blow her off the stage, and they'd find some excuse to dump you by the third date, I guarantee it. Now, I was chatting with Sebastian the other night, and this is totally hush-hush, but there is talk of a Skid Row reunion. It might be an unplugged thing or maybe a whole tour, they don't know, but I'll stay on it. Let me work on this and get the perfect combo, all right? Meantime, are you guys writing any new tunes? I've got a boatload of publisher demos we can start going through, but I'd rather you come up with the hit. It means more dinero for all concerned, right?"

Danny Cocktail pulled a cassette out of his jacket pocket. "I've got some country songs I've been working on. No real melodies, they're more like those macho talking songs, you know."

"All right, Double, let me check them out," said Uncle unenthusiastically, "but see if you guys can start brainstorming. Remember, we can always bring in a song doctor to punch it up later. Moving right along, I need you each to sign the back catalogue agreement. Candy has the paperwork on her desk, so be sure to do that before you leave. I think Roc's finally on the same page, and the good news is that the label isn't asking for a reduced royalty rate, doubtless influenced in no small part by your current status on the charts, gentlemen." Uncle flashed a conspiratorial smile before adding, "And I talked to Warren Blade in special products this morning. He would like you guys to be featured more prominently in the packaging as well. This is going to get a major holiday push and can only help your record go through the roof. Everybody happy?"

He stood up, signalling the end of the meeting, and wrapped his arms around the three leftovers, trying not to inhale the stench of smoke, booze, and Mexican food that permeated them. He lowered his voice and ratcheted up the sincerity. "I am so proud of each of you. Even when you doubted yourselves, I knew this day would come. Now get some sleep, you knuckleheads, and don't forget to sign each copy."

Twelve

Roc stayed up late into the night making lists. Uncle had insisted that no appearance of preparation was crucial, no goodbye notes, no tidying up of business. Still, Roc knew there'd be some essentials he'd need to have stashed in his little hideaway — guitars, clothes, favourite CDs, etc. There were people he needed to write to before he disappeared, without letting on why he was writing all of a sudden. Things to ask Uncle about the parachute stunt. It was sounding too easy, and Uncle knew that Roc couldn't swim. He'd convinced his nervous client that this was critical to the success of the plan. He'd told Roc that boating accidents and drowning in general was definitely the way to go if you wanted to disappear. All you needed was to have an article of clothing wash ashore. "If someone spots you later, it'll just be another Elvis moment," he joked.

In his mind, Roc wrote a letter to Bobbie over and over, but what could he really say? *I'm going to die next week, but don't worry? Have a nice life? I did write "Swan Dive" for you, and just about every song on this bloody record, to be honest.* At this, his heart hurt, but then he stopped himself and went down to the bar for a drink. The bartender was closing up but asked him what he'd like.

Settling in with a Dos Equis, Roc was absentmindedly munching on bar peanuts, thoughts far away, when he heard giggling as two cute young women, looking a little drunk, teetering on impossibly high heels and leaning on each other, came into the lobby. He recognized Marie and her girlfriend and reasoned that between them they could have caused a serious silicone shortage in Beverly Hills. Roc swung his chair around so that they wouldn't see him in the bar as they passed.

"Why not me, Julie? Uncle says I don't have to so much sing, but just to be cute." Roc recognized Marie's unmistakable accent and breathy tone.

Her friend Julie was looking for dirt. "So you're getting it on with that old Buddha, are you, Marie?"

Marie giggled and said as the elevator doors opened, "He likes it when I lick his head."

"Eeeuuww, barf," her friend replied as they fell into uncontrollable laughter, and the elevator closed, leaving Roc shaking his head in revulsion. Just as unsavoury was the idea that Uncle now bought into the current wisdom that talent no longer mattered, that cup size, collagen, and snappy choreography could mask all manner of shortcomings in the musical department. Roc couldn't blame Uncle for staying ahead of the curve, or at best right on it, but it was a reminder that he wasn't in the same game as he used to be. He decided to go up to his room and surf the real estate sites for property in Big Sur, maybe download some photos if he saw something he liked to show Uncle tomorrow.

Thirteen

Uncle was at his office in the little Spanish bungalow on Wilshire Boulevard early the next morning. His plate was indeed full, and he was buzzing with focused intensity as he prioritized his day while lying on the floor with his head nestled into his meditation cushion. Lately he'd been having lower back pain, and he had to save the lotus position for maximum effect in face-to-face meetings. He pushed "play" on the remote, and a crude drumbeat accompanied by a spaghetti western guitar came out of the giant quad speakers. Uncle was sipping an espresso when the vocal kicked in, and he practically gagged with laughter at the sound of Danny Cocktail's speak-sing delivery, his voice back in his throat with a canyon of reverb on it.

> "There's a fella stands tall on his board
> Swims with the surfers and walks with the Lord
> Rides the waves like a rodeo champ
> Toes on the nose don't get his boots damp
> He's a cowboy dude
> Don't give him no 'tude
> He's a cowboy dude
> Wetsuit and Stetson a bible and a tan
> He's a cowboy dude a wild west coast man...."

Uncle had been holding back his laughter so that he could hear the words, but now he was almost crying at the hilarity and incongruity of it all. He was picturing Danny forcing his voice deeper, delivering this stuff seriously, with the background singer, who Uncle guessed would be Danny's long-suffering girlfriend Gwen, adding "whoas" and "cools" during the chorus. At this moment Uncle's secretary and office manager, Felicia Kane, known to all as Candy, came in and walked over to where Uncle was lying on the floor. In a facial tissue-sized skirt, she stood over him with a pile of papers and a raspberry Danish on a plate. "You're in early this morning. Who was that?"

"You mean the song?" Uncle was still grinning at the lyrics.

"Yeah, it was cool. Surf country, what a concept."

She put the Danish on the floor beside Uncle (while he looked up her skirt), dropped the papers on his desk and was about to leave when he replied, "Danny, from The Cocktails. You dug it, huh? Hey, do we know any real live country singers? What about the guy who covered Roc's 'Untangle You' a few years ago?" Candy furrowed her brow, not remembering. "You know, the calf roping video?"

Candy nodded. "Right. Randy Rawhide and the Haywires. I think his career tanked and he went Celtic."

Uncle had a sudden thought. "Hey, Candy, did you see that hayseed hanging out front when you drove in? A real shitkicker in jeans and a checked shirt?"

"Hard to miss. He's been lurking for the last two days; right now he's chatting up two teenage Cocktails fans from Idaho who are showing him their autograph books. Why?"

"Just a crazy thought. See if he's still out there and ask him if he wants to come in for a soda or something, and then I'm going to casually pass through the lobby and listen to him talk."

Delray Jackson couldn't believe his luck when Candy invited him in for a cold drink. "Well, thank you ma'am. It's hotter than

Madonna's panties out there. Say, do you know her?" Candy handed the zit sisters some scribbles on a piece of paper, bringing on a major case of the vapors. "I'd take a Lone Star, a forty if you got one, but hell, anything cold to wet my whistle right about now. Delray Jackson at your service."

Candy grinned slyly at Uncle over Delray's shoulder as she handed him a Corona in a can. "Mmm-mmm." He drained his beer and looked hopefully in the direction of the fridge. "Madge's gettin' up there, but I wouldn't kick her outta bed for eatin' crackers."

"Uncle Strange," said Uncle, crossing the lobby and offering his hand to Delray. "Come into my office, I want you to hear something. Candy, would you send out for a case of Lone Star?"

A quarter of an hour later, Candy called over the intercom, "Roc on two, can you take it?" Uncle excused himself to head into an adjacent office, leaving Delray to practice the lyrics to "Cowboy Dude." Delray made sure Uncle was out of the room before leaning over the desk and flipping through Uncle's Rolodex. He wrote a number and an address on his hand and sat back down, amazed and gratified at how the Lord takes care of his own.

Fourteen

Roc sat munching chips and guacamole, sipping a Mango Strawberry Delight from the room service tray. He looked again at the photos of properties in Big Sur arrayed on the coffee table. He'd replied to his mother's email, authorized direct deposit of Emma's cheques, deleted the penis enlargement enticements along with Justin Savage's message, and knocked out a quick greeting to Danny from The Cocktails, congratulating him on Gwen's pregnancy and the record. He couldn't resist titling the email "rock 'n roll as usual," echoing Frankie's lame comment during the MTV interview. He was now wishing he hadn't so quickly deleted Bobbie's last few messages, but he still believed nothing would have changed. Some things are just too hard to forgive and forget. His attorney, Max Stone, had copied him on the latest version of the catalogue agreement with his changes handwritten in the margin. It looked signable. Every once in a while he'd re-open his desert island discs page and add another title or two. This time it was *Steal Away* by Charlie Haden and Hank Jones, along with T. Rex's *Electric Warrior*, strange bedfellows to be sure.

The coast of California had held a special magic for Roc ever since that first family trip west when he was fourteen. He had done everything in his power to get out of going, the thought of sharing the back seat with his brother who could pass wind on command and his parents' choice of music on the little record player that sat balanced between them being two very good reasons. He'd gotten his best friend's parents to offer to take him to their fishing cabin, feigned car sickness for months in advance, even spoken enthusiastically of enrolling in summer school to pick up typing, all to no avail. He'd stayed in sweltering hotel rooms from Bismarck, North Dakota, to Missoula, Montana, playing his guitar while the rest of the family splashed in the pool; he'd heard his dad threaten "I'm going to have to separate you two" a few hundred times as they made their way from Duluth across the top of America along I-94 to I-90 through a major heat wave with no air conditioning, and he'd cursed his rotten luck the whole way. It all changed when he saw the Pacific Ocean for the first time. His mother had put on her husband's favourite Chuck Mangione record, rolled down her window, and coyly suggested they get off the interstate for a while south of Portland to look at some waves. Disneyland could wait an extra day if need be. And that was it.

Roc picked up one of the photos and recalled marvelling at the rock formations along the coast, his first sighting of a real lighthouse and the reflections of the cliffs in the coves below. He'd written his first song on that trip, a very unmemorable ode to a Sequoia tree, but the feelings never left. They'd ganged up on his dad, who was notoriously "all business" when it came to family trips and convinced him to spend one night in a tiny cedar cabin a short walk from the ocean. That first sunset had sealed it. Roc promised himself that someday he'd live in a place like this. Maybe now was the time to make good on that promise.

He was feeling a nervous excitement that had the effect of pushing aside his ongoing doubts. He hit speakerphone to call Uncle as he sat with a guitar on his lap, strumming lazily. "Hey, are you in all day?"

"Swamped. And just getting started. Can we meet later instead of lunch at the Ivy?"

"Yeah. No problem. I hate it when we're going over contracts with all those big ears around anyway. Listen, why don't I come by the office. I've got something to show you."

"Cool. A soft three?"

"All right," Roc replied and hung up. He could never master Uncle's business speak, no matter how immersed he felt in their common affairs. He put down his guitar and clicked on the virtual tour of San Luis Obispo County. He could almost smell the ocean.

Fifteen

The coolness of the Sunset Lagoon parking garage was mighty welcoming to Delray Jackson after his walk from Uncle's office on Wilshire Boulevard. His permanent farmer's tan was deepening, his hands, face, and neck starting to turn a deep chestnut shade after a couple of days of walking around L.A. and Santa Monica. He was glad that he'd dyed his buzz cut blonde before leaving Farcry. Originally, he'd hoped it would help convince Bobbie that he was a real contemporary guy now, not just some local dickweed like his buddies back home, but now he felt it would also ensure that he wouldn't be taken for a spade, what with the way his skin was getting dark. Delray was reciting the lyrics to "Cowboy Dude" as he dug around in the kitchen dumpster for remnants of something that once walked. He settled for some kind of grilled chicken, wiping off the gooey vegetable matter stuck to its underside. He hated the things they did to bread out here, putting little seeds on it and whatnot, but all in all, the pickings had been downright generous. If this is what they left behind here, think of what they must be putting away in those hundred-dollar hotel rooms upstairs.

That bald weirdo had turned out to be pretty accommodating. He'd asked for Delray's number, which had created a rough patch in the conversation, but had suggested they cut a vocal next week on this song after things chilled a bit with his other projects, whatever the hell that meant. Anyway, he'd given Delray a business card and a couple of cold ones for the road. Most importantly, though, he'd given Delray something he didn't know he had parted with, the phone number and address of Roc Molotov's hotel in Hollywood. And now, as clear as Delray was about his purpose in coming to California, he had no idea of what he would do or say when he finally came face to face with Mr. Roc Molotov, Mr. Big Fucking Rock Star.

Delray was just about to cruise for some dessert when he heard footsteps approaching. In the shadows of the parking garage, it didn't look like the valet parking guy he'd seen the last few times picking up a Beemer or Land Rover. Not realizing that Roc shunned valet parking, unlike most guests, Delray took his good fortune for granted as he became aware that he'd spotted his prey in the flesh. He watched silently from the side of the dumpster and thought that Roc looked a lot skinnier in person, kind of pathetic if you got right down to it. He pulled his Alabama toothpick out of his jeans and stepped into Roc's path just as he reached his Lexus. Seeing the knife, but not noticing the hunk of chicken on the tip blunting Delray's menace, Roc froze, keys in hand.

"Roc Molotov," Delray announced as sternly as he could manage.

Roc had never heard anyone pronounce his name like it rhymed with locomotive, but he simply replied, "Yes?" trying to keep his terror of celebrity violence under control and maintain the ability to reason his way out of this nightmare.

Delray leaned closer to Roc's trembling face and flashed the blade dramatically, unwittingly flicking the morsel of chicken breast past Roc's ear. This was all it took to temporarily derail Delray, and he sputtered, "Chicken, are you?"

Roc gathered his thoughts. "What can I do for you? I've got cash, a watch, that's about it. Here, take the car." He offered the keys.

"I don't want but what's mine to begin with," Delray hissed. He tried to think of something cool to fill the momentary silence, but nothing sprang to mind, so he went straight to the point. "Bobbie Jean Burnette, that's what I'm here for."

Roc was speechless, but a distant notion tugged at him. Bobbie had told him about some of the guys she had dated in Alabama, in particular one peckerwood, as she referred to him. The name escaped him, but the description of the prom date who had passed out in his own truck before they made it to the dance suited the hillbilly standing in front of him now.

"If you think a little pussy boy like you's gonna come along and take her from me, I'ma have to convince you otherwise." The hick added something he thought Jack might have said in one of his cooler movies, "Do I make myself perfectly clear, little man?" but it didn't come out right.

Roc rapidly took stock of the situation and found himself opening his palms Uncle-style. "Man, you've got this all wrong." Now he was starting to sound like he was reciting film dialogue. Maybe Cagney or Edward G. "I make no claim on Bobbie. Can I go now?"

Roc started to ease toward his car, but Delray wasn't going to let his glorious moment of complete intimidation pass so quickly. "What do you mean by that, fuckwad? You messin' with me, I'll slit your little carcass like roadkill."

Roc was starting to feel like this was going to end with threats, but not taking any chances, he hastened to add, a little vehemently, "No man, I'm serious, I haven't got the slightest interest in Bobbie. She's all yours."

An uncertain look appeared on Delray Jackson's face, and he unthinkingly licked the edge of his knife. "You sayin' she ain't worthy of a little dipshit like you? You should be thankin' your lucky stars you can breathe the same air as Bobbie Jean Burnette."

Roc was wondering what Bubba here would say if he'd heard the sounds bouncing around his beloved's car the other night, when they both noticed an approaching vehicle. Roc gave a jaunty wave to Hector, the valet parker, but Delray panicked, and in trying to conceal the knife, accidentally sliced through Roc's shirt, drawing blood. Not noticing his injury, Roc got into his car as quickly as possible and eased out of the garage, stomach trembling and hands shaking as Delray beat a hasty retreat to the dumpster, bloody knife in hand.

Sixteen

On the short drive to Uncle's office, Roc felt like he'd gone to hell without knowing how he'd gotten there. Seeing his bloodied sleeve had, if anything, brought him back to reality. He replayed the Delray confrontation, imagining how he might have responded — more outrage or challenge maybe, but the guy did have a knife. He didn't even consider calling the cops, not wanting to deal with officialdom at any time. And if this moron knew Bobbie's family, for instance, it was even more complicated. In his agitated state, Roc had accidentally cut off a pony-tailed suit in a vintage convertible Benz. The driver had pulled up beside him and tossed coffee down the side of Roc's car before miming pointing a gun at Roc's head. He'd taken a shortcut down 3rd Street and gotten stuck in a shoot for a network cop show that he recognized. By the time he realized and tried to back up, the people behind him were out of their car, taking pictures of actors covered in fake blood and pointing at him, and all he could get on the radio aside from commercials was "Ring My Bell" on the oldies station and a screaming caller on a talk radio program arguing that "the NRA has done more for America than the ****ing United Way ever will." The host agreed.

He'd actually been so disturbed by Delray Jackson that he'd dialed Bobbie moments after leaving the parking garage. He'd pulled over on Santa Monica Boulevard, trying to control his breathing, unsure of whether he was looking for sympathy or wanting to rage at her for ever having had a boyfriend like Delray. Once he heard the anonymous sounding "You have reached the voice mail of ..." that was Bobbie's new message, it didn't matter, and he hung up. *Just as well*, he thought as he dug through an unopened first aid kit for gauze and tape.

He walked past the nuclear nail polish site that was Candy's desk and into Uncle's office before collapsing into the couch. The beer and sweat stench was no improvement, so he opened the window as Uncle greeted him silently in mid-call. He picked up the newest issue of an industry rag from Uncle's desk and immediately saw a piece entitled "Tails Wag Roc," comparing the relative status at radio of his single to The Cocktails' "Stop Before I Start." Uncle got off quickly, reading the distress on his old friend's face.

"Sorry, Roc, I would've put that thing in the trash where it belongs if I'd known you were here."

"It's not that." Roc's voice had an alien sound to it.

"You don't look well, my brother." Uncle hit the intercom. "Candy, no calls for the moment." He finally noticed Roc's bloodied sleeve and recoiled slightly. "What happened there?" He came around from behind his desk for a closer look. "Can I get you a drink?"

"You could get me a bodyguard." Roc was getting his voice under control. "The fucking weirdest thing happened to me in the garage at the Lagoon. I was attacked by this deranged blonde hillbilly with a knife the size of a guillotine."

Uncle buried a wave of dread as the very real image of an armed Delray came to mind and quickly transferred it into deep concern. "My God, Roc. What did he want?"

"Nothing. I mean, not money or anything. He said he was there for Bobbie."

"How twisted is that?" Uncle's mind was spinning. "You must have been terrified. How'd you get out of there?"

"I spotted Hector the valet and got out while hickweed was drooling on himself. Man, I did not need that today. All the years I've been in public, and never has anything like this happened. I mean, I really thought my number was up when he jumped in front of me and put that blade in my face. Yeah, I will take a drink. Thanks."

Uncle pulled a couple of Lone Stars out of the mini fridge in his office and poured one for Roc, who looked a little quizzically at the can before taking a sip. They commiserated for a while, and Roc replayed the scene in the parking garage until all the details were exhausted. After a few moments of silence, he was starting to unwind a bit. Uncle spoke quietly. "I'm sure you don't feel like going over contracts now. You said you have something to show me?"

"I'll be okay, just give me a minute. I actually feel better already. The arm looks more dramatic than it is." Roc took the photos of the Northern California coast out of his bag and smiled for the first time since he'd gotten there. "Check these out, Uncle."

With exaggerated grandeur, Uncle said, "This could all be yours." He swept his hands dramatically over the pictures. "Gorgeous. I've never been there, but JJ calls it God's country. You're really thinking about this whole thing, aren't you?"

Roc smiled again, this time revealing a youthful enthusiasm that Uncle hadn't seen for a long time. "Yeah, I am. When I think about getting out, it's like a beautiful trap door into a world totally different than this one. And I'm really sick of this one, Uncle. I mean what have I got to lose? Whoever gets a chance to start again?"

Uncle put his hand on Roc's shoulder. "We've got a lot to do, my good sir. Let's start with the easy stuff. Max tweaked the catalogue deal, and the boys signed off on it yesterday. I didn't bother them with the details, of course. So, whenever you're ready, ink it." A pen conveniently appeared alongside the stack of papers.

"I've got Eddie's brother set up with a rescue chopper, and there's a helipad in La Jolla that's totally private."

Roc nodded along with Uncle's recitation as he initialed the pages of the agreement in front of him. He gave Uncle a list of things he'd need right away, and Uncle stopped to look over the desert island disc list. "Okay, I'm there with the Jobim and the Firebird, but Debussy's Preludes? Aren't we getting sophisto?" The two laughed, and Uncle continued, "*Back in Black*! You've restored my faith."

"So Eddie's going to be in on this, Uncle?" Roc asked.

"We need him, amigo. And not just for the escape, but I was thinking you could hole up at the studio apartment till we get your permanent Valhalla in place."

"Yeah, that makes sense," Roc agreed. "And Eddie'd be there whenever I wanted to record something new. But ..."

Uncle cut him off. "Don't worry, we'll get a new carpet and couch by Thursday. Too many memories, right?"

Roc laughed and nodded. He recalled many a night crashed on that couch after a session that might have lasted for days on end. Cigarette burns, spilled drinks, and salsa were layered like ancient civilizations into the furniture at Eddie's place, known in those days as "Reel Oddio." Mostly he remembered good times and great music.

Uncle brought him out of his reverie. "Adult thought. You'll need to give me power of attorney. And I'm still executor, right? Let's backdate it for appearances." He paused to let this sink in. "I know it's weird to think of, but there are going to be some serious probate issues to deal with. And by the way, you have to be missing seven years to be legally dead, which would hold up inheritance." Uncle looked pensive for a moment. "Mind you, it's only four years in Minnesota. Of course, in Nevada they divvy property provisionally after three years. I'm just saying ..."

Roc thought about Tabby's request that he redirect Emma's payments as he raised his eyebrows in wonder at Uncle's natural deviousness. "Let me guess, it's a fortnight in Madagascar, so maybe we talk to MTV there …"

Uncle laughed a little too robustly. "I'm just thinking out loud here. I do think we should keep Max's hands clean on this thing."

A shiver flicked through Roc's shoulders but passed quickly. "Who else am I going to trust?" He smiled. "Do you worry at all about people being suspicious?"

"See it from the public's point of view. You have no debts, you're not wanted for anything illegal, you've got a rock star top-of-the-world lifestyle. Why would you want to escape?"

Roc shrugged, "Yeah, I guess that's all true."

Uncle rolled on. "The press will love this story. Hey, I read about this guy who slowly but surely built up a credit history for his dog before he disappeared. It was so easy." Uncle saw Roc glazing over. "All right. I'll get the paperwork drawn up by a guy I worked with in New York a few years ago. Now, on to more important matters. I think you should come with Marie and Julie and me to dinner then maybe the Roxy for old times' sake. You've seen Marie; well, her bosom buddy Julie's got a set on her that could move furniture at fifty paces. What do you say?"

Roc grinned at Uncle's perennial adolescence. "All right. I could use a night out. I know when I'm licked."

Uncle gave him a strange and bemused look at this last remark and hit the intercom. "Candy? Would you make a reservation for four at Maple Drive at nine? Thanks."

Seventeen

The maitre'd at Maple Drive escorted Roc and Uncle to a booth on the far side of the main dining room, an ideal place to see but not be seen. Marie and her friend Julie were already engaged in launching a bottle of Perrier Jouet, and the mood was clearly festive. Taking a seat, Roc was introduced to Julie; he didn't acknowledge that he'd almost met her in the lobby of the Sunset Lagoon the night before. He watched Marie go through a breezy series of little kisses on either side of Uncle's skull, and it wasn't until his second glass of champagne that he could erase the lurid image of her licking that big bald head. Marie, it turned out, was quite witty and seemed to have Uncle Strange's number in many ways. He was clearly in thrall to that breathy accent, among her other charms, and he shrugged sheepishly when she referred to him as her *Monsieur Propre*, a reference to the French version of the well-known cleaning product and its bald symbol. Julie, it emerged, was a trust fund baby whose grandmother had invented Teflon, and she and Marie had gone to school together in Switzerland. Roc found himself enjoying the company in spite of his usual social discomfort.

"My father is Jean Luc Solange," Marie explained. "Maybe you are knowing his films, *O, P,* and *Q*. It is his trilogy, very famous in France, of course, where each line of dialogue begins with the letter in the title."

Uncle was nodding far too seriously at this. "I'm sure that *Q* must have been his most challenging work."

"Yes, until now, that is. He has been brought to Hollywood to work in English for the first time, you know. In this new picture, the child of Dr. and Madame Bovary would be unhappily married to a plastic surgeon, you see." At this point, Julie leaned close to Roc, ostensibly not wanting to interrupt her friend, and whispered a request for champagne, brushing her lips against his ear. Uncle noticed and took the opportunity to fondle Marie's thigh under the table.

The dinner became louder and looser, and Roc actually laughed out loud in public for the first time in a long while when Julie threw her hair back and thumped her chest, imitating the faux swagger of the latest reality starlet on Fox. Roc referred to her caboose being mightier than her engine, and Uncle looked genuinely surprised. Roc went to get up and had to grab the edge of the table to steady himself. The girls, noticing, giggled in unison, and Julie said with authority, "Time to go dancing."

Marie added her *oui,* but Uncle was still pressing for the Roxy. Roc cast the deciding vote, again to Uncle's surprise. He'd spent enough hours in the Roxy for one lifetime. He wouldn't dance, of course, but a change of scene would be fun. Uncle just shrugged and grinned and made a quick call on his cell.

The Swerve Club was loud and dark, and they were led to a corner table lit by candlelight. The DJ was doing an eighties and nineties mix, and Roc was surprised at how well the Clash, Human League, the Black Crowes, and Howard Jones got along.

Of course, a change of beverage had led to more hilarity. Julie was doing an excellent impression of Marie's accent, asking directions "to the water closet if it please you" and Marie in turn was passably impersonating Uncle, holding her palms out and crossing her legs in a lotus position, saying, "Problem. Empty glass. Solution. Another drink." A photographer suddenly appeared and took a quick shot of Roc and Julie; she nestled in close and smiled at him, forcing a shy smile in return. Uncle and Marie were happily snogging and sharing a seat when Julie grabbed Roc in the middle of a conversation about the dos and don'ts of leather pants and pulled him onto the dance floor. "Black Velvet" was playing, and Roc moved tentatively but was soon distracted as Julie ran her hands down his sides and grabbed his hips during the sultry opening bars of the song. She began moving him back and forth in time to the swaying of her body, and she looked into his eyes with flamenco intensity. He caught his breath and thought how easy it would be to let this night go where it was clearly headed. His heart wasn't in it, but another part of his anatomy might be telling his heart to go home early. Julie was writhing about an inch away from his body when the song ended, and they stood on the dance floor in one of those "there's no one else here" moments. A camera flashed.

Everyone agreed it was time for some fresh air, so Uncle paged Roscoe, his driver for the night, and they headed unsteadily into the street. Uncle insisted on playing the new CD in the limo, and in the silence after "Swan Dive," Julie said wide-eyed, "That's so beautiful. Did you write that for someone?"

Roc shrugged enigmatically, his normal response to that question, and the moment passed. He felt a twinge of what — regret? Uncle opened a bottle of Armagnac and handed glasses around. Julie stuck her nose in the glass. "Mmmm, way pruney."

Uncle was warming the glass with his hands. "Another exquisite French export." He leered at Marie. "Prune, vanilla, and a touch of violet, *non, mon amour*?" She nodded and giggled into her glass.

With the sunroof open and the tops of the palm trees blurring past, Roc closed his eyes for a moment as he slouched on the seat. The next time he opened them, Julie was asleep, curled at his feet, and out of the corner of his eye he saw Marie looking lustily at Uncle's glowing dome. He asked Roscoe to take him to the hotel and rested his eyes for just a minute.

When he came to the next morning, there was an inferno in his mouth and a war raging in his stomach. He opened his eyes just enough to know that he was in his room at the Sunset Lagoon, and not in Cedars Sinai hospital. He felt a moment of panic and said a small prayer before looking to his left in the bed. He sighed with gratitude to see that he'd slept alone. *Did I really tell Uncle about Bobbie?* He felt like a detective trying to reassemble bits of last night like a torn up photograph. There was a picture, he vaguely remembered. *And I danced in public,* he recalled with pained amusement.

Eighteen

To: Warren Blade - v.p. special products
  cc: Uncle Strange
  From: Roc Molotov

Warren: Nice to hear from you. The new mastering sounds great. I haven't listened to some of those tracks in a very long time. Ouch! Send me your ideal running order & I'll give you my thoughts. You probably remember as much about all of this as we do but I think your idea of recollections from each of us is perfect for the compilation. Here's what I recall ... R

When we first came to L.A., we were a bunch of awkward corduroy kids with hair in our eyes, from the wasteland of northern Minnesota. We'd won a local radio station battle of the bands with a song I'd written called, I think, "Black Sky Birds Cry," that mercifully has been lost along the way. My closest friend and soon-to-be manager Uncle Strange, known then on his driver's license as Karl Breit, gave the song to a Styx soundman, and it eventually led to our first record deal. We cut the record at Sowndz Ear on Fairfax above a bakery, and at night we'd hit every bar that featured a band. We made a lot of friends on those nights, and some of them played on that record and the ones that came after. You can check the credits; they're far more reliable than my memory. Hollywood was weirder than we could have imagined in those days and the scene on the street outside the Whiskey, the Roxy, and the Rainbow was something we could hardly wait to tell our friends back home about. The endless parade of flashy cars doing the slow cruise down Sunset, the outrageously dressed party people, the Santa Ana winds — it all stirred up the restless awake-all-night side of each of us, and we'd often go back to the studio and work till the caffeine finally wore off.

Listening back to those songs that came so incredibly easily, I feel a mixture of envy of my younger self and the effortlessness of it all, and nostalgia for the days when coming up with a cool song was all that mattered, leavened with a healthy dose of embarrassment at some of what I wrote. I know that we can't leave "Dreamland Feel" out of this collection, but I'm grateful for my remote right at this moment. Did I really write the words "Staring through my window blanking/ Every broken star I'm thanking"? And to those of you with headphones on, yes — Danny, Frankie, and Barry were singing "wanking" in the background bit. But I'll leave it to you to discover or rediscover whatever alchemy brought us all to where we are today. Much is lost, but here's the best of what remains. To the guys, here's to the most brilliant times of my life and to you, thanks for taking us along.

Love, Roc.

Uncle sat at his desk and smiled as he read Roc's liner notes before dashing off a quick reply.

R - Groovy notes. The teflon tart is talking about a swan tattoo — you haven't lost it!

Breitly yours, Karl

He hit the intercom and asked Candy, "Have you got an address for Bobbie Burnette in your Rolodex?" He wrote it down on a large brown envelope and looked again at the lusty expression on Julie's face in the picture from last night before popping the photo into the envelope. "And Candy, would you call Rabbit Courier and send them in when they get here? Thanks."

Bobbie leaned back in her seat in the parking lot of the Griffith Park Observatory and took a deep breath. Her customers were weird and funny at the same time; the animal names she gave them helped her to depersonalize them and keep better track of their individual fetishes. From purring like a kitten to reprimanding like a displeased schoolmistress, whatever worked was what she delivered. Fresh from pacifying the Pasadena hyena followed by a horn-polishing session with the divine rhino she realized she was exhausted as she got out of the car and walked over to the barrier that overlooked Los Angeles. The Santa Ana winds had blown away all the smog, and the city was crystalline, as it must have been in its glory days. She remembered coming here with Roc on one of their first dates and him telling her that the Planetarium at the Observatory was where Sal Mineo as Plato gets aced at the end of *Rebel Without a Cause*. His affection for the darker side of Hollywood was thrilling to Bobbie, particularly since it was so different from his quiet personality. His Hollywood landmarks — Belushi's last stand at the Chateau Marmont, Bugsy Siegel's living room, the fictional haunts of Philip Marlowe from Raymond Chandler's *The Long Goodbye*, and Musso and Franks, stayed with her whenever she was out driving, which was often, given that her business had been thriving of late.

A bunch of school kids came pouring out of a bus and raced over to the lookout before their teacher could rein them in. Bobbie saw one little boy, obviously the loner, quietly observing her through the chunks of hair that hung over his glasses. He turned away, reluctantly following his class, and Bobbie had a flash of a childhood version of the man she loved. She strode back to her car, got in, turned off the cellphone, and headed for Santa Monica, determined to get him back — tonight.

Roc was prepared to curse his snail-like accountant when he opened the email from miaoumiaou@hotmail.com.

Roc,

Thanks for handling the banking thing so quickly. This is a bit weird for me, especially by email, but I have a large confession to make. It is entirely my doing that you haven't met your daughter. After our break-up and the time that followed, it was just easier that way, and of course she thought for a long time that James was her father. I had to tell her eventually, and I did so years ago, but she just acted like I'd mentioned that I was running out to the store for a minute. I know where you think she got that iciness from, but after that it seemed like a dead issue, so I let it lie. Until last night while I'm crazed trying to pack etc. & Emma announces that she wants to meet you. She came down from school to see me off, and while I was pulling things out of closets she found those stories you wrote for me, the miaou miaou ones with the funny drawings and poems. What do I do? I can't deal with this. I want to just say no, but that doesn't fly anymore.

I'm sorry. I'm sorry.

Help.

Tabbie

Help indeed, Roc thought. *Just like Tabbie to be totally in control until one thread comes loose.* It was a big thread, and Roc could see her unraveling as the email went on. Well, he'd make it easy for her.

T- I agree with you. It's too late.

R

This sounded so ominous, that he added a p.s. before hitting "send."

p.s. Give my best to Botticelli.

Never meeting Emma was a regret he'd have to live with, but he didn't know if he could disappear without at least saying goodbye to Bobbie. After writing and deleting a series of unsent emails, he went to the bed and picked up his guitar.

Uncle was whistling "Stop Before I Start" when Stan Smiley waved him into his office. He could barely see Stan between the towers of CDs on his desk. The walls were layered with posters of acts new and old that Stan had worked with, and the "deli shots" of Stan with his arm around thirty years of stars were everywhere in evidence. "I hope they're working on a follow-up real quick," barked Stan. "I think their fifteen minutes might get reduced for dumb behaviour. That video is the worst piece of crap I've ever seen. Lovely guys though, Uncle."

Uncle knew that Stan was referring to The Cocktails and just grinned. "You got that right, my good sir. Yeah, they've got some great new songs in the works. What are you liking for the follow-up? It's not too early."

"Absolutely. Well, the devil's child wants 'Say It Don't Spray It,' but we all know his taste is up his ass. And Trey's been testing the record with his surfer buddies, and he says they don't like anything. Of course, they have the collective attention span of a newt, so take that for what it's worth. Me, I think 'Cross the Line,' but a remix would help, and I wish to hell the chorus didn't remind me of something else I can't put my finger on."

"What do you want?" said Uncle breezily. "There only are twelve notes, and most musicians are still in single digits, so don't sweat it. A remix is spot on. I've got to speak to Jason anyway, so I'll mention it."

"You want some garlic or a silver cross if you're heading there now?" grinned Stan. "So, it looks like we're a go for the *Beach Blast* thing. Trey set it up with Chad Sparx and the producer. They shoot in the morning, so it'll probably be a bit cloudy, but they say no problem picking up the chute if it's red or something. Is Roc cool with this? I couldn't tell the other day, he doesn't say much."

"Roc is totally there," said Uncle. "He wants to do whatever's necessary to make this record happen. It's personal."

"Great. I'd hate to see this one go the way of the last two. It's a killer record, but the market for anything with a shred of intelligence is pretty damn sad. I guess I don't have to tell you that." Stan shot Uncle a knowing look.

"Stan, you the man. As always. And Roc really appreciates your commitment." Uncle stood up. "All right, I'm outta here."

He continued down the hall to a corner office that was guarded by a secretary decked in Prada executioner black with eyebrows that could cut glass. "Strange. I've got a three o'clock with Jason."

She glanced at the appointment book. "Have a seat. I'll let him know you're here. Can I get you a drink?"

Uncle shook his head and sat down. His knees had really been bothering him lately, so he didn't bother assuming the lotus position, hoping that Jason wouldn't notice. Jason did and smiled knowingly as he greeted Uncle from the doorway to his office. "C'mon in, my brother." He seemed to take pleasure in imitating Uncle's phony Zen-speak.

"So, The Cocktails go gold this week, I'm told." Jason smiled approvingly. "We're still debating the follow-up. There are so many potential smashes, it's going to be hard to choose."

"Stan mentioned maybe doing a little remix on 'Cross the Line.' What do you think, Jason?"

"Stan is so fucking prehistoric. Those CDs on his desk look like Stonehenge. He just loves to spend the company's money, something he fortunately won't be doing much longer. We're grooming Rebecca for the gig. What do you think?"

Uncle recalled with barely disguised pleasure the sight of Rebecca Stanton's ass swaying as she left last week's meeting. "Oh, I'd be behind her all the way. Good call." He pulled himself back to the present. "Listen, I'm working on a new project that I wanted to offer to you first. Her name's Marie, she's French, but she can sing in English. Check this out." Uncle pulled out an eight by ten of Marie that was dominated by cleavage and pouting lips. "She's kind of Claudine Longet with major gazongas."

"Colour me interested," said Jason, looking over the photograph. "You got anything on tape?"

"Not yet. Still in development." Uncle gave Jason a leer. "But if you've got any writing and production teams that you think might be good for this, let me know."

"I definitely will. Listen, one more thing, and I know you're not going to want to hear it, but this Molotov disc is D.O.A., man. The promo team can't get arrested with this thing. Has Roc signed off on the back catalogue deal yet?"

Uncle nodded and extended his palms. "Favour. Give me another week. You can float it. Milky Way will chart if you send them over a box of paperclips. Let me do the *Beach Blast* thing, and if that doesn't work, kill it."

"All right, my good sir." Jason offered a reptilian smile. "Your credit's good around here. But one week is all the juice we've got, okay?" He got up to see Uncle to the door. "Keep me in the loop on the Marie thing. I'm there."

Uncle eased his aching knees into the back seat of the car. "Eddie, back to the office, please. Listen, I need your help on something Roc-related. And it means maximum discretion, which is why I'm talking to you."

"Anything for Rocco, man. What's up?"

Bobbie had a ripe mango and a small box of strawberries flying around in the blender as she added an extra spoonful of clover honey to the mixture. She opened the door of the little oven to check on the peach pie. As she popped it shut to give it a few minutes to brown, she checked out her reflection in the door and gave her hair a little poof. The pink workout suit and the Jimmy Choos were a strange combination, but whatever floated his boat was hunky dory with her. She had her speech all prepared and had herself convinced that given the opportunity, Roc would surely understand that a girl has to get by. If he asked her to quit car phone sex, she would hang up her cell, just like that. She applied a last-minute layer of lip-gloss and was heading for the parking garage when her doorbell rang. She thought of not answering, picturing Delray or one of those tree huggers from Greenpeace, but in the end called out "Who is it?" When the answer came back, she opened the door to the courier and took the brown envelope after signing the slip. She almost put it down on the hall table for later, but it was anonymous and somewhat mysterious looking, so she put down the pie and smoothie and opened the envelope. The first thing in the photograph she recognized was the shirt that she'd given Roc for his birthday this year. She stared at the bimbo pressing her boobs into a smiling Roc and hyperventilated.

Bobbie gathered up the goodies she'd made for Roc, along with the photo, which she held onto by a corner like it would infect her, and dropped them into the dumpster in the garage on top of a growing mountain of Lone Star empties. The familiar hand-crushed cans gave her an extra wave of nausea. She got in her car and drove to the gym. If anyone thought it was odd that she was wearing shades and Jimmy Choos while she beat the daylights out of a punching bag, at least they couldn't see the mess she'd made of the makeup around her eyes.

It was around three thirty when Roc mixed down his new song on his laptop. He'd added a few touches to the basic vocal and guitar part that he'd recorded in a performance straight from the heart. A melody that lifted step by step led to an odd chord that created a perfect rub on the word "strange." A high harmony in the chorus and a little shimmering second guitar part was all it needed. When he had started writing in the afternoon, he hadn't known where it was going. That's how it worked with songwriting for Roc; what wasn't at all clear beyond a tangle of emotion and some indistinct but powerful urge gave way to something coherent in committing it to paper or tape. He'd been flat creatively lately, and he felt at peace as he listened to the playback of "Yours Truly." The opening line sounded like it came from some old country song, but they didn't have a lock on the naked emotions, did they?

"I remember everything I meant to say …"

And the final chorus was as straightforward as anything he'd ever written:

**"Now I don't wonder how I feel
Where we're going or if it's real
It's too late to change things now
But I'm going to tell you anyhow
I was yours truly yours truly
Yours truly goodbye."**

The pause before the final "goodbye" seemed kind of melodramatic, but he decided to leave it in. In songwriting terms, it was the right choice.

In some ways, it wasn't until this moment that he realized how complex his feelings for Bobbie were. He'd taken their relationship, a word he hated, lightly, and that had felt like the magic of it. The lightness and the ease of being together, things that he had never felt before and no doubt had taken for granted, had been the joy of it. Maybe he had driven her to be unfaithful to him, through carelessness and coolness. Why did it have to be now that it finally dawned on him that the words unsaid, the ones he "meant to say," were heart-wrenchingly true?

He took a deep, tired breath and attached an mp3 of the song to an email, typed in Bobbie's address and sat back to pause for a moment before sending it. Was this fair, knowing that a few days after she received it, he'd be gone, truly gone as far as Bobbie was concerned? Trust the feeling, he decided, and hit send.

Unfortunately, Bobbie had no idea how to open an attachment to an email, and later that night, angry and confused, just stared at the blank space in the body of the letter before closing her computer and going to bed.

Nineteen

Roc felt like he might have been a little heavy-handed with the eyeliner, but he didn't know how close the MTV cameras were going to get, and he wanted to look good. Dressed to kill, he thought wryly as he pulled on his black jeans, waiting for his hair to dry and the Midnight Velvet colour to settle. He tossed the bottle with his face on it into the trash and looked around the room. Uncle had stressed that he had to leave everything as it was in the hotel room, but he had a sports bag with his portable studio, his latest song book, his favorite antique watch — the six-sided Illinois — and two photos, the baby shot of Emma that Tabbie had sent him eighteen years ago and the one of Bobbie hiking in Big Sur. He put his Martin D-28 into the case and snapped it shut, shuddering at the unavoidable coffin image as he did so.

Uncle grabbed the guitar and bag, and they left the hotel, past a dozy all-night desk clerk and into the cool pre-dawn darkness. Eddie smiled in the mirror as Roc sank back into the seat with his eyes closed and his mind racing.

"I'm guessing you didn't have any breakfast," said Uncle, handing Roc a cold Mango Strawberry Delight. "You all right?"

"Yeah, this is just a whole new kind of weird for me," said Roc in little more than a whisper.

"Nick has been flying choppers for years," said Eddie. "Used to work for the Coast Guard. He's done the whole air-sea rescue thing countless times. He says being able to plan it is a luxury he's not used to."

"Just focus on the freedom, my brother," Uncle added.

"I just wish I was already there," Roc replied and closed his eyes again.

They pulled into a sedate, gated architectural home in La Jolla as the sun started to slant down on the Pacific Ocean just beyond. Once the iron gates closed automatically, the hush returned to the grounds and Eddie pulled the car up to the edge of a heliport. It was surrounded by rich landscaping and offered a dramatic view of the sea. Roc could feel the butterflies dancing and tasted the sour return of the fruit shake he was sorry he'd drunk.

Nick opened the limo door ceremoniously. "Thanks for flying Air Play. Let us give you a spin." He shook hands with Roc then Uncle as they emerged from the car. The morning sun sparkled on the gleaming blades of the helicopter sitting on a logo designed to look like an old 45 rpm record. Little flying music notes decorated the side of the craft. "Nice to finally meet you, Roc. How's tricks, Uncle? Let me show you the set-up."

"I'm just going to check out your rig while you brief Roc, okay?" said Uncle.

Nick patiently went over all aspects of the jump, cheerfully explaining the equipment and what Roc had to do with it. "Now, normally, you'd have been practicing all this beforehand, with tandem jumps and so on, but we're going to keep it simple today. It's more a hop and pop than a real jump. You'll be on a Telesis 2 harness with an automatic opener on the main and reserve parachutes. You'll also be attached to this baby; it's a Lucas three hundred pound external hoist. You'll be going out at around thirty-five hundred feet, and we'll hover just above the cloud cover, ready to reel you in. Okay?"

Uncle glanced over at Roc and Nick conferring. He ran his hand over the rescue cable and felt his breath shorten. It was a fine line between faking a disappearance and actually disappearing, wasn't it? He looked back again and saw Roc nodding, trusting as always.

Roc asked if there was anything dangerous about all of this. Nick smiled reassuringly. "I'm sure Uncle told you how long I've been doing this. Most accidents happen because of someone improperly folding their chute, but I took care of that for you." He slipped the gear onto Roc's back and strapped it into place. "If you want to get fancy while you're out there, you can use these control knobs. They spill air out of one side or the other, increase or decrease the lift for turning, but I'm guessing you're not going to be doing much of that, right?"

Roc nodded mutely as Nick handed a headset to him. "It's kinda loud once we get going, so you'll need these." Uncle put his arm on Roc's shoulder and turned to Nick. "Give us a moment, would you?" They stepped away from the chopper as Nick climbed in and started it up.

Roc looked terrified. "What if this doesn't work? Or no one buys it? Like me, right now."

The roar of the engine and the rush of wind from the blades made it hard to concentrate, and Uncle had to shout. "Listen, the viewers won't see much. *Beach Blast* shoots this early to avoid the heat and the harsh light." He gestured toward the ocean. "That morning haze out there serves us very well. Once you're on your way up, it'll look like you got caught in an updraft or a chute malfunction."

Roc blanched at this, and Uncle continued, seeing him faltering. "It's cool. Worst case, you land, do the show … look, the MTV shooters are hand-held and are used to zooming in on beach volleyball butts." Uncle put his hand on Roc's shoulder. "Not to denigrate that, of course." Roc smiled thinly.

"You look great, man. No worries. Once you get close enough to be recognized from the ground, they'll start playing the track for 'Swan Dive,' anticipating your landing, and the kids will start to sing along. That'll be the cue for Eddie to haul you in. I've hired a couple of extra shooters to make sure we get the whole thing in case the network guys are asleep. I'm going to cab it to Malibu to meet Marie and Stan and the rest of the crew, and I'll see you here as soon as I can get back. All right?"

Roc nodded and blinked away the dust from his eyes during Uncle's instructions, feeling like everything was moving dreamlike, just beyond his touch. He mumbled, "Thanks, man." Uncle patted him on the back and gave Eddie, who was waiting beside the car, a thumbs up.

Inside the chopper, the roar was tremendous, and Roc immediately put on his headset. "Ladies and gentlemen, please make sure your seat backs and tray tables are in their full upright position, and that your seatbelts are securely fastened at all times during takeoff." Nick turned and grinned at Roc and Eddie, continuing in a melodious voice. "We know you have an option, and we thank you for choosing Air Play, the Rock of the Sky." It struck Roc as perhaps not the most reassuring of company slogans. Nick's spiel reminded him of the ridiculous intros that Eddie used to insist on in the studio when they were cutting tunes in the old days, and he smiled at the memory.

Nick ran over the parachute equipment one more time, and Roc was glad he did. A lot of it sounded as if he'd never heard it before. A few minutes later, they were circling about a half a mile south of the MTV *Beach Blast* location, waiting for the signal from Uncle, who was on a two-way radio. When the moment came, Roc felt the top of his helmet and ran his shaking hands down the straps on his parachute. His throat was incredibly dry, and tears from the wind blurred his eyes as he tried to find the beach through the surrounding clouds. He wondered briefly how Nick could tell where anything was and how he would know exactly when to tell Roc to jump. Just at that moment, he heard Nick's voice in his headset. "Okay, flyboy, are you ready for your close-up? You'll be clear before the chute pops, but don't worry, it will."

Eddie had his arm around Roc and was saying something that Roc couldn't make out, and the next thing he knew he was in the sky in freefall. Moments later, he felt the chute open, and an invisible hand seemed to jerk his body back into place. Instantly he could make out the water and the beach and tiny figures below. He felt a rush of excitement and a strange sense of joy and freedom as he got used to his perspective on the planet. He was short of breath, but it seemed as if the terror of anticipation had been replaced by an unbelievable exhilaration.

The scene below was coming into focus, and he could see the volleyball nets and the little stage where MTV was expecting him to land. He saw camera people moving into position and an excited looking scrum of beach babes and hunks gathering near the stage with its *Beach Blast* banner flapping in the wind. To one side of the set, he could make out Uncle's shining dome and beside him Marie — and was that Julie? He felt a smile pressed onto a face that no longer felt like his own as he drifted slowly toward the target. Now he could make out the faces and hear the track for "Swan Dive" booming out of the speakers mounted behind the stage. At that instant he felt himself being yanked again, and his head tipped forward involuntarily. His body jerked back and forth hard before he felt the upward tug of the winch from the chopper. He tried to steady himself and accidentally pulled on one of the lift controls, sending himself wildly to one side. He stretched his arms out to his sides to try to right himself, and he tilted backwards so that he was looking up into his parachute, which seemed to be losing its shape. He could just make out the light blue cable that was attached to him and felt another wild jerk upwards. He straightened out long enough to see the expressions of the people below turning from cheers to surprise as he rapidly ascended. He saw camera operators scrambling to get shots of his departure and Chad Sparx pointing up at him. The rest became a blur as Roc was pulled back into the chopper above the clouds, and he didn't really have a sense of the drama until watching later on TV. Eddie was madly hauling in the parachute as the hoist took care of Roc's body, dancing like a marionette below. When he was pulled into the chopper, he felt a disarming dizziness, and all he could do was crawl shivering to the open door and dry heave into the clouds below.

PART II

Am I falling through the trapdoor
As you watch me disappear.

Twenty

Emma walked into the catastrophe known as her dorm room in her usual state of twitchy fatigue after a day spent in lecture halls and a library cubicle. She'd taken a wind-down walk by Sunset Lake on her way back from the College Center but hadn't taken in much of this windswept fall day. She'd been absorbed in listening to *Higher than Heaven* with intense interest, something she wouldn't admit to.

Emma had seen her mother off to Italy in the customary Hurricane Tabbie style — a swirling vortex of arms, scarves, and hair accompanied by broken fragments of instruction and reminders. Tight as the two were, Emma always felt a rush of relief when the taxi drove away, late again. Weirdly, it also gave her more time with the father she'd never met. Lately, she'd been looking him up on various search engines, getting into his music and seeing then not seeing a resemblance in his photos.

Roc's music was far from anything else she listened to, like Doves, Turin Brakes, or Björk, but it brought her the closest to him, and his new solo record gave her the feeling that she could see into him in a new way.

Tossing her book bag on the bed, she dropped the headphones around her neck and grabbed a Diet Coke from the fridge under the desk. She booted up the Mac and yanked an oversized plastic clip from her head. Flyaway slices of sandy hair framed a face that revealed her genetic debts — her father's cheekbones and her mother's Chagall-blue eyes. She spun slowly in her chair, decompressing, sipping on her drink, and waited for the Earthlink welcome page to open.

In the midst of her mom's frenzy, Emma knew she'd been dropping a depth charge into Tabbie's day when she'd said she wanted to meet her father. She'd tried to explain that she felt this primal urge to go to California. Maybe she should've left out the part about taking a semester off from Vassar. She didn't know when, but it had to be soon.

When the screen came on, she glanced past the first two headlines: "Mars Scandal Paints White House Red" and "Amtrak Worker Admits To Goat Prank," but the third one stopped her cold. With a catch in her breath, she clicked on "Rocker Vanishes Over Pacific" and found herself staring at a photo of her father and reading "Skyjinks Lead To Tragedy: Roc Molotov, 38, Presumed Dead." She felt fingers pressing on her throat and moving quickly to her heart as the details unwound. She fought back the burning in her eyes as she clicked on "MTV" from "Favorites." She watched the footage from that morning's *Beach Blast*, followed by host Chad Sparx going on about how uncool death is, man. She stared unblinking, uncomprehending, at the shaky images of the parachute and its occupant flapping and dancing, then receding into the clouds.

Emma refused to accept what she saw and read. She knew she had to go to California, as if by going back those three time zones, she could somehow prevent the inevitability of Roc's death.

Through her tears, she stabbed at her keyboard. Burbank on Southwest at 9:50 a.m. That would work. She entered her credit card info then closed her eyes, sitting perfectly still as her mind careened wildly. The sky had darkened by the time she sent an email to her mom, knowing it would be received after her departure.

I'll call you when I get to L.A.
Love,
Em

Twenty-One

A brisk ocean breeze kept blowing out their candles, but a few hundred fans, illuminated by TV lights, huddled together with towels draped over chilly shoulders, spirits undaunted, singing the best-known of Roc Molotov's songs. The group was getting help with forgotten lyrics from a teleprompter mounted on a volleyball net. In the foreground, *Beach Blast* host Chad Sparx assumed a sombre tone as he took his cue.

"Wow. Thanks, Cleava, for that exclusive 'Rocwatch' report from our Northern Blast Headquarters, like a few hundred miles up the coast in Half Moon Bay. Here in Malibu, dudes and babes alike are really just dealing with the weirdness, asking 'like how' and 'like why' as we realize how totally uncool death is. And in case you were completely partied out all day and missed it, here's what happened this morning on *Beach Blast* when rock legend Roc Molotov was about to drop in. Check it out!"

Uncle and Eddie collapsed in howls of laughter, shouting "totally!" at the same time. Roc, wrapped in a thick sweater and wearing a tired grin, was wedged between them on the old sofa in the lounge of Eddie's studio. On the TV, the footage of Roc's descent and ascent played yet again, and he watched with fascination, recalling the bizarre sensation of being suspended over the beach. Boxes of Chinese take-out, glasses, and three mostly empty bottles of Beringer Pinot Noir crowded the well-stained coffee table. Uncle tried to relight one of the three partially smoked cigars in the ashtray, succeeding only in spilling red wine on his cream-coloured caftan.

"Remember the take-out from the Lucky Star on Ventura?" Uncle dug into a box of shrimp chow mein.

Eddie made gagging noises. "That was the place with those gross red balls, right?"

"Nothing an over-the-counter ointment couldn't take care of," mumbled a slumping Roc.

Uncle laughed and farted simultaneously while pointing at the screen. "Like how! Like why!" he and Eddie bellowed, falling into each other again like a couple of wasted frat boys. Eddie grabbed the remote and turned it up midway through a "Rocwatch Exclusive" interview with some uncomfortable-looking dude on the set of the show.

"… normally the wind moves a body south." The shorthaired interview subject wore a windbreaker and a hat with a state logo. He gestured to his right. On the screen he was identified as Glen Claire of the Coast Guard. On MTV, his delivery sounded especially terse, almost military. "But a coastally trapped wind reversal would have carried the body west and out to sea."

Chad Sparx looked like he was listening to a lecture on the twelfth century origins of papal infallibility but still managed the right question. "But the body would still be happening on the surface, wouldn't it, man?"

Glen Claire nodded, looking more than a little suspicious of his interviewer. "Except in this case, the weight of the harness could've prevented it from floating. It could've been lodged in a kelp forest on the sea floor."

"Hard to fathom, dude," replied Chad with a spacey expression as he set up the next music break.

Uncle muted the opening chords of "Stop Before I Start," which seemed to run after every segment of *Beach Blast*. "Oh man, I gotta pull myself together. I've got a suite booked for ten to start the edit on 'Swan Dive.' Justin was on my cell screaming for it practically before flyboy here was even back in the chopper. And I'd better buzz by Marie's; she'll be flying her bikini top at half-mast in sympathy, and to ignore that gesture would be so wrong."

Eddie grinned. "Listen, everyone thinks we're down for repairs, so the place is all Roc's till whenever, okay? Anytime you want to start recording, just say the word, Rocco."

But the first-time skydiver was asleep between them, dreaming of watching the dolphins from above.

Twenty-Two

Bobbie sat up blinking in her bed. The TV was still on and the curtains were open enough to admit spikes of sunlight from an unwelcome morning. She swept two empty peanut butter fudge ice cream tubs onto the floor and sank back down as the sickening feelings of the day before returned. It was a while before she realized that the nausea was being accompanied by the repeated ringing of her doorbell. Peering through the window, she spotted a Santa Monica PD cruiser parked in front and heard voices outside the door.

"I'd suggest you zip it, young man. If Ms. Burnette doesn't assume responsibility for you, very little is going to seem amusing."

"Ah, hell, officer, I was just funnin' about borrowin' your spare uniform. Besides, hillbilly funk don't last but a month or two."

Bobbie opened the door a crack against all her better judgment, but after all, it was the law leaning on the buzzer.

"Ms. Bobbie Jean Burnette?"

"Uh-huh."

"Jeez, Bobbie, you look like you got dragged by a mule down forty miles of bad road, what the …"

The officer shot Delray a silencing glance. "I'm Officer Farina, Santa Monica PD. After receiving a complaint from an elderly patron, Mr. Jackson was apprehended at the Pico Kwik Kleen Laundromat this morning ... in his underwear."

Delray, wrapped in a police blanket, his skinny white legs sticking out of a pair of cowboy boots, flashed Bobbie his best homegrown "you know me" smile, but quickly straightened up as Officer Farina continued. "I've taken possession of a hunting knife that Mr. Jackson admits is his. That can be claimed by someone fully dressed at a later date, but for the moment, I understand that this is Mr. Jackson's temporary residence while he vacations in California."

Despite this last statement sounding more like a question, Bobbie opened her mouth to speak, but nothing came out. Delray pretended to be distracted by the neighbour starting his lawnmower as the officer handed Bobbie a form. "Okay, Ms. Burnette, just sign here and I'll be on my way. I'll leave it to you to explain the difference in wardrobe standards between California and Alabama." Unwrapping the blanket from an unrepentant Delray, the officer headed for his car. "Good day."

Waving feebly at her now-curious neighbour, Bobbie allowed Delray to slide past her into the apartment. "Man, that cop made me leave my favourite Wranglers and that brand new Fruit of the Loom v-neck at the damn washeteria. What kinda hospitality is that?" He made for the bathroom while pulling his wedgie back into place. "I mean, who knows where that blanket's been, right, honey?"

Bobbie glared at Delray as he ceremoniously wrapped a towel around his waist. "Wouldn't want to frighten you, baby, you look a little wrung out." He smirked and headed for the kitchen. "What's on the menu? I need a little something for the old breadbasket, and it's been slim pickins in that dumpster. I had to bum change 'fore I had enough for a box of Lone Stars."

"Don't call me 'baby,' you no count lowlife peckerwood. As soon as that cop is outta sight, you're gonna vaporize and never come back, you hear! Just for the record, what were you doing hangin' around the washeteria in your skivvies and boots? And what were you thinkin' tellin' him you lived here 'temporarily'? I think your brain is on permanent vacation, you deep-fried lummox."

"Hmm. Grolsch, what's that, health food beer, hon?" Delray stood in front of the now-open fridge while Bobbie leaned on the doorframe and tried to collect her thoughts. "Funny-lookin' beef jerky you got." He pointed warily at a package of sun-dried tomatoes and winced as he tore a strip of skin off of his finger trying to twist open the beer. "You got any baggy pants I could loan for a bit? I only had but the one pair. 'S why I was half naked at the Kwik Kleen. I wouldn've bothered washin' them, but I fell into the dumpster tryna reach this big ole taco." He leered at Bobbie and nodded. "Those might do, they look a little generous. I'll turn th'other way while you slip 'em off, all right, junebug? Just kiddin'." Delray leered in the direction of Bobbie's midriff. "Hey, you getting' a little pooch on you, sweetheart?"

"Delray Jackson, they sure drained the gene pool when you jumped in. Of all days for you to show up at my door. I've met pitchforks with more sensitivity." She closed her eyes and put a hand on her forehead, rubbing slowly.

Genuinely stumped, Delray did his best. "Is it Zippy, that little pet rabbit of yours' birthday? If it is, I'm sorry, I plum forgot."

Bobbie hardly knew where to begin. "His name was Flippy, and, no, that's not it. Have you been sleeping under a truck for the last day?" Delray shrugged guiltily as she stared, seeming to wish to turn him to stone.

"Listen, honey bunny, uh, sorry, I was gonna tell you about my bunkin' in the ga-rage, but you didn't give me much of a chance and ..."

Her voice came out like a broken whisper. "It's Roc ... he's dead ... and I didn't say goodbye, I was angry ... oh sweet lord, Delray, I don't know what to do, I ..."

"I swear to you on Floppy's grave, Bobbie Jean Burnette, I did not do it. I was only tryna throw a bit of a scare into him with that little old knife of mine, you gotta believe me. There wasn't much blood. I wouldn't ..."

"What are you on about, Delray?" she sobbed. "He died in a helicopter accident. It was on the TV and everything."

Barely managing to hide his delight at this news, Delray tried a little awkward humour. "Sorry, mine's been on the fritz, baby." He put his arm around her shoulder while she explained through her tears.

"He was promoting his new record, and it all went wrong. At first, I thought it was part of the stunt, but ... oh I just know he wrote that there song for me ..." At this point, words wouldn't come, and Delray did his best to comfort her while he grinned over her shoulder.

"Well, what do you say we step out for a bite of something, june bug? Eating something hot and greasy always picks me right up." Delray let the towel slip to the floor. "Of course, I've always got other ways to make you feel better."

Bobbie stood back in disgust and disbelief before slugging Delray square in the nose and pushing him out the door with surprising strength. He stayed on the porch moaning for a while and ringing the bell until he saw Officer Farina's car rounding the corner. Bobbie ran her hand over her tummy before closing the curtains and climbing back into bed.

Twenty-Three

Roc slept late, the sleep of the dead, he thought wryly as he looked around the tiny bedroom above the studio. How many years had it been since he'd crashed here after an all-night session, too tired to drive, or more likely planning to wake up and jump back into work. He saw his guitar propped up in a corner underneath a poster from the first UK tour with the Hammersmith Odeon date in bright orange letters, the O representing the olive in the cocktail glass logo. Eddie had always been fastidious in his swag collecting, and Roc spotted an ancient "Pet Roc" from the first Japanese tour on the wall among the "All Access" laminates and limited edition t-shirts.

These would have to go soon if Roc was going to live in the present or whatever place in time he was inhabiting. The desert island discs were lined up beside a blaster next to a stack of towels under one of Eddie's trademark post-it notes.

Welcome to the afterlife! Coffee and supplies in the kitchen. Check out your new patio.

Roc pulled on a pair of black jeans and a t-shirt and followed the smell of coffee. He recalled Eddie telling him last night about a warning light system he'd installed in case someone dropped by. It had sounded a bit like a Bond fantasy, but Uncle and Eddie would love that. At the height of last night's drunkenness, they had gleefully described their trip to the spy shop on Sunset, and Uncle had proudly displayed his voice disguiser and monocular. The kitchen had more post-it notes about cup rinsing and the location of paper towels, and the fridge was stocked with Roc-friendly fare. Grabbing a coffee, his notebook, and guitar, he followed the note marked *Patio — this way >>>*, as if there was any other possible location than the roof.

Eddie had definitely gone to some effort in anticipation of Roc's arrival. Surrounding a lounge chair, table, and umbrella ensemble was an arrangement of palms and jasmine. Purple bougainvillea covered the redwood fence that encircled the patio. Roc spotted a cellphone, a jar of pens, a remote, and another note from Eddie on the table pointing toward the plants. He hit "play," and from speakers in the shrubbery came the opening of an old song of his called "Sky Child" from the second album, or was it the third? He listened till about the bridge, and recalling Frankie's first experiment with the electric cello, muted the rest of the song, laughing.

The San Fernando valley had always represented "the other side of the hill," and since the band had stopped recording at Eddie's and Uncle had moved his office from that glorified treehouse in Laurel Canyon, Roc hadn't seen too much of the valley. It was notoriously ten degrees hotter in the summer, with constant air quality alerts and a tacky bleakness that kept the chic-at-heart away. With few exceptions, fine dining was with a plastic fork, the parks were to be avoided, and the same five action flicks played at every mall. In short, a cultural wasteland and the ideal place for an allegedly dead rock star to disappear. That said, Eddie's studio was tucked away in a quiet and green corner of Toluca Lake. A giant magnolia tree combined with the jasmine to do battle with the hydrocarbons that hovered over the valley like airborne sewage. There were hummingbirds and butterflies and fresh lemons most of the year. A distant siren was drowned by the beep of a trash truck backing up, then a plane landing at the nearby Burbank Airport. *Relatively peaceful*, thought Roc, as he listened to the sound of his breath and felt the clutter of recent days fall away. He picked up his guitar, noticing that Eddie had changed the strings, and strummed aimlessly, finding that place where ideas and emotions mingle, and sometimes become songs.

Roc's songwriting reverie was broken by the purr of the cellphone on the table beside his notebook. Seeing Uncle's ID, he picked up. "Eddie's Afterworld. Better late than never."

Uncle chuckled hoarsely in his "been on the phone yelling all morning" voice. "My brother, your career has never been this vital. I've only got a minute, but check this out — the label had two hundred thousand units of the CD on order before the business day began. They're working on a commemorative limited edition of the single with a platinum-embossed swan on the label. The old Casey Kasem special from '98 is bumping *ER* next week, and you won't believe how cool this video is looking. The beach footage rocks. We've got a freeze of you spread-eagled just before you were wound back up, and it spins and floats like a butterfly. And I found a cutaway of Julie and Marie staring up at the sky, bosoms heaving with concern, that'll break your heart. Anyway, I gotta jet, I want to prime Nick before the coast guard questions him, and I've got to start planning the memorial. Let me know if you have any thoughts. Listen, this is the only number I'll call you from, okay? Later."

Replacing the cell on the table, Roc leaned back in his chair, guitar still on his lap, and watched a hummingbird feeding in a bougainvillea blossom. He'd read somewhere that their wings flap about fifty times a second. *How do they suspend themselves like that, seeming not to move in midair?* he wondered.

Twenty-Four

Working his way through Santa Monica, down back alleys, in and out of doorways, through parks then crossing the vast Veteran's Cemetery in broad daylight in his underwear had taxed all of Delray's wild hog hunting skills. The only troublesome incident had been in a yard big enough for the Crimson Tide to practise in, when that maid had chased him around the pool and into the hedge with a mop. Screaming "Fire!" in the rear door of the Kwik Kleen Laundromat had been an unfortunate necessity, and he had needed every minute it took to locate his still-damp jeans and t-shirt before the Santa Monica Fire Department's finest showed up. He gave his name as Guy Hunt, figuring correctly that the SMFD boys wouldn't recognize the name of a disgraced former governor of Alabama.

Air-drying as he walked, admiring himself in car windows and with a mighty thirst on, Delray found himself pleased with the new circumstances of his life as he approached Uncle's office on Wilshire Boulevard. With Roc out of the way and a chance to get into the business himself, he figured he'd give Bobbie a couple of weeks to get over it, then he'd slide back into her life smooth as an oil spill. In the waiting area of Uncle's office, where all hell seemed to be breaking loose, he tried a little Elvis sneer on Candy, the receptionist, but he ended up looking like he'd smelled something funky. "Hillbilly alert," she whispered into the intercom.

Inside Uncle's office, a morose Danny Cocktail sat on the couch drumming on his lap, while Uncle sat cross-legged on the carpet, surrounded by phone messages, an untouched Flora Kitchen take-out container next to him. "Oh, shit, I forgot. Order in a half dozen Lone Stars and see if he can hang in. What else?"

"The Savage kid is begging for the video today. MTV is saying they'll waive the rights to use of the *Beach Blast* footage for the other networks in exchange for a seventy-two hour window and exclusive rights to shoot the memorial."

"Tell him I've got my best man on it." Uncle grinned at the thought of Justin clamouring for Roc Molotov's work.

"A Detective Hancock wants to talk to you about the chopper stunt, and Nick says everything was cool with the Coast Guard interview. He gave the dude a copy of the pre-flight photo; says it'll go from evidence to eBay in no time."

"Get the cop's number, and I'll call him from the car. Any word from Max Stone?"

"I was just about to tell you, he's on four, and he doesn't sound happy."

"Thanks, Candy. See if you can keep numb nuts out of trouble while I deal with this."

Uncle rubbed his hand in circles on his head and closed his eyes momentarily before looking up at Danny like an indulgent parent. "Danny-boy, *I* believe you, but that's not the point. No one is going to care if you've never heard *Revolver*. You wrote 'Cross the Line,' and it sounds like a rip of 'Good Day Sunshine.' Let's see what Max has to say." Hitting the flashing button on line four, Uncle called out to the speakerphone, "Heyyy, Dr. Maximum, what's up?"

"Uncle. I'm stunned about Roc. Have they really exhausted the search that quickly? This was one of the good guys. I just can't believe it. Condolences on your friend. On The Cocktails plagiarism thing, I've got nothing but bad news. The publisher wouldn't even discuss the idea of calling it a co-write with Lennon/McCartney. How the hell did this get by, surely those morons must have had some clue while they were …"

"Yeah, Max, I've got Danny with me here, and we all feel kinda dumb about this."

Danny, red-faced and standing, pointed a finger at the phone. "Okay, Mr. Five bills an hour, I'm sure you didn't think I was a moron when you were doing our publishing deal, did you?"

"Danny, I'm sorry, I didn't realize you were … I mean, look, I'm sure it was unintentional, but of all the catalogues you had to dip into …"

Danny's lip was quivering at this point, and Uncle got up and started massaging his shoulders. Shaking him off, Danny leaned into the speakerphone. "Easy for you to say. What? You never lifted someone else's paragraph three, clause (b) or whatever …"

"Danny, that's called precedent, and it's what you're supposed …"

"Okay, okay, well what about 'Twinkle Twinkle Little Star' and 'Baa, Baa, Black Sheep'? I'm gonna be a dad soon, and I've been learning those songs. Have you ever noticed how close they are? It's ridiculous, but no one starts talking copycat there, do they? Well, do they?"

"I think we're likely into public domain with those particular copyrights, Danny, but we're getting a little off track. Bottom line, Uncle, they want all the publishing, two points on everything to date; you have to agree to drop the song from all future pressings, and issue an apology in *Billboard* next week."

Uncle saw Danny winding up and getting ready to kick the phone, and he gently steered the disgruntled Cocktail back to the couch. "I don't have a problem, Max, if that'll make it go away. The label is already onto 'Say It Don't Spray It' for the next single, and there's going to be quite a bounce for the boys once the box set comes out."

"I thought that wasn't coming out till Christmas." Here Max paused, and his voice got quiet. "I don't suppose Roc signed off before ..." he trailed off.

"As luck would have it, Max, he did, just before the uh ..." Uncle replied soberly. "And, Warren emailed me today that they want to move up the release. I think they feel it would be comforting to the fans."

Danny was staring out the window, biting his lip as Max brought things to a conclusion. "I guess we shouldn't be surprised. Well, listen; I'll do the paperwork on the 'Cross the Line' thing, and Danny, good luck with the baby. Uncle, you're going to have your hands full with probate issues surrounding Roc's uh, demise, if that turns out to be the case. Did you want someone in our office to handle that for you?"

Uncle's tone became unnaturally breezy. "All in good time, Herr Stone, but *danke schön* for all the good advice." Hanging up and turning to Danny, now sounding positively paternal, he smiled. "Problem? Solution. Listen, before you split, there's someone I'd like you to meet. I think he might be perfect for 'Cowboy Dude.' Did I tell you how much I like it? I mean, surf country could be huge." Hitting the intercom, he said, "Candy, would you ask Delray to come in?"

The bumpkin swaggered in with a band-aid on the bridge of his nose and a Lone Star quartet buzz, nodding along with an imaginary song in his head, and slapped Uncle on the shoulder. "Yo, Telly, how's it hangin'?"

Uncle gestured at Danny. "Delray Jackson, Danny from The Cocktails, writer of 'Cowboy Dude' and drummer extraordinaire for America's hottest band."

"Hot damn. You wrote that tune? Nice work. I'm fixin' to put my stamp on that baby and make us all some serious green. What do you say there, Dan the man?"

Nonplussed at Delray's cockiness, the drummer instantly regretted extending his hand once the handshake ended with a loud crunch of his metacarpal bones. "Hey."

Uncle had an inspiration. "Listen, Danny, why don't you take Delray back to your studio and put the vocal on there? You've got the master, and Eddie's place is down for repairs for awhile." Without waiting for a reply, he motored on, "I can't wait to hear what you two wild men come up with."

"Me three, Daniel, I'm itchin' to have a shot at that tune. It's a monster, man. Say, mind if we make a little brewski stop on the way? I need a little lip lube, know what I mean?"

Uncle escorted the twosome to the door and returned to his place on the carpet, putting his head back on the embroidered pillow and sighing deeply. The phone lines kept flashing, and he was just about to dial Marie's number on his cell when Candy cut him off. "There's an Emma Hoffman on two. She won't tell me what it's about, but she's real insistent. You want me to blow her off, Uncle?"

Uncle paused. Although he'd known it was coming, he hadn't expected it quite this quickly. He'd never met Emma Hoffman, only seen the name on legal documents, tax returns, that sort of thing. "I'll take it Candy, thanks." *This should be interesting.*

Twenty-Five

Three days later, Emma sat in a red leather booth at Musso and Frank's at Hollywood and Cherokee waiting for Uncle Strange. The reptilian waiter refreshing her water looked like an escapee from the Wax Museum down the street. She knew this place was famous but had a hard time imagining Marilyn or Douglas Fairbanks cozying up to the bar across the room. She'd read the *L.A. Weekly* cover to cover, laughing at the personals:

— *Clooney lookalike seeks dazzling blonde with silver dollar nipples into Proust, barbeque, and moonlight walks.*

— *Busty iconoclast with cascading black hair and full lips looking for SWM donor into museums, cats.*

— *Chunky Christian Bi wants hairy Middle Eastern sophisticate who can do foot massage.*

"Emma? Sorry to keep you waiting." Uncle, wearing an aquamarine caftan, used his most soothing tone as he slid into the seat opposite her. "I wish we'd been able to get together sooner, but …" He smiled and gestured with upturned palms. She winced when she heard his feet bang into her backpack, which held her laptop and camera.

Uncle watched as she brushed her hair out of her eyes. Even in the slanting late afternoon light, he could see Tabatha nineteen years ago, when a smitten Roc had introduced them backstage at the Beacon. The same deep calm, the almost placid expression, but with intense activity beneath the surface. Warm but untouchable at the same time. Uncle was intimidated by women like this, instinctively knowing that they were immune to his conman charisma. The uncomfortable silence ended with the arrival of the prehistoric server in red vest and black bow tie.

"I'll have a diet Coke, please," said Emma.

"Would you ask Juan if he'll do a chamomile on ice with a dash of sarsaparilla? Anything to eat?" Uncle looked up at Emma, wondering if she'd always be pencil-shaped.

"A salad, I guess."

"Bring the young lady the Musso mesclun." Uncle dismissed the waiter and shifted uncomfortably while Emma sat watching him. "This hasn't been a great year for sarsaparilla, but they don't carry the Siberian ginseng anymore." He rearranged the salt and pepper and sugar containers, not used to feeling the dynamic of the moment being out of his control. "Supposedly Chaplin got the idea for that scene in *The Gold Rush* while eating a baked potato here." The tour guide charm rang false, and he felt it. "The driver found your place okay? Blue Jay Way is kinda tucked up there in the hills, isn't it?"

Emma nodded and sipped on her drink. "It's my friend Megan's parents' place. They're sailing around the world and writing about it for *Conde Nast Traveler*."

"Seriously?" Uncle shifted again, drawing in a long breath. "George Harrison wrote that song there, you know. 'Blue Jay Way,' I mean." He continued after a silence. "Emma, I understand you wanting to come here, but realistically ... I mean, I'm sure this a very difficult time for you. Did your mother discuss any of the probate issues we'll be dealing with? As you may or may not know, Roc ... your father ... is considered 'missing' at this time."

"My mom is in Italy somewhere on an archeology tour with the museum. I can't reach her. She probably doesn't know I'm here, but I need to know what happened, and you're the only contact I have. Uncle …" She grimaced slightly. "It's too weird for me to call you that. Do you have another name?"

"Well, legally, but no one uses it anymore." He paused, seeing that wasn't going to satisfy her. "It's Karl."

"Hmm. Karl? Yes, that's better. Karl, you're my father's best friend. I know his songs, his career; a couple of months ago I even found some really cool letters, more like stories with illustrations, that my mom kept, but I don't know anything about him. I got gifts on my birthday and direct deposit cheques and that's about it. But I guess you're aware of that."

Uncle saw an opening to go into raconteur mode, something he was comfortable with. "We met in the schoolyard at P.S. 131 in Duluth. Your dad was about to get beaten up for wearing these blue checked pants and mirror belt, and even though I was terrified, I had size working for me, and I took his side."

Two hours, a dozen touching anecdotes, and a bottle of Chardonnay later, Uncle walked Emma to the sidewalk as the early evening scene on Hollywood Boulevard got underway. "Call me any time. I'll have the office send over passes for the memorial concert. Can I drop you somewhere?"

Emma said no thanks, and Uncle put his arm around her thin shoulders. "I'm glad we had this time. Emma, Roc was a brilliant man and a wonderful friend. I wish you'd known him the way I did. I'm so sorry about your dad."

As his car pulled up, she held Uncle's focus for a long, unblinking moment. "Why be sorry, Karl? We both know he's still alive." She pulled on her backpack and disappeared into a group of tourists on the sidewalk.

Twenty-Six

"Dick Edwards comin' at you with a brand new smash from the Roc of Minnesota." Roc couldn't help grinning at Eddie's well-practiced DJ routine on the talkback as he adjusted his headphones. Surrounded by candles and hunched over his guitar, he strummed through the chords for his newest song, written that afternoon on the patio. The days were beginning to blend together, and Roc found himself curiously calm, despite the storm of activity around his name outside the walls of the studio. Eddie's voice interrupted his concentration. "We've got company. Hang on, Rocco."

A blue light flashed above the door, and moments later Uncle burst in with a smug grin. "Hey, it's the high priest at work. I have an offering for you." He held up a VHS tape and bowed ceremoniously.

They went to the lounge, and Eddie popped the tape in. "Okay, it's a rough cut," Uncle said. "Sorry about the time code. But, check this. Tonight at eight p.m., it's an MTV exclusive, and they haven't seen it yet!"

The video began with a swirl of swan-shaped clouds that immediately gave Roc goose bumps as the opening wash of guitars ushered the song in. A montage of old concert footage treated in a silver colour accompanied the first verse, and you couldn't tell that it was from a different song. Roc was impressed, and Uncle was in his glory. When the chorus of "Swan Dive" began, the concert was overlaid with waves in slow motion then the distant image of Roc in his parachute harness. He squinted like a kid watching a horror movie, but Uncle made calming motions with his hand. Diving swans and leaping dolphins took over until the second verse. Uncle could barely contain his glee at the reaction shot of Marie and Julie on the beach, mercifully in soft focus. More waves, beauty shots of clouds, and a freeze frame of Roc in midair spinning slowly skyward brought the video to an end. An expectant Uncle looked at Roc.

"It's cool. You know I hate these things at the best of times," said Roc. "It's especially weird watching that skydiving stuff, but I'll get used to it, I guess." He shrugged and turned off the TV, preventing Uncle from playing it again.

"Too bad you couldn't have landed on those luscious dunes waiting below, mmm?" offered Uncle.

Eddie chuckled at this, but it flashed through Roc's mind that it could be awhile before he spent time with a woman again. He recalled that weird night with Marie and Julie, but then, quickly, his thoughts moved to Bobbie again, so he got up abruptly. "Listen, I'm in mid-masterpiece, so I'll catch you later, okay? Eddie, you want to go back to work?"

As Eddie headed back into the control room, Uncle turned to Roc and lowered his voice. "Congrats on having the hit record you deserve, my brother." Roc nodded, smiling, as Uncle continued. "I've got a favour to ask. You remember I told you I was trying to get something going for Marie? Honestly, I'm not sure how much hang time the Cocktails thing has got, and I think this would be a great time to launch some new projects." Roc's suspicions grew as Uncle's tone turned a bit sheepish. "She's all over me to …" he smirked, "I mean aside from that … to have one of your songs." Seeing Roc stiffen, he continued quickly. "Hey, relax, she knows there's lots of great stuff in the vault. She could do a duet with you, I mean with your supposedly late self, and what a great way to launch her career. What do you think?"

Roc stood silently and began slowly shaking his head. "Man, you have done some outrageous things over the years to get it wet, but this might be the *coup de grâce*, Uncle. Call me when the drugs wear off." Without waiting for a reply, he passed through the door back into the studio, leaving Uncle with open palms and a sad sack expression.

Twenty-Seven

Bobbie stood in the kitchen doorway, surveying the wreckage that her life had become in the last week. The curtains were still drawn; the light on the phone continued to flash, ignored, and the garbage overflowed. The capper was the empty Sara Lee box on the counter and the reek of sour cheesecake. Taking a deep breath, she went to work cleaning up before heading back to the bedroom and putting on a fresh pink tracksuit. She grabbed her iPod, dialed up Lucinda Williams, and headed for the street. On her way out, she ran into the super and asked casually, "Y'all haven't seen a goofy looking guy with short blonde hair hangin' around, have you?"

The super nodded. "There was a cowboy-looking fella singing and riffling through the trash a few nights ago, but I threatened to call the cops, and I haven't seen him since. Was he bothering you?"

"No, I'd just noticed him around and wondered, that's all. See you later." Bobbie headed down the street and broke into a jog, feeling better already. Returning about forty-five minutes later, and having attracted more than her share of male attention, she felt ready to surface again. Showered and changed, she picked up an iced mochachino and plugged her dead cell into the charger in the car.

"Hey there, my funky skunk, did you change your stripe while I was away?" She giggled, pulling onto the PCH. "I love that kooky accent. Call me your little cauliflower again."

Delray came into the garage studio in a Cocktails t-shirt, bobbing his head as he handed Danny a can of Lone Star. Danny grabbed it with a lurch and laughed as the foam spilled into the console. "Dig this, big guy!" He hit play and cranked the speakers to Richter scale levels. A spaghetti western guitar line moaned over a steady drum and bass groove until the vocals kicked in. A major shit-eating grin enveloped Delray's face as he listened to his voice bathed in deep reverb.

"There's a fella stands tall on his board

Hangs with the surfers and walks with the Lord …"

"Awesome. What d'ya think, Danny my man, is that cool changing it to 'hangs' instead of 'swims'?"

"I don't give a rat's ass. It's a fugging smash, DJ. I played it for Gwen this morning, and she was blubbering by the end of the first verse. 'Course she's preggers, so that might not count for much, but I think it seriously rocks."

"So, when we gonna play it for Telly? You figure he'll be stoked?" Delray played air guitar behind Danny's chair.

"Hell with Uncle. With him it's all about Roc and that fucking memorial he's planning. I know who to send it to. That record company dude, Justin, he really gets what we're doing. I'll send him an mp3; it'll just take a second." Danny took a slug of his beer and fumbled with his keypad, but not enough to prevent the song from heading for Justin Savage's inbox.

Uncle lay on the floor in Marie's bedroom face down while she polished his head slowly and tenderly. "I would not assume that l'Occitane made this for the head of the man, but it smells as some lavender, no?" Uncle rocked his head slightly in agreement. Marie inhaled deeply. "There is always so much busy in here." Uncle groaned. Letting her hair fall around his face, she pressed her breasts into his ears. "But maybe there is a little place for *moi*, no?" Uncle purred deeply in reply. "I would sing for you if I had some song, my big man. Did you find what you promise, mmm?"

"Oh … no, but don't worry, my little *bonbon*, there are so many songs, and I'm sure you could sing anything you set your mind to." Uncle was emerging from his torpor and attempted to redirect the conversation to more carnal matters. "Why don't we perform a little duet before I have to go."

Marie tossed her hair back and slipped on a bathrobe. She picked Uncle's cellphone up from the bedside table. "You know, *monsieur*, I see a number that you call so many times, and I wonder if I am your only and one, eh?"

Uncle awoke in a hurry and hastily grabbed the phone from Marie, who shot him a wicked look. "It's one and only, my sweet, and don't you be concerned, I'm sure I can work out something regarding your career. Leave it with me."

Twenty-Eight

Emma soon realized she was the only pedestrian in this part of the city. A security cruiser slowed, and the uniformed driver peered out of the window. "Lost, ma'am?"

"No." She smiled quizzically at the young officer. "Just walking."

"Okay. It's just that I've never seen anyone walk in Beverly Hills before. It's not illegal or anything." She shrugged and waited until he put the cruiser back in gear. "You take care now. Sure I can't give you a lift somewhere?"

She shook her head and carried on down a series of winding streets lined with palm trees, musing about the city planner, who must have been a closet ornithologist. Blue Jay Way led to Warbler, Mockingbird, and Skylark, before she approached the throb of Sunset Boulevard down Doheny. A couple of emaciated guys in leather pants and sunglasses emerged from the liquor store on the corner and stared at her until she felt slimed.

It was everything she'd expected, which wasn't much, and different somehow. The strip hadn't aged well, she imagined. Sure, a few new layers of neon were in evidence, based on the old photos she'd seen. But it was sleazier than she had anticipated, even more so than Hollywood Boulevard in some hard-to-pin-down ways. There were the clubs she knew her dad had played when he was starting his career, and that made her smile. She pictured his name on the marquee above the Roxy, or maybe the Rainbow Room. Scantily clad girls clustered outside now, smoking, trying to look cool rather than just cold. Guys in Italian clothes sauntered by, checking them out, trying to look sophisticated rather than just old. Every car played a different tune, like an ad for its inhabitants. Everyone was on the make.

Across the street she excitedly spotted the sign for the Viper Room, Johnny Depp's place, where well-known bands would show up under assumed names, where River Phoenix had died. Her thoughts drifted again to her dad, and she realized that it was probably some early sign of grief that had led her to claim that he was still alive as she left Uncle the other night. Or just a desire to mess with Karl's oiliness. She'd read the accounts and knew that the coast guard was calling it a probable death by drowning after interviewing the helicopter pilot and searching up and down the Malibu coast. Sure, something in that footage was weird, and she couldn't put her finger on it, but it was beyond wishful thinking to assume he was anything but gone. She realized she'd been standing on the corner of Larrabee and Sunset for too long and decided she might as well check out the Viper Room. She didn't recognize any of the bands on the marquee, but a cold drink in a loud room was definitely the best idea of the moment.

Once inside, she instantly regretted her decision when she saw that the room was wall to wall with the same types she'd tried to avoid making eye contact with on Sunset. Determined to get something for her eight dollar cover charge — "a buck a band" the sign had said — Emma sat on a stool with her back to the wall and ordered a glass of wine. No doubt the only patron in a sweater and sneakers, she calculated she might be the only girl with her real hair colour and god-given flat chest. The latest band was just taking the stage, and a monotone voice introduced them to the indifferent crowd. "Ladies and gentlemen, please give a warm Viper Room welcome to Maureen's Ankle."

A table of, she guessed, band friends cheered too loudly, and the rest of the room barely glanced toward the stage. Maureen's Ankle started with a couple of droning minor chords and proceeded dirge-like through a repertoire of almost identical songs that elicited a feeble response from the cooler-than-thou crowd. There was a dreamy quality about the music that Emma kind of liked, and she ordered another drink, nodding along until their short set ended with applause that suggested relief rather than appreciation.

A couple of small buildings with tattooed arms began to clear the stage immediately, and the crowd carried on as before. She noticed a cute guy she hadn't seen earlier noticing her, and they both looked away before looking back at the same time and laughing at being caught. She realized that he was the drummer in the band she had just seen. He had a torn denim vest over a scrawny chest and hair with a mind of its own. She stopped noticing the earring collection once he smiled awkwardly and asked if he could sit down.

"Sure. Hey, I like your band. Have you guys been together long?"

"Kind of on and off over about six months, but the singer's in two other bands, so, you know …" He trailed off and smiled again, shrugging.

"Cool. I'm Emma. Want a drink?"

"Yeah, thanks. I'm Stick Neff." He pronounced it "Steek" and noticing her suppressed grin, added, "It's a band name thing. My real name's Richard."

"There must be a story to go along with that," she said teasingly and waved at the waitress.

"Well, okay, you see, Christopher Guest played this character called El Supremo, right? I know this is obscure, but he wore a fez and a neck brace and said in this weird accent how he always had a 'steek neff.'" Hearing Emma giggle, he continued, embarrassed. "I had this accident on my bike and … you asked."

"What is it with the pseudonym thing here? I feel incomplete without one. What do you think I should change my name to?"

Stick paused before answering, "I wouldn't change anything about you." Realizing that the sincerity of his tone sounded out of tune with the room, he tried to keep the conversation going. "You don't look like the usual Viper Room type. Where are you from?"

"New York via Boston. Can't you tell by the crease in my pants?" She smiled. "I'm staying at an old friend's place near here, and I just wandered in. This place is sort of famous, isn't it?"

"Yeah, I suppose so. We're just hoping some of the lustre rubs off on us, but they didn't seem to be too into our set." He took a long slug of beer while Emma sipped her wine.

"Well, I really liked it. Have you guys recorded anything yet?"

"Nothing for public consumption. We did some demos in my dad's studio. He's a recording engineer. Our sort of manager says we should post them on the Internet, but I'm not sure we're really ready yet."

The lights were going down as guitars were being placed on stage for the next band, called the Love Cats, judging by the sign on the bass drum. Emma looked back at Stick, thinking how vulnerable he seemed when talking about his music, and she blurted out, "I'd like to hear your demos."

"Really? Well, I'd like to play them for you sometime," he said, shifting uncomfortably on his stool. "I mean, anytime you want, really."

"How about now?" Emma realized that the third glass of wine was emboldening her. She also had a strong feeling about the person she'd just met and trusted her instincts completely.

"Yeah, okay." He hesitated visibly.

"Not if you don't want to," she added quickly.

"Oh no, I do. You see, the tapes are at my dad's place, and it's under repair and the studio is down for a while, and he's all weird about anyone being in there now … I think it's some insurance thing."

Emma tried to read through his hesitation as the next band took the stage to a chorus of cheers from the room. Love Cats was an all-girl outfit that looked like they needed chaperones, but the crowd was primed for whatever they had to offer.

"Oh, hell, let's go. I've got a key. We'll just have to make sure my dad's not around. He's paranoid, really bent out of shape lately, too much weed in his youth, probably." Emma grinned. "The studio's in the valley. I've got an extra helmet for my bike."

He said a few goodbyes to the other band members and friends who were opting to stay for the Love Cats. In the alley behind the club, he handed Emma the helmet, and they climbed onto his bike. "The studio's small, nothing upscale or Hollywood or anything, but it's cool. My dad recorded all the early stuff by that guy Roc Molotov and his band, The Cocktails. Heard of them? He's the guy that just died. He was a good friend of my dad's."

Emma wondered if the flush she felt rising up her neck to her face registered in the dim light of the alley behind the Viper Room.

Sensing her discomfort, he paused. "You sure you're up for this?"

"Definitely," she replied seriously and managed a smile as she pulled on her helmet. "As long as I can call you Richard."

Twenty-Nine

Perched on an embroidered orange cushion in a booth at Matsuhisa, Uncle Strange pushed the tiny boat-shaped eggplant around his plate, enjoying the moment and nodding at Justin Savage. As soon as he'd read Savage's enthusiasm for Danny and Delray's cockeyed collaboration, Uncle had hastened to take credit.

"I'm loving this surf country hybrid. Totally, pardner." Justin took another sip of sake, obviously amused by himself. "So, we'll shoot the video for 'Cowboy Dude' and the new Cocktails the same day, so the band can be in both. We'll wardrobe them up for Delray. Nudie suits like the old Burrito Brothers look, with a little splash of Beach Boys. What do you think — should we call him Del Ray and leave it at that?"

"Uh-uh," said Uncle. "Too beachy sounding. Remember, this guy's all hush puppies and beef jerky. I'll tell you, though, based on what I read in the eyes of the women who've met him, this Bubba's got it goin' on."

"Go figure, man. He actually referred to the 'git box' playing in the song."

"I can believe it. But check this; he flat-out refused to do a song at the memorial. I mean, I don't give a shit. No one knows him from a hole in the ground, and we've got the immediate world crying for a spot on the bill, but still ... by the way, did business affairs get all the waivers for broadcast and the concert album?"

"No worries," said Justin. "We can probably hit them with a full stat rate if you want to push it. None of that reduced 'controlled composition' shit. It's our ball. Blade wants this one for 'Special Products' 'cause so much catalogue is involved. Cool with me, but I'd like to grab exec producer credit, put my personal stamp on the thing, if that doesn't mess with you, oh supreme keeper of the flame." Savage laughed a little too loudly, and the waiter pointedly ignored his "more drinks" gesture. He continued without giving Uncle a chance to reply. "Listen, a little closer to home, I don't suppose you could set me up with Marie's bosom buddy for the concert?" He narrowed his eyes and leaned conspiratorially close to Uncle, who held his hands out and grinned smugly.

"Consider it a fearsome foursome, my brother." Uncle paused dramatically and lowered his voice to a serpentine level. "Can we celebrate Marie's label deal after the show?"

Justin leaned back in his chair and nodded with a smile of admiration. "Uncle Strange — ever the negotiator — and always ..." he paused to raise his empty glass, "always, my brother!"

Uncle poured half of his sake into Justin's glass and clinked them together as the two laughed in unison. Uncle saw Roc's number displayed on his cell and excused himself to go to the restroom.

"Don't be in there too long, or I'll know who you're talking to," smirked Justin as he grabbed the passing waiter's sleeve and handed him a pair of Ulysses S. Grants.

Thirty

"*Beach Blast* has been following the Molotov mystery from day one, as you're, like, totally aware. In new developments, we've learned that a turquoise bracelet, identical to the one Roc was wearing in this photo from the '92 'Magic and Mayhem' European tour, washed up on Zuma Beach. Check it out, right?"

How in God's name did that get there? Roc puzzled. Uncle — of course — he'd given the bracelet to Uncle, who'd wanted it to impress some hippie chick working the merch table.

"So this morning I was trying to scope the chopper that Roc jumped from, right, so I went down to La Jolla, where the surf was crankin', by the way ... and we were shooting through this mondo privacy gate when this assmunch starts going ballistic at the camera. 'Course, when he spots yours truly and the *Beach Blast* mike, he chills right out, so I asked him some questions."

Roc sat up when he saw Eddie's brother, Nick, and the helicopter in the background.

"Whoa, bitchin' chopper dude!" Nick's smile looked strained as the mike was thrust between the bars of the gate. "Is that a Gulfstream?"

"No, it's a Twin Otter ... made by DeHavilland. They're used a lot for skydiving."

"Righteous! Chad Sparx here from *Beach Blast*. You're the dude who flew the Roc Molotov ultimate flight, right?" Nick nodded soberly as Chad continued. "So was Roc wearing a turquoise bracelet that day or what?"

"I, uh, didn't notice Mr. Molotov's jewellery that morning I'm afraid, why?"

"One of our regular beach bunnies found it, and I recognized it from my research." Nick appeared momentarily startled. "So, we were waiting on the beach when Roc went aerial and got all rag dolled. Like what happened, man?"

Nick paused before answering, "Well, it was initially pretty straightforward from my point of view. We were flying IFR, that's …"

"You mean Instrument Flight Rules? For flying without seeing where you're going, right?" Chad's permanently stunned expression belied the directness of his line of questioning.

"That's … that's right, Chad. Let me be clear, we met the minimums for a shallow IFR approach. We didn't know anything had gone wrong until I got radioed just as I was landing back here."

"Like, do you buy the coastally trapped wind reversal theory of how he got cashed, dude? Sounds bogus to me."

"That's not for me to say." Nick's gaze turned distant. "It's a tragedy, I know that much."

"For sure, man. Thanks." Nick smiled and was turning away when Chad Columbo'd him. "Oh, one last question, bro … did you know Roc Molotov couldn't swim?"

Nick looked like he'd swallowed a cockroach. "No, I wasn't aware of that. Listen, I've got to check my flux capacitor, all right?"

"Solid! Just like in *Back to the Future*. Cool."

As Chad signed off and intro'd the "Swan Dive" video, Roc felt he could live without seeing it one more time and walked out onto the deck. The interview had left him uneasy. He hadn't thought much about the possible repercussions of this deceit being uncovered, but it was out of his hands. The bracelet ruse reminded Roc of Uncle's ease with deception. He'd been glad of this capacity in the past, why not now? More than ever Roc felt like Uncle was operating in two versions of the same reality.

Closing his eyes, he inhaled the sweet smell of an orange tree; it seemed to take the edge off his hermetic world. He knew he was getting restless — it was inevitable, Uncle had warned him, and Eddie tried to be resourceful in the diversions department, arriving back daily with menus from the city's best restaurants, an archery set, a candle-making kit, old Justice League of America comics, and in an unthinking moment, a remote controlled helicopter.

Roc's mind wandered once again to the upcoming tribute concert, and his curiosity spiked. Uncle had listened to his suggestions for performers and promised to leave certain songs off the list of possible choices. He had respectfully noted Roc's concerns over staging, visuals, and keys for the songs, but refused to clear the speeches beforehand, claiming impracticality. "You can't write your own eulogy, my friend," Uncle had said. It was hard to disagree, but it prompted a series of queasy images of rants and tributes and overwrought versions of his songs by people swaying and holding hands.

He wandered back inside and watched the news segment about The Cocktails plagiarism settlement, shaking his head then turning the sound off. That never would have happened when they were together, Roc thought, realizing how long ago that seemed. He was refining a riff, leaning over the guitar, when he looked up and saw something startling on the screen — his mother with an MTV mike in hand, standing outside the family home in Duluth. He quickly hit the mute switch.

"... used to play catch on the lawn right here." She gestured from the weed-infested patch that fronted their home to the drive on her right and the garage door. "He broke that window with a slap shot one time. He wanted to play for the Huskies when he grew up, but once he got that guitar ..."

Roc got up and hovered over the television, staring in shock. As the camera panned past a group of curious kids and neighbours behind a rope, she continued. He noticed she was wearing her ever-present bunny slippers.

"C'mon in and I'll show you his bedroom. We never moved a thing, you know." Knowing this to be a blatant untruth, Roc clamped his hands on his head in disbelief. His mother passed through the living room, which must have been seriously redecorated in recent days. In place of the old tweed sofa was a tacky tan-coloured leather sectional that looked like it had just arrived from the IKEA showroom. "Yup, right behind that couch, him and his little brother would do skits for the family at Easter and Thanksgiving. He was just adorable in that turkey get-up with the paper feathers." Afraid to blink in the face of this travesty, Roc stood numbly, inches from the screen. "I often thought about those times when I'd see him in the music videos. Hideos, we call them around here. Hah hah!" she cackled. The camera followed Roc's mother down the hallway of the family home, and he found himself craning as if he could see outside the frame to locate things remembered from his past, even as that past was being skewered for any curious viewer with a remote in hand.

"What the fuck?" he blurted at the screen as the camera found his room, now done up like it was when he was six years old, or how his mother would want to imagine it. There were cowboy curtains, model sports cars, and plastic monsters everywhere and on the bed, a red toy ukulele. It was all so K-Mart Graceland, he couldn't absorb what he was seeing. He was momentarily distracted by the sound of a motorcycle revving down beside the building, followed by lowered voices, but his attention was drawn back to the horror on the screen.

"And here's the words to my little guy's first song." His mom got weepy as she held out a crumpled sheet of three-ring paper toward the camera. He could just make out the title, "Sequoia Sunset." Where the hell had she found that? "Of course, that was just the beginning," she said, regaining her composure on cue, "and by the way, we've got a numbered limited edition of the 'Sequoia Sunset' lyrics which you'll be able to order at the end of this program." Roc felt his stomach turn over. "Along with some rare guitar picks, also numbered." *I never used one then*, he thought in disgust. "Now, we can't make it to the concert in Los Angeles, but we're going to have our own hometown candlelight vigil over by the Lift Bridge, and Roc, honey, if you're out there somewhere, we miss you." She artfully wiped an imaginary tear from her eye and perked up as the camera pulled back to reveal a giant "Roc Molotov Home" sign behind her. He watched his mom wave to the departing camera and yell "Go Huskies!" before the screen began displaying the parade of merchandise available through MinnieMall Enterprises.

Teeth clenched, Roc had just picked up his cellphone to call Uncle when he heard music blasting from the studio below, and he froze, phone in hand.

The studio didn't look at all like the high-tech wonderland that Emma expected a musicians' sandbox to be, but Stick had prepared her for the fact that this place was pre-digital, pre-midi, pre-virtual everything. In fact, it looked more like a beach shack with instruments and equipment, housed in a couple of reasonably small wood-panelled rooms. There were framed posters of Roc Molotov and The Cocktails on most walls, and Emma fought to subdue her curiosity during Stick's tour.

"So the control room is through that glass, and that's where the engineer sits, and in here, the musicians and singers do their thing. It actually kinda looks like it did when I was a kid hanging out here, with the mikes set up and all the candles and guitars and stuff."

"And what are these little walls for?" Emma gestured toward dividers of various sizes around the room.

"Oh, those are baffles for isolating the musicians so there's not too much bleed between the tracks when they're recording." He pointed out a drum kit tucked into the corner of the room, surrounded by baffles and screens. "That's where I sit when I'm recording. A lot of studios have a separate drum booth, but my dad likes all the players in the same room, for the 'vibe,' as he calls it." He did a little yoga hand position, and they both laughed. "C'mon, I'll play you some of our stuff."

They passed through the double doors into the control room, where Stick dimmed the lights and pulled a disc from a shelf. "I don't know what's up with the repairs. Doesn't look like anything's been done; 'course that shouldn't surprise me. But it's weird, everything's still on." He loaded the disc and hit "play" as he positioned Emma in the oversized engineer's chair midway between the speakers. She tucked her feet underneath her and closed her eyes.

The same sound that she'd heard at the club rolled out of the speakers, but instead of sounding like droning and crashing, it took on a stark beauty as the music rose and fell. The lyrics were buried in the mix of guitars and drums, making it hard to tell what was being said, and the songs evoked a similar feeling as they went by; but at the end, Emma sat very still, feeling massaged by the sound. She didn't speak for a while, not wanting the spell to break. Finally, she turned the chair around and looked at Stick. "Amazing. Your music is beautiful."

"Thanks. I'm glad you like it. My dad says you can't hear the vocals, but I kinda like it that way. It's the Maureen's Ankle sound."

"I wouldn't change a thing." Emma smiled teasingly. "It's like a meditation to music or something. Does the singer write the songs?"

"No, I do. Most people think drummers don't write, 'cause we bang on things and don't play chords, but as you might have noticed, there aren't too many chords involved." He grinned shyly at Emma. "You want to go?"

"In a minute. The 'vibe' in here *is* pretty cool," she said, looking around at the old tape machines and the sprawling console with its tiny coloured lights in rows in front of her. Easing off the engineer's chair, she peered at the room through the glass. "So, how do they communicate with the musicians?"

"Like this," he replied, hitting the talkback button. "Hey, all you cats and kittens, it's the Stickman on K-ED radio, hoping you got a smooth groove goin' on tonight." They laughed at his suave DJ voice, so incongruous with his personality. "That's my dad's thing. He always cues the band like he's on the radio. Kind of a senior fantasy, I guess."

"It's working for me." Emma grinned. "Can I go back in the studio?"

"Sure," Stick replied and held the door for her.

She walked over to where an empty chair sat in the centre of the room, a couple of mikes placed in front of it. There were candles partly melted down arranged on a small table with a half-empty water glass; a music stand with some lyrics sat nearby. "So, when Roc Molotov recorded in here, where would he sit?" She turned back to Stick.

"Well, it's been a while ago now, but probably right about there, actually. I mean, I was a kid and usually more interested in what the drummer was doing. Once I fell asleep inside the bass drum and woke up screaming when Danny gave it a giant kick. They all thought it was hilarious, but I didn't ever do that again. Still wanted to be a drummer, though."

Emma, not really listening to Stick's anecdote, picked up the lyrics and read them to herself before putting them carefully back onto the stand. She pushed a finger into the soft wax of one of the candles. "What was he like?" Her voice had descended to almost a whisper.

Regarding her quizzically, Stick replied, "Roc? He was cool. He didn't try too hard like most people do with kids." He could see that he had her complete attention. "I mean, he never would have done that thing with the kick drum, you know." He paused, noticing that she wasn't looking at him. "Quiet I guess, but funny in a quirky way. A lot of the time he was absorbed in his writing, even when the rest of them were partying madly around him. It was like he just tuned them out or something. Frankie and Barry used to want to borrow me to go to the park to pick up chicks, but like, not Roc." He walked awkwardly around the mikes so he could see her face, and as she turned to look at him, he saw tears on her cheeks. "What is it? Emma?"

She paused a long time, trying to find her voice. "He was my dad."

"Roc? Roc Molotov? Wow. Cool." Stick took her hand and led Emma toward the exit door. "Let's go, okay? Tell me all about it later."

Once the panic had subsided, Roc brought his breath under control and considered what to do. Eddie had taken his annual drive to Twenty-Nine Palms to chill by the pool at the motel and soak up some desert air, having topped up all of Roc's supplies before he left. So what was going on? Burglars? Not unless they had a key and the security code. He fiddled with Eddie's tiny chrome inter-cam, but never having used it was able only to get a rotating image of various locations in and around the building, with no sound. For one maddening instant, he could make out two figures in the control room, but just when one of them passed close enough to be seen, her hair fell in her face and the screen jumped to the kitchen. The feeling of being trapped gradually gave way to a curiosity about what he was hearing. He couldn't make out the vocals through the floor, but the band had a kind of noisy majesty to it. Almost like a meditation to music, he thought when it ended about twenty-five minutes after it started. Then he heard nothing. He could briefly make out a young girl sitting in his chair in the studio, but then someone else's back stepped in front of the camera. After trying to reach Uncle for a while, he heard the roar of a motorbike in the alley and saw that the alarm had been reset.

Thirty-One

Uncle found Roc on the patio, surrounded by scribbled notes, absorbed in his music; he stood at the doorway watching his old friend in a familiar pose before announcing his arrival. In the light of day, he could see the bits of grey spiking through the black mop as Roc's head bobbed in time to the song he was trying to find. He'd been shaken by Roc's call last night concerning the intruders in the studio, and he knew that he was going to have to be at his reassuring best to accomplish his number one mission today.

"Hey!" Uncle strode onto the patio and saw that he'd completely surprised his friend. "Sorry, brother, do you want me to give you a little time? I can wait inside."

"Oh, hey. No, no ... I was just ... you know. Lemonade?" Roc indicated a pitcher on the table.

"Sure. Thanks. What are you working on?" Uncle played to Roc's vanity.

"It's just a fragment right now. Maybe it'll become something, maybe not." Roc played a restless riff on his guitar and sang in a world weary tone:

"A makeshift day the colour of rain
Did they scrape the light off the sky

> The hours roll past like cars on a train
> And I watch the world go by
> I can't feel the spin but I know it's happening
> Can't feel change or blood or anything."

"Then I've got another section, not sure how they connect; but remember in 'Hollow Hand' it was choruses from three different songs, and in a rehearsal we jammed them together because they were in the same key." Roc flipped the guitar on his lap and banged out an intense groove while half humming, half singing something that sounded like,

> "I hear voices
> How'd they get my number
> I read the news
> Words written on water."

Roc looked up at Uncle and laughed. "I don't know what the hell I'm writing about. The last line refers to Keats' gravestone, 'A name writ on water,' I think."

But Uncle could feel the ripple of anxiety beneath the surface of the lyrics that he'd just heard. "Very cool. I'd love to hear it when you're done. Listen, I'm sorry about that surprise visit last night. I'm going to redo the security set-up. Do you like pit bulls? Seriously, when Eddie gets back from Joshua Tree, we'll go to the spy shop, get it right, okay?"

"You two going to wear your invisibility cloaks?" Roc gave Uncle a skeptical smile. "Maybe pick up some cool matching night vision goggles?"

"Just want to protect your ivory tower, my man. So, do you want the good news first or the good news?" Uncle asked smugly, palms aloft. Roc put down his guitar and waited. "Your video is number one most requested and broke all records for one-day phones. Oh, and by the way, your album is platinum as of this morning." Uncle didn't try to hide his satisfaction at being the bearer of this news.

"You're kidding?" Roc knew he wasn't. "Amazing. And all I had to do was die. All right, you're a genius, I admit it." He reached out and shook Uncle's hand, and the two laughed together, glorying in the moment.

"I'm meeting with an agent this afternoon. I'm thinking about relocating the office, and she tells me she's also got some Big Sur properties for us to check out, in case you were wondering how to spend your *Higher than Heaven* royalties."

Roc smiled, nodding and thinking that this sounded good. He'd been yearning for the ocean lately and often fantasized about a life in northern California. His picture of this life was as foggy as the coastline he loved, but he could fill in the details later. The reverie passed. "On the subject of real estate, what in God's name was my mother doing on MTV? She got over my earthly departure awfully quickly," he added bitterly. "Did you see it? And who the hell is MinnieMall Enterprises?"

Uncle flashed a grin of resignation. "She got me at a bad time. I gave her the merch rights so she wouldn't ask too many questions. I'm not going to bore you with the mountain of probate issues on your future 'old' songs, but this was an easy way out. It's limited to the home tour stuff, and I think it's her way of handling her grief, keeping busy." Knowing Roc really didn't want to deal with this, Uncle moved on, his voice dropping into the obsequious register. "Listen, I know I caught you off guard the other night when I brought up the Marie thing, but," smelling resistance, he pressed on, "it's different this time. Yeah, Marie's got a rack you could start a religion around, but there's more to her. She's elegant, funny, smart. And she does this thing to my head." He involuntarily rubbed his gleaming dome. "I'm in love." Seeing Roc's bemused expression, his voice became urgent. "Wait, stop, I know you've been through all this with me, but … I think I want to marry Marie."

Roc eyed Uncle like he was waiting for the punch line that didn't come. "Marry? As in, I promise to honour, cherish, and fondle?"

Uncle smiled sheepishly and shrugged. "All right, I wouldn't be opposed to a see-through wedding gown." They laughed. Roc got up and put his arm around Uncle's shoulders.

"You're full of surprises today. I don't think I've ever heard you use the word 'elegant' before. And let me guess, you'd like my engagement gift to be a song for the bounteous bride, right?"

Uncle didn't reply but eventually nodded. Roc sighed, slowly shaking his head. "You're relentless. All right, why not? But no duet from the grave. You'll have to find someone whose vital signs would allow them to appear in the video."

Uncle laughed in nervous relief. "Most excellent. *Merci, mon ami.* I really appreciate this. Now, she doesn't have much in the way of vocal range, but she'll make up for it in attitude."

"I'll do my best to work that in. Keep the pout quotient high." Roc found himself amused that he had caved in to this most ridiculous request. Then he had a flash. "Just one condition. I want to go to the memorial." He locked his gaze on Uncle, preparing for the evasion that was sure to follow.

"Roc, that's not fair. You know that's impossible." Uncle looked deflated.

"Nothing is impossible, remember, Mr. Übermanager." He was sounding more determined, to Uncle's alarm. "Listen, this set-up is totally cool," Roc said, looking around the patio, "and I'm having a ball, cutting new songs as I write them, free from scrutiny by some pimply label hack. But, it's confining at times, and I know Big Sur's going to take a while to become a reality. And, frankly, I'm curious as hell and need some excitement."

"A couple of kids breaking in and playing music in the studio in the middle of the night wasn't enough of a buzz for one week?" Uncle failed to hold back his sarcasm. Even as he was working it out in his mind, he threw the question to Roc. "So, how do you propose we pull this one off? You want to strap on some wings and just kind of hover over the Wiltern Theater?"

"Use your imagination, big boy, unless Marie's sucked it dry. I don't know, maybe another trip for you and Eddie to Spies 'R Us. C'mon. Wheel me in inside an equipment case; rent a security guard uniform, nobody notices those poor sods. You don't have to come up with it right now, but I want to go, Uncle."

"Yeah, I can see that. All right," Uncle said wearily, "leave it with me. Just no stopping people in midsong and correcting the lyrics like at that Boulder folk festival." Uncle couldn't resist tossing out a memory painful for both of them.

Roc frowned and rolled his eyes. "Hey, one other thing. Do the security cameras record what they shoot? I'm awfully curious about who the hell was here last night. The band was pretty cool, for what it's worth."

"I'll have to ask Eddie. Okay, platinum pal, I'm outta here. Good luck with the writing." Uncle paused, taking in the setting. "It is nice here, isn't it? Well, you'll need your creative mojo working. Savage is already asking what's in the vault for the next release. Not many artists get to decide what direction their posthumous career is going to take."

"You're right," Roc smiled. "Hey, what do you think of this, a kind of grunge Maurice Chevalier thing?" He began slashing at his guitar and singing, "Every little breeze seems to whisper ... Marie," before coughing with laughter.

"You need to get out more," replied Uncle, shaking his head. "Just kidding. See you."

A few minutes later, Roc returned from the kitchen with lunch and fresh lemonade and sat down with his notebook open. While grabbing his guitar in the studio, he'd noticed a new post-it note beside the drums. *Against the ruin of the world there is only the creative act. — Kenneth Rexroth* Not really Eddie's style, he thought on his way upstairs. He tried to come up with a germ of an idea for Marie, but the whole notion seemed ludicrous. Nevertheless, he'd pretty much committed himself, and it was best to get it over with. After downing an avocado sandwich, he picked up the guitar and strummed aimlessly, watching a butterfly on the railing flapping its wings. Supposedly, they came back to the same place every year. *How do they know?* he mused. Relying on an old trick, he tried to picture the video before the song existed, but he kept seeing Marie playing an accordion on a bicycle with a baguette sticking out of her purse; Marie as Edith Piaf in a spotlight on the stage of the Olympia Theatre in Paris; Marie, with a cigarette holder sipping Pernod in a café in the rain. If he'd known what this song would lead to, he might have not bothered to write it at all.

Thirty-Two

Approaching the Wiltern Theater at the corner of Wilshire Boulevard and Western Avenue (hence the theatre's name), traffic was stalled in all directions. Overdressed music biz dudes in leather, denim, and cowboy boots, accompanied by underdressed dates in fishnets, bustiers, and too much jewellery, climbed out of limos and walked the remaining block or two to the venue, the 1930s deco movie palace that was hosting the Roc Molotov memorial concert. Fans clogged the streets with signs begging for tickets; bootleg t-shirt hustlers moved through the crowd hawking cut-rate memorabilia, cashing in on pre-concert enthusiasm before customers reached the legit vendors inside the hall. A pair of scruffy kids with guitars was standing on two newspaper boxes bellowing out a punky version of "Damn Straight" to the approval of no one. Flashbulbs popped when anyone vaguely recognizable emerged from a stretch with sunglasses on, waving. Most of the performers had been in the hall for hours, but among the glitzy latecomers, Jack and Sheryl arrived arm in arm, Susan and Tim followed minutes later, and the wow factor swelled with a sighting of Justin and his surprise date, Hilary. Publicists, politicians, and celebrity chefs had called in favours to join the "Song Celebration," as it was being billed.

Bobbie had followed the build-up to the event on MTV, wondering if she was going to be able to handle watching, knowing she couldn't bring herself to call Roc's manager, the unctuous Uncle Strange, to ask for a ticket. He'd only ever been cordial to her, but she always felt slimed by his gaze. When a courier arrived at her door with an envelope containing a ticket, she was surprised, but stunned wouldn't describe her reaction to the note inside.

Hey June bug,
Don't say I never did nothing for ya.
Peace, DJ

DJ? Delray? Peace? How could that be? Dumpster diving one day, showing up in his skivvies with a cop the next; and now he'd got his hillbilly mitts on the hottest ticket in L.A. No one else called her "june bug," that was for sure. Staring at the ticket, Bobbie realized how badly she really did want to be there, as though it somehow might get her closer to Roc one more time. What would *he* want her to wear? She started tossing wardrobe possibilities on the bed, humming "Swan Dive."

Emma and Stick locked up their motorcycle helmets and walked through the crowd, getting caught up in the buzz. Glamour-free, they passed easily by the camera crews and paparazzi into the theatre, stopping only for a quick security search, before taking their tenth-row seats. Emma clutched Stick's arm nervously as she took in the opulence of the hall, lit by giant vintage chandeliers. In this sea of L.A. hipness, she felt like an alien and was glad to have her new friend in the next seat.

An ambulance backed up to the rear of the building through a tight wedge of fans. The doors to the backstage opened, blocking the crowd's view of two masked medics who made their way quickly past security, accompanied by a scene-stealing Uncle Strange in a Stetson and black caftan.

"Overdose in the nosebleed section," he said with authority to the guard at the stage door, flashing an all access pass as they hurried up a small set of back stairs, medical kit in hand.

Bobbie gave her hair one last toss and locked her car. She smoothed the chiffon skirt she'd chosen (after much deliberation) over her jeans and walked quickly to the Wiltern, barely noticing the street scene she wove through. She was directed to her seat in a VIP section close to the stage and smiled at the young couple sitting next to her as she picked up the glossy black program on the seat. Noticing the place next to her was vacant, Bobbie looked down the row to an aisle where she spotted, to her horror, Delray in a white suit with giant roses embroidered up the sleeves and mirror glasses wedged in his heavily moussed coif. He was being slapped on the back by a slick young Hollywood hipster and chatting loudly with a matching pair of pouty bimbos. When she recognized one of them as the girl in the photo with Roc, her stomach flipped, and she turned away quickly, closing her eyes to gather composure for the long, uncomfortable night ahead. Picking up the program and looking at the cover shot of Roc, avoiding the camera as usual, provided no relief, so she let her hair fall in her eyes, blinking rapidly.

"Yo, june bug!" It had to be. Delray Jackson squeezed down the row toward the seat next to her. He flashed a peace sign to the silicone sisters, who were mercifully settling in at the end of the row. "Wassup, sugerplum?" he added as he kissed her airily on both cheeks. Bobbie was too taken aback to offer more than a vague smile in reply. The new Delray was as jarring as anything that she'd dealt with early in this evening; someone had scraped the shit off his aura and tweaked his swagger in the weirdest way. "What do ya think of the new duds, Bobbie Jean? Speechless, baby?"

"Thank you for the ticket, Delray. That was very thoughtful of you," she replied tensely, wondering how he'd pulled it off.

"No sweat, sweetheart," Delray grinned and leaned in conspiratorially. "Listen, I know this could be a bit rough on you, this whole tribute thing, so if it gets to be too much, we can always slide back to my new pad and work through any grief issues you're hankering to deal with."

Bobbie noticed the young girl next to her suppressing a laugh and digging her partner in the ribs at this overheard tidbit from the nouveau hick who was hovering over her. "Oh, I think I'll be all right, Delray. You just keep those healing hands on your side of the armrest, and I'll hold up just fine. What in the blazes is going on with you anyway?" She lowered her voice to a whisper. "All duded up like this and talking like them mister cools at the Starbucks all of a sudden?"

"Please turn off all cellular devices and two way pagers for the sake of your fellow patrons. The Wiltern Theater and Strange Savage Productions thank you," a deep voice intoned from above.

"Hang on, hunny bunny," said Delray, reaching into his pocket to extract a flashy new chunk of colourful technology. Squinting at the keypad, he randomly pushed buttons unsuccessfully, until Bobbie took the phone from his hand and switched it off.

"Gracias, gorgeous," he grinned, slipping the phone back into his pants pocket. "I'll just keep that little puppy next to my heart now."

As the lights dimmed, Bobbie noticed the silhouette of what looked like Uncle in a flowing outfit and cowboy hat sliding into his seat between the babes at the end of the row. As he sat down amid a flurry of greetings, one girl leaned over, removed his hat, and kissed the top of his head. The night got stranger still.

In the pit in front of the stage, a pony-tailed conductor in a silver lamé tux stood up and gestured dramatically with his baton. The room quieted, and the orchestra began a medley of Roc's best-known songs. Faces in the crowd lit up with smiles of recognition and perhaps at the absurdity of it all. An usher pointed a flashlight at an old couple bending over and sharing a little wooden pipe, and latecomers hustled into the few remaining seats.

When the hall darkened, a curtain parted on a private box that overlooked the room from a point near the arched ceiling. It was impossible to make out the two figures seated far back from the railing, but Eddie Dyck and his associate in a black toque and shades had an excellent view of the stage below.

"I knew this was going to be weird," said Roc, "but I feel like I'm in that Pink Panther movie where Clouseau attends his own funeral."

Eddie chuckled quietly, adding in his best bad French accent, "You want to know what is strannnge, I will tell you."

"Check out this program, the cover should have a doorknob on it, Ed."

"Yeah, that's Warren Blade's doing. It's pretty cool; I'm even in there in one of the studio shots, well, my left arm is, anyway. I think he used a lot of the shots they put together for the box set. All taste no waste."

"Man, that medic outfit was hot and itchy as hell. If CPR failed, they could pop the vic in, zip it up, and steam him back to life."

"You want a drink? Much as I'm enjoying the medley," Eddie smiled, "I think this would be a safe time to slip down and grab us a couple of lagers."

"Yeah, that'd be great. I'll tell you what you missed." Roc smiled back as he quietly closed the door to the box.

The medley ended to loud applause, and a spotlight hit the centre of the stage. Nervously twirling his drumsticks, Danny Cocktail walked to the mike in front of the curtain. He cleared his throat loudly, and it shook the room; this occasioned a ripple of soft laughter. "Uh … hi … good evening, ladies and gentlemen, and welcome to a 'Celebration in Song.' Umm … usually you can't see me through my cymbals, but I'm Danny from The Cocktails and …" Interrupted by a burst of warm applause from the house, Danny flushed but seemed glad of the chance to catch his breath. "I'm glad to be here tonight with you … I mean I wish I wasn't … but it's my … privilege to honour the man who gave me and the other guys their start and who wrote all the great songs you'll hear tonight … and who had really cool hair."

The encouraging laughter throughout the room broke the tension, and Danny continued. "I guess like most of you, I can't really believe he's gone, and I know it's a cliché, but while we're playing tonight, I feel like he'll be looking down on us and reminding me to hit my bass drum a little harder so he can hear up there." Smiles greeted this attempt at humour, and Danny braved on. "Thanks in advance to all the incredible performers who are going to be on this stage tonight, to MTV — you'll see their cameras everywhere, so behave yourselves — to all of you who supported us through the years, and most of all …" here he faltered and the crowd held its breath as if to help him along, "my best friend," Danny's voice dropped to a whisper, "Roc Molotov." The crowd roared, partly in relief, as the curtain parted, revealing the other two Cocktails wearing the Edwardian suits from the first album cover. Frankie leapt from atop his amp and hit the opening riff from "Main Street Serenade." The crowd got to its feet, clapping along. Danny jumped behind his drums and slammed into the groove as a grinning Simon LeBon raced to the mike and sang the opening lines.

> "It used to be a carnival but now it's a parade
> Listen to the Main Street serenade."

Delray grabbed Bobbie's hand and gave her no option but to join the standing crowd. Either Roc's demise or Delray's newfound status had enabled him to appreciate Roc's music wholeheartedly, and he pumped his fist in the air until the solo drove him to an unrestrained air guitar performance. Eddie and Roc were standing grinning in the private box, and Uncle fondled Marie in time to the song. A string of artists paid tribute in their own way as the evening went along. Bryan Ferry's ultra-slow version of "Sky Train" was one of the night's true musical surprises, and was topped only by a Meatloaf and Susanna Hoffs duet on "Deep Down" that had the entire Wiltern Theater singing along. Courtney Love's nude spoken word performance behind a screen of "We've All Got a Way to Fall" was bizarrely fascinating until she tumbled into the screen, sending it and her naked self into the orchestra pit. Intermission was announced silently by Jim Carrey, who transcended laryngitis by holding up a series of cards à la Dylan in *Don't Look Back*.

When the lights dimmed for the second half, a pious Uncle Strange welcomed a well-lubricated audience back with a gauzy anecdote about the first time he'd heard Roc singing in the coat closet of Mr. Golubchuck's music room. In the upper box, Eddie turned to Roc. "Heard this one. Do you fancy another pint, mate?" Roc nodded and turned his attention back to the stage. He'd heard the story before, but it was always interesting to note Uncle's newest embroidery on the old tale. Suddenly Eddie's phone rang, and it echoed through the hall, momentarily throwing Uncle off his mark and causing heads to turn upward.

"Shit!" Roc lunged for the phone and hit "answer." Panicking, he held it up to his ear and said a quiet "Hello?"

"Roc?" a familiar but distant voice said. "Roc, I need to talk to you. Roc?" Tabatha.

In desperation he affected a sort of caveman Slavic accent. "No Roc. He gone."

"Please, Roc, I have no time for this. It's Tabby. I'm on this dig in Umbria, and I've been out of touch for a while. Roc, are you listening?"

Curled in a ball on the floor of the private box, he pulled the medic's jacket over his head as he heard Uncle droning in the background. "Roc dead, lady. Sorry."

"Roc, have you been drinking? That's the worst accent I've ever heard. Listen, it's about Emma, she emailed me a week or so ago, and I just received it. She says she's coming to see you. Has she made contact?"

"He no is, madam. Oh, oh, not hear you." After making a series of static sounds with his mouth, Roc hastily hung up and switched off the phone. He worked to calm himself down. The thought of never meeting Emma caused an ache he'd have to get used to; file that along with some other regrets. Down below he could see The Cocktails picking up their instruments in front of a giant screen showing him singing "My Next Life" with acoustic guitar. Cheese factor aside, the combination of his solo performance on video with the band live was pretty cool, and he was starting to forget the Tabbie call when Eddie reappeared, drinks in hand.

"Your beverage, sir. Did I miss anything?"

Roc smiled weakly and nodded toward the proceedings below. Archival footage of the band — in the studio, goofing off in a hotel pool, opening for Kajagoogoo on their first concert tour — rolled on the screen while The Cocktails thundered away on an extended jam at the end of "My Next Life." Roc's guitar, in a moment of ultimate kitsch, rose dramatically on a stand, from beneath the stage, as the lights narrowed to a single spot and held for prolonged applause. Roc looked away, and Eddie spilled his beer while laughing heartily. A long line of guest singers romped through the song catalogue, and again, it was a surprise duet, this time Morrissey and Joan Jett, that stole the show. The obligatory finale featured members of The Black Crowes, Counting Crows, and Sheryl Crow on stage for the first time together.

As the weary audience headed for Wilshire Boulevard, Roc looked at Eddie, shaking his head. "I don't know what to say. I do know that I have to whiz desperately."

"Hmmm. I have specific instructions from Uncle to hang here till it empties out completely. Getting you in was one thing, but ... hey, could you pee in this bottle? Pretend it's a check-up or something?"

Backstage, The Cocktails, looking drained, were assembled on a couch in the glare of TV lighting. Chad Sparx had shed his t-shirt and boardshorts for a black linen suit with no shirt.

"Epic show, dudes. Danny, bitchin' opening."

Danny nodded. "Yeah, I meant every word. Roc did have the coolest hair."

Frankie jumped in. "He never acted superior, and you know he coulda pulled all the chicks."

Chad turned to Barry, who clearly wished to avoid any attention. "Roc convinced me to exchange my recorder for a bass when we started the band. Our sound would've been totally different."

"Well put, amigo. So, the show, the DVD, the CD ... you guys must be easing the pain with a hefty share of mechanical royalties for this extravaganza." The camera panned across a trio of blank faces. "Clearly a stricken trio, but one who will continue on their own musical path wherever that may take them." The host paused and put his hands in a prayer position. "Thank you, Cocktails, for a wonderful and memorable evening."

A few feet away, Justin made gagging motions at Uncle, who shrugged and raised his palms. Marie and Julie returned freshly sprayed and glossed and clearly ready for the real party to begin.

"I'll meet you revellers at Onyx. We've got the whole upstairs. Have you got your passes? I've got something to take care of."

Marie pursed her lips and held up her laminate, featuring the squiggle of a rock with a fringe of hair on it and the words "Afterlife Afterparty" on it. "Don't be too long, my 'airless genie. You are leaving us with some savage, you know." Justin beamed at this reference, took the girls' arms, and headed for the line of limos along Western Avenue.

Upstairs, Uncle let himself into Roc's sanctuary. "Amazing enough for you, gentlemen?" He hugged Roc. "And it was all for you, my brother. What a show. Man, I'm thirsty." Uncle grabbed the first bottle he could reach and took a swig before Eddie or Roc could stop him. "Yech, nothing worse than warm beer. Tastes like piss." Roc couldn't look at Eddie. "I'm going to page Nick in the ambulance, then we'll head down to the backstage door. He'll let us know when it's clear. Once you guys are in, he'll take off. I'll see you later; I've got some business to take care of." Seeing Roc's disgust at the uniform, he added, "Hey, it's a paramedic, not a parachute." Roc just shook his head and pulled on the white jacket and mask.

From inside a white stretch limo with an open door, Delray was beckoning to Bobbie. "C'mon, sweetness, I feel you blocking me with that dang negative energy. There's room to roam back here."

She started down the sidewalk in the direction of her car. "Delray, I do appreciate you inviting me to this concert, but I've got a mess of laundry waiting on me. I'm happy about your new career and all, but it doesn't change a thing between us."

Delray jumped onto the sidewalk with a forty-ouncer of Lone Star in each hand. "Ah, hell, Bobbie Jean Burnette, you just gotta purge some of your toxins is all. You know you can't resist me." She retreated into the thinning crowd.

The ambulance was stuck in a throng around the stage door after Eddie and Roc had climbed in the back. Roc peered out the window to the crowd on the sidewalk as a young couple passed and looked in casually. "Eddie, hey, come here, that's the couple that were in the studio the other night, you remember I told you about them."

Eddie looked out the window just in time to see Emma and Stick fade into the crowd. "Those two? I don't know the girl, but that's Rich, my son. I wonder how he got tickets. He's got a new love interest and he's being kinda mysterious about her. This is weird, like watching him on TV or something. Is she cute?"

Roc kept his thoughts to himself. "I couldn't really see her, sorry, Ed. Speaking of weird, I forgot to tell you that I picked up your phone while you were getting beers for us." Eddie arched his brow and waited for the rest of the story.

Thirty-Three

"It wasn't as bizarre as I expected. What am I saying? It was utterly bizarre, but a lot of the time I forgot it was me they were carrying on about and just enjoyed the music." Roc leaned back into the old studio sofa. "So they're going to do a tribute album, I guess."

"They being Strange Savage Productions. I love that name. You're lucky, you haven't had to witness the secret handshake and the weird growly thing they do. You want another beer?" Eddie moved toward the fridge as Roc nodded. "So you're sure it was Tabatha?" he asked, returning to the hot topic of the phone call.

"Oh yeah, and I blanked and answered in this Neanderthal voice — 'No Roc, he gone.' I panicked when the phone rang while Uncle was doing his spiel. Guess who was the strange savage at that moment?"

Eddie was laughing at the absurdity of it all, now that the seriousness of the security breach had receded with the last beer. "I suppose Mr. Clean doesn't have to know about this. I couldn't take another Zen reprimand."

"Not without laughing my ass off. Did you notice the other day that he kinda got stuck in his lotus position in the studio? I think that little cushion at the office must be spring-loaded."

"Maybe his butt fell asleep. Does that ever happen to you?" At this moment, Roc became aware of how many Tuborgs into the night they were. "When did all that master of time and space crap start anyway?" Eddie said.

Roc paused to recollect before answering. "I remember Uncle studying tai chi at the Y, and when we were at parties, he'd all of a sudden get up in mid-conversation and do this thing he called 'repulse the monkey.' Looked like he was operating a set of pedals with his hands in slow motion. No one really paid much attention, but some of the girls took to calling him Elvis, and he eventually stopped."

"Hey, check this." Eddie picked up the remote and unmuted MTV. Some dork in a Porter Wagoner outfit was balancing on a surfboard with a couple of babes, obviously shot on bluescreen in a studio, singing, 'He's a cowboy dude, don't give him no 'tude.'"

Roc peered at the screen, not quite believing what he was seeing. "What the fuck? Eddie, that's the weirdo with the knife from the parking lot at the Sunset. Remember I told you about him?"

"You're kidding. Is it just me, or does that look a bit like Barry gone Nashville?" Eddie gestured at the TV and at the rotund bassist crammed into a white suit with little appliquéd slices of pie floating around on it.

"Wet suit and Stetson, a bible and a tan
He's a cowboy dude, a Wild West coast man...."

The bikinied girls crossed themselves in time to the music and cozied up to the grinning singer as he delivered those lines.

"That's Barry all right, and check out Danny in the little scarf behind the drums. This must be Uncle's idea of developing new projects. Sad. I think I chose the right time to bail from the music business."

They both watched mesmerized as the surfboard morphed into a bucking bronco carrying the singer, identified as Delray Jackson, and his backups, the Rayve-ups, into the horizon.

"You know, I heard about some hick who was cutting a song Danny wrote. This must be him," said Eddie, still staring at the now-muted TV.

"As long as a song is all he's cutting. This is bizarre. I love that I have to watch fucking MTV to find out what fearless leader is up to," Roc added grimly. "Anyway, I've got a song that wants to be written, so I'll see you tomorrow, Ed."

Emma flicked off the remote and tossed it on the bed, dumping a bowl of corn chips in the process. "I felt sorry for that guy's date at the show; you know, the new age come-on bullshit and then the air guitar solo. Now the rest of the world has to put up with him."

"Hangs with the surfers and walks with the Lord!" Stick was standing on the bed, pretending to surf. Emma pulled him down, sending the chips, the remote, and a pair of drumsticks to the floor. She kissed him, and they lay nose to nose, sharing a pillow.

"Was it too weird for you to hear all those people talking about your dad?"

"I was proud of him. I realized that I knew almost all of those songs, even though most of them were popular when I was a little kid. The guitar rising out of the stage thing was absurd, but that guy in his band made me want to cry. I'm so glad you were with me, Richard. Thank you."

"Hey. Yeah, I know those songs too. I can remember some of the early ones being recorded at my dad's place. I'm not a big fatalist, but I have to admit that us being here together is pretty out there. So, Emma, did it make you wish you'd gotten to know him or even met him once?"

Emma smiled enigmatically and went over to the bureau for her laptop. Climbing back into bed, she booted up and leaned on Stick's shoulder. In the silence between them, a car passed nearby, and they both stared at the city below through the bedroom window. Emma's voice was low and serious. "I'm taking, or was until a couple of weeks ago, a course called 'Exploring Multimedia' at college. We're combining text, audio, photo, and video images, and it's based around the ideas of Walter Benjamin."

"Was he Grandpa on the 'Real McCoys'?" Stick asked without breaking a grin.

Emma punched him gently in the arm. "Walter Benjamin examined the relationship between modernity and everyday life. He had a really cool way of looking at things. He said, 'Strength lies in improvisation. All the decisive blows are struck left-handed.' You're a drummer; you must be able to relate to that?"

Stick nodded knowingly. "Of course. I mean, was it Descartes or Ringo who said, 'I like to sit in front of the telly and go bang bang'?"

She regarded him as an indulgent mother might. "Richard. Oh, never mind. Just look at this." Emma pulled up the QuickTime box with the footage of Roc's descent from the clouds toward the *Beach Blast* set and ran it top to bottom with audio and commentary, such as it was, from Chad Sparx.

"Now, there's a thinker," said Stick, indicating the show host. Emma, ignoring him, reran a segment without audio and froze a frame of Roc spread-eagled with the backdrop of the parachute. Stick, intrigued, leaned closer to the laptop as she clicked off single frames and enlarged one to fill the screen in which the parachute momentarily flapped to one side.

"There," she said, pointing at a blurry line rising up from the rear of the harness into the clouds above, "what does that look like?"

"A bad root canal, I don't know."

"To me, it looks like a cable attached to the chute."

"Don't those things have cables galore to support the sky diver?" Stick suggested, clearly puzzled.

"Not one going above the parachute itself." Emma indicated the white line that continued to the top of the frame. "I know it's pretty grainy, but this doesn't look like any video glitch I've seen. The way the sun bounces off it, I'd say it's heavy-duty metallic cable, like you'd use in a rescue operation." She skipped ahead a couple of frames, and the parachute flapped back to fill the space it had formerly occupied. "Easy to miss, but once you've seen it, hard to ignore."

Thirty-Four

Art is the holy spirit blowing through your soul. — Jack Kerouac.

I'll drink to that, thought Roc as he poured himself a strawberry mango shake while reading the post-it on the cupboard. The note on the other door, *Roaches love crumbs*, demanded less thought. Roc was in that wonderful creative haze where the physical world was manoeuvred on autopilot while musical fragments floated through his head, seeming to want to push their way into life in the open air. Often they did, and songs were born. He was in a different musical phase now, and while not wanting to examine it too closely, he realized that the work was unlike anything that had come before; and the idea that it represented some earlier, cruder career phase was ridiculous. Still, Uncle had been calling, reminding him of the upcoming label meeting to discuss the first *Echoes* release. Glad to no longer be part of that world, Roc was enjoying his unassailable creative freedom. The only thing nagging was the Marie song, the one he hadn't started and that she was scheduled to sing in a matter of hours. Eddie had wired up his bedroom so Roc could have audio and video contact with the control room, to effectively produce the track from the grave.

He wandered into the studio, confident that inspiration awaited. Things had been moved around again, but the mystery had been solved. Eddie's son, Rich, alias Stick Neff, had been sneaking into the studio to work on his music. Roc hadn't mentioned this to Eddie because, truth be told, he was now enjoying the intrusions. It was forcing a change in his sleeping patterns, and he'd had to beat a quick retreat from the studio a couple of times when he heard the system being disarmed, but he was fascinated by the music. And he was curious about Rich's girlfriend, who always seemed to be just out of range of the security cameras or curled up in a corner of the studio, reading, with her hair falling in her face while her boyfriend moved restlessly from drums to bass to piano and back.

Roc found himself making the same circuit as he tried to get a start on the Marie song. Finally, he decided to see what the percussion closet would yield. There was a post-it note on the door.

I couldn't go pop with a mouth full of firecrackers. — Waylon Jennings

Roc smiled as he pulled out the old Scandalli accordion. Perfect. He dusted off the keys and flashed back to his father playing those pieces he called musettes — wobbly, gypsy-sounding waltzes that Roc and his brother used to dance to like marionettes while his mother leaned in the doorway looking dreamy-eyed. After working up a wheezy squeezebox riff, Roc headed back to the control room. He patched in an old Roland 808, one of those early eighties drum machines that they used on "Sexual Healing" and "In the Air Tonight," and dialed up a primitive groove. After adding some strumming Spanish guitar and the two chord accordion pattern, he looped it so it repeated infinitely, grabbed a studio notepad, and scribbled:

> "I'm your *negligée*
>
> You're my *matinée*
>
> I'm your *tarte aux pommes*

> You're my *chocolat bombe*
> Oh *mais oui*
> It's just you and me."

Greatly amused, Roc glanced at the clock and dashed off a chorus lyric:

> "Ooo lala, ooo lala
> *C'est moi et toi*
> Ooo lala."

No time for editing, he thought as he hastily recorded a guide vocal, or whisper, more accurately. Processing the vocal up to girlie range, he did a quick one-pass mix and left the disc, marked "Edam and Weep," where Eddie would find it.

A short time later, he was refining one of the new "old" song lyrics when a glowering Uncle burst in. "You're kidding, right?"

Roc held his gaze and paused. "Aren't you?"

"C'mon, man. This is serious. I've been counting on you."

Roc couldn't suppress a smile and saw Uncle trying to fight one back. Roc sang quietly, "Ooo lala. *C'est moi et toi.*"

"Shut up!" Uncle laughed out loud at this point. "Okay, it's funny, but Marie's not a comedy act, for God's sake."

"Doesn't she like it?"

"She loves it, but she grew up on a diet of French disco." Uncle shook his head slowly. "All right, but you've got to help us through this."

"Tell Ed to keep his phones on and use talkback 2 for me and 1 for Marie, okay?"

"Yeah, all right," Uncle sighed. "I'd better get back, or they'll wonder what the hell I'm doing."

"They?"

"Julie's here too. Remember Julie?" Uncle arched his brow and departed.

The session went remarkably well. Marie proved to be a quick study, and the talkback system worked perfectly.

"Have her replace 'think' with 'wink,' it's coming out 'tink,' and I'm not sure what that means." Eddie nodded in reply to the camera, which caught Julie over Eddie's shoulder. She almost seemed to be posing for him, running her hand through her hair and fixing her lipstick while she encouraged her friend. Roc told Eddie, "Have Marie get closer to the mike. Really work it. Imagine it's little Uncle. Oh, and could you move your chair about six inches to the left, you're blocking my view of Julie."

Eddie suppressed a smile and hit the talkback. "Okay, one more pass at the chorus. We need to stack it. Keep it breathy, Marie, here we go. Comin' at you goin' strong, it's K-Ed, the rock of Toluca, and a brand new sexy smash from sweet Marie."

Julie smiled straight into the security camera.

Thirty-Five

Uncle sailed through the label's lobby with fresh authority and a lusty grin for the saucy new receptionist. There was no "Do you have an appointment?", no long wait, sunk in a couch, rehearsing the pitch, no "Hang on, let me get rid of this call, man." It was Uncle's show now, and oozing false humility, he revelled in it. Posters of Delray bronco-busting a move on a surfboard stared at Cocktailmania black and whites of the sullen pageboy trio. Advance copies of *Roots and Pebbles*, the now four-disc retrospective (expanded from two, including the Beacon Theatre concert DVD and an interactive stroll through downtown Duluth in the eighties), sat like vinyl bibles on every desk. The two discs Uncle carried in his satin Tibetan shoulder bag would take him to the next level of dominance, he was convinced.

Justin greeted him with a conspiratorial grin and their new secret handshake, which concluded with soft growling and a whispered "strange savage" in unison. No one laughed.

The boardroom circus, plus or minus a few clowns from the last show, was in full swing. Uncle drank in their raucous welcome, palms up, with a "what can I say" expression.

Justin brought things to order and quickly ran down the "Swan Dive" radio stats and overall *Higher than Heaven* album sales, which, although everyone knew them, were impressive enough to bear repeating. The buzz on Delray was building, and two young publicity tarts argued about who was more suited to accompany the newest stud on his debut promo tour. Enthusiasm was lavished on the latest Cocktails single, "Say It Don't Spray It," as details of the video launch at an Orange County waterpark were tossed around. The CD single package in the form of a stained cocktail napkin was lauded as genius.

Circling the table and putting his hands on the old man's shoulders, Savage announced, "As you all know, this is Stan Smiley's last hurrah with the label, and what a hurrah it's been."

The cheeriness was in contrast to a sober Stan, who looked around the table and began in his rusty voice, "First of all, because I haven't had a chance to say this publicly, Uncle, I am truly saddened by the death of one of the nicest, most genuine, and genuinely talented people I've ever worked with. So, let's be glad of our success and be proud to help deserving music be heard, but not forget the loss of an artist and a friend, Roc Molotov."

A rumble of sincere sounding "yeahs" and "rights" and a raising of Evians followed. Uncle cast his face downward to compose himself and adjust the pillow on his chair.

Stan picked up the tone quickly. "Yeah, I'm gone at the end of the year officially, after thirty-six years in this nuthouse, but for all intents and purposes, this is it for me, and I'd like to reintroduce you to someone." A young hipster in a gunmetal Dries suit and tangerine t-shirt, who looked vaguely familiar to Uncle, smiled coolly in the seat next to Stan. "This is Trey, who wants to be known as Trey Suave now, and he will be assuming the title of head of national promo immediately, while I rummage through my desk for my Van Halen backstage passes to sell on eBay." In the ensuing laughter, Uncle recognized the kid who had come up with the chopper idea. Uncle supposed that kissing him might be thought gauche, considering the presumed outcome of the event.

"Trey's contacts at *Beach Blast* and his ability to spot the next wave make him ideally suited for the most important and meaningless job in the music industry. The floor's yours, Mr. Suave."

More laughter and applause greeted Trey, who nodded coolly. He'd been purged, Uncle noticed, of virtually all vestiges of his recent geek past. "All right, Stan. Hey, music lovers. I just want to say how stoked I am to have this gig and amazed I didn't have to blow anyone to get it." This was delivered in a nasal surf twang, and Trey waited for the approving laughter to pass. "Kudos to the smartest suit in the biz, Justin Savage, for taking a chance on me, and I'm pumped that we're all on the same side. It's all about the music, folks, but I wanna shift units till they can't count that high." Uncle zoned out, daydreaming about Maria's video wardrobe, until he heard Justin introducing him. "... manager, mentor, and man of the hour, Uncle Strange."

With his best sense of ceremony, Uncle had the lights dimmed as he played three songs from Roc's first release from the *Echoes from the Archives* series, set to roll out every six months or so. These, of course, were the three newest songs that Roc had recorded, and he'd in fact been putting the finishing touches on them till the early hours of that morning. Uncle assured him that they were expected to be rough, but a perfectionist's work is never done. A hushed reverence greeted the three songs, much nodding and silently mouthed "wows." Accompanying these and other unheard gems were to be some supposed early demos of older songs. In fact, they were new recordings, giving Roc a chance to improve on the originals in a stripped-down style.

Uncle smiled and tapped out a brief text message while he passed an unmarked disc to the front of the room. "And now, *mes amis*, the *coup de grâce*, from the land of Bardot and Deneuve, the hottest little croissant on the rack, Marie Ladurée."

Justin slyly opened the door to the boardroom as the music began, and in rolled Marie on cue, riding a bicycle, wearing a beret, and fondling a baguette. Smiling demurely, she dismounted, stretching her vintage striped Dubonnet ad sweater tourniquet tight. Perhaps torn between hilarity and outrage, the boardroom erupted in "bravos" and whistles. Marie pout-synched her way through the song, at one point dramatically yanking off her beret. Making her way around the room, she mouthed the lines into the ears of each listener, pausing to perform the first chorus on Uncle's lap. By the end, the room was singing "ooo lala" and thumping the table, yelling "encore" as Marie exited with a twirl of her skirt, revealing a pair of *fleur de lis* panties.

When the room emptied, Uncle and Justin exchanged bows. "I'd say that went passably well, wouldn't you, Monsieur Savage?"

"*Bien sur, mon oncle,*" smirked Justin.

"Listen, I have to confer with my client in confidence, but I did want to mention that Marie's father has agreed to direct the video. He's going to break from the Bovary shoot next week just for us and has a brilliant concept."

"Whatever you want, *mon frère,*" replied a giddy Justin as the two growled "strange savage" in unison before parting, laughing.

Uncle was massaging his knees in the parking lot when his cell rang. "Hey, Stan, sorry I didn't say goodbye; I think you were in the little boy's room."

"Listen, oh strange one, you must have passed around the Kool Aid before I got to the meeting. I've been through the archives with Eddie Dyck, and I don't remember any of those songs."

Uncle covered quickly. "Oh, well, they're mostly leftovers from the 'Higher' sessions."

"And did you say Roc wrote your little *bonbon*'s slice of *fromage* years ago? Bunkle! Maybe I start my day with Bobby Darin, but my ears still function. That vintage brie of hers sounded pretty *au courant* to me. Lots of auto-tune and some pretty cool pitch variation tricks in the chorus, eh, *mon ami?*"

Uncle silently celebrated the ancient promo chief's imminent departure. "Oh, I suppose Eddie did a bit of tweaking before it went out the door. If you've got it, use it, I guess."

"My guess is you got some wannabe at a songwriter's night at Highland Grounds or some underling at McCann to do your evil bidding."

Uncle spotted Marie changing out of her outfit in the back seat. "Listen, Stan, I gotta major meeting waiting for me. Great to see you as always."

"Don't hurt yourself, genie." Stan hung up as Uncle climbed into the limo and closed the privacy curtain.

Thirty-Six

Bobbie felt like her days were spent on a rollercoaster; the night of the concert had been an entire amusement park. She needed some peace — not to forget, that would be impossible. But some temporary equilibrium would be welcome. Medicating — not her style. She didn't want to confess to anyone, although she did break down on the phone with her mama, who signed off with "Y'all come home, Bobbie Jean," a slightly better choice than her usual "Why buy the cow when you can get the milk for free" warning. Exercise was good, but how many hours a day could a girl spend on a Stairmaster? The calls from Delray weren't helping; she'd just about jumped out of her skin when the call display indicated "The Sunset Lagoon — x222" as the source. Her hands hadn't stopped shaking till long after she'd gotten rid of Delray, whose swagger had reached epic proportions. She'd been fascinated, admittedly, seeing his video for the first time, but now it just seemed supremely stupid. The fact that he was hooked up with Uncle Strange was too twisted to believe. What really did her in was hearing "Swan Dive" on the radio, in Backpages Bookstore, in the cereal aisle of Earth's Bounty, and in her bedroom with the curtains pulled at any time of day or night. Her life was in that song, and reliving it brought out the best and worst of emotions.

Work, of course, turned out to be the best distraction. She increasingly saw herself as an actor, an improviser, writing as she went along in the course of her car phone sex calls. The clientele was growing, and she felt strangely creative in her work of late, adding new detail and variety to each fantasy. Stuck in traffic on the 405 or passing the exit for Carpinteria, Bobbie wove details of exotic locations into her seductions — the bat cave at Griffith Park, the caboose at Travel Town, the Palisades Library copier room. Tantalizing references to kiwi fruit and taco sauce were added to taste as she sipped on an ice-blended mocha frapp. Like a travelling DJ, Bobbie mixed Nepalese trance music with Berlin cabaret and Nova Scotian jigs at will.

Exhausted from a call featuring an elaborate fantasy involving a slow drive through a midnight car wash in a convertible Rolls filled with rose petals, Bobbie pulled off Sunset into the Heavenly Blessings Garden and Meditation Center. Breathing in a combination of evening jasmine and salty air, she made her way to a little stone bench in a secluded part of the gardens. Eyes closed, her mind attuned to her breath, her heart all but stopped before pounding violently at the sound of that well-oiled voice. "Did you enjoy the concert, Bobbie?"

"Hells bells, you pretty near scared me to death." She hadn't heard Uncle approach, but Bobbie was keenly aware that no one else was in sight. "What are you doin' sneakin' around here anyway?" She wrapped her arms across her chest as if the temperature had suddenly plummeted.

"Sorry I startled you. This is my little getaway from the madness." He smiled warmly, and she could hear the cellphone pulse in his pocket. "How are you doing since ..." he left it hanging, "Bobbie, I feel badly that I didn't get to know you better while.... I mean, I was the manager and you were the girlfriend." This was punctuated by that ridiculous Buddha palms gesture she'd seen before. "Are you … is everything all right? This hasn't been easy for any of us, least of all you, I'm sure." He seemed to be toying with her.

Bobbie couldn't rid her mind of images of the spider and the fly, and every pore was alert to the risk that she felt in this moment. What could he do? It didn't matter; she felt vulnerable and afraid. "I'm fine. We were … Roc and I were about done anyway…. I mean, I miss him something terrible … but I've got my friends, my work."

"What do you do?" he asked abruptly with something indefinable in his eyes.

"I drive … I mean it's a car job … you know, the valet girls who park cars at swanky parties … just till I find something else … it's fun. It's all right, you know." She could hear the defensiveness in her own voice.

"Cool. Have you got a card?" His eyebrows arched unnaturally.

"I suppose, let me look." Bobbie dug into her purse and in the dim light didn't notice the one she handed Uncle. "Listen, I was just about to head out. I'm plumb mellowed out."

"'Swan Dive' was for you, wasn't it?" Bobbie felt like she'd been stabbed. Uncle looked away toward the little man-made lake as if expecting a swan to swim by on cue. The wind passed through nearby chimes.

"I don't know." She remained frozen, her voice faint.

"Songwriters." Uncle grinned as though it was the final word on the matter.

"Yeah." The breath burst out of her.

"So, Delray to Roc. You've got interesting taste in men." For this comment she would always despise him.

"Yeah, well, Delray, bless his pointed head, was the prom date from hell. Or would've been, if he hadn't passed out in his truck while I was getting ready."

"Why do I find that totally believable? A waste of good crinoline, I imagine too." He did that weird thing with the head tilt and hands up like he was blessing the damn flock.

"Well, you know, when a hillbilly gets lit, that's it."

Uncle smiled again and seemed to put away the blade. "I'll walk you to your car." He stood motionless above her.

"Obliged."

As they circled the lake, Bobbie's breathing settled, and they passed a few other early evening visitors. The fear she'd been feeling was changing into something else, and she stopped at the edge of the parking lot as a realization hit her. "You sent me that photo, didn't you?" Uncle's face was hidden from the light. "The one of the girl with Roc in the shirt I gave him for his birthday."

"Why would I do that?"

"I don't rightly know, Uncle." She spoke his name like it described something stuck on her shoe. "But from what I understand, you don't do anything without a reason."

He grinned as she strode away, looking at the card that read "Hot Wheels" with a number and no name.

Thirty-Seven

"… twelve-car pile-up on the Pasadena Freeway near the Huntington Gardens exit … nothing new on the jewellery mart hostage taking … we're reporting a 4.1 quake just north of the Simi Valley … *he's a cowboy dude, don't give him no 'tude'* …."

"Yeah, leave it there. Thanks, Roscoe."

The warmth of the late afternoon sun calmed the activity level in Uncle's head to a low drone. As the limo pulled off the Hollywood Freeway at Highland, he noticed the statues in the fountain, designed by George Stanley, the sculptor who had created the Oscar statuette, and found his daydreams turning celluloid. Why not? Marie had the look; she was even shaped like an Oscar. The famous-in-Europe director father. A hit song on the way, written by the hottest dead rock star *du jour*. Easing up the hill to the Hollywood Bowl, the site of Marie's video shoot, he thought of last night's dome polishing and how Marie's gratitude could find new peaks in a future that contained movies too.

He passed craft services tables surrounded by members of the Hollywood Bowl Symphony Orchestra in tuxes and formal dresses, laughing in groups, smoking, noshing on *crudités*. He walked slowly up the hill, deciding to leave Marie alone in her trailer, no doubt receiving last minute fussing-over by hair and make-up.

Unconsciously humming "Ooo lala," Uncle came in sight of the Hollywood Bowl, one of his favourite California landmarks. He stood silently, admiring the magnificent curved white shell and watching the enterprise that centred on the stage. Taking in the elegance of the white tablecloths, champagne, and tiny bouquets on each table, he reflected on impresarios past and began to consider his place in the lineage. A giant crane was being positioned in the centre aisle of the box seats as extras filed in. Slowly the orchestra members took their seats, and as a small, bearded man in a Daft Punk cap pointed to a spot at centre stage, Marie appeared in a stunning translucent cloud of a gown with glowing red shoes emerging from underneath.

Insects and the odd chopper buzzed through the midday heat, and Uncle settled in the back row to watch. Eventually, playback began and the orchestra played soundlessly as the audience swayed in their seats, singing along. There was something odd, weirdly discordant about the whole thing that Uncle couldn't pinpoint. Maybe it was just the usual music video disconnect, he was thinking, when a voice called out, "Could she be any more gorgeous?"

Uncle smiled at Julie and kissed her on both cheeks as she sat down. *"Impossible,"* he replied in his worst French accent. "Was she nervous this morning?"

"Not at all, big boy. In fact, she had quite a nice glow on at six this morning when they started working on that Marie Antoinette wig thing she's wearing." Julie gave him a salacious look.

Uncle noticed the giant hair for the first time but saw that the crane camera seemed to be pointing at Marie's feet at this point. "Covering all the angles, I see." He nodded toward the stage.

"If you've got 'em ... hey, I'm just curious, Uncle, did Roc really write that little slice of *fromage*?"

"The band never cut it." Uncle shrugged uncomfortably. "It was left over from this United Nations fundraiser thing." He looked at Julie, but she was watching the stage. "They went with 'Say No More Mon Amour' by Max Caulfield." His reverie well and truly broken, he decided to go back to the office. On stage, two men were circling Marie with what looked like oversized dustbusters, causing her gown to billow dreamily.

"Tell Marie I was here, will you?" Uncle kissed Julie again quickly. "And that I want to drink bellinis from one of those little red shoes."

Unable to get comfortable twenty minutes later, he was lying on the floor of the limo staring through the sunroof. "Candy, can you see if I can get an hour with Dr. Pook, my knees are killing me."

"Too much praying? I'll call now. Listen, Delray's been trying to reach you for hours. Where've you been?"

"I guess the cell didn't work at the Bowl. What's up?"

"He and Danny have been recording all night, and they're all in a lather about their new song. But listen, if he tells me one more time that he's hotter than a horn toad in a microwave, I may have to have him killed. Don't say I didn't warn you."

Uncle laughed. "Okay, I'll call him. Anything else?"

"Uh-huh. Max says you have to set up some trust accounts ASAP for Roc's royalties. I didn't know he had a daughter. He's at the Ojai Valley Inn but says he'll take your call."

"Thanks, Candy. Call me back if Pook's got time."

Uncle decided to drop by Danny's studio and see what the Narf twins were up to. When he got to Westlake Village, there was no answer, so he went around the back to where the studio was located. Danny was passed out on a deck chair, and Delray, in a leopard print Speedo, was trying to balance a small TV set on a blow-up dolphin floating in the pool. Sensing imminent disaster, Uncle raced to the side of the house and yanked the extension cord from the wall, just as the television launched itself in the air and into the pool with a cruel splash.

"Dang!" Delray dove in and was swimming to the edge, TV in hand, when he spotted Uncle. "Danny's gonna bulldoze my nuts for this one. I already singed his Stratocaster fanning the barbeque today."

Uncle took the set from Delray and placed it on a towel in the sun. "I'm sure it'll be fine in a few hours." He eyed a snoring Danny. "I hear you two have been hard at work."

"A few hours? But *Disasters of the Century* is on the History Channel, followed by *Licence to Grill*."

"Look, I know how you feel. I missed Pamela Lee guest hosting *Comfy Couch* this morning."

"No, shit. Hey, Daniel," Delray picked up the hose and drenched Danny for several seconds before he came to, "the swami's here to check out the new tune."

In the studio, a rolling train groove set the song in motion until Delray's now distinctive drawl sang/spoke,

> **"Six pack and a *Playboy***
> **I'm in for the night**
> **99 channels and a La-Z-Boy**
> **Well that sounds about right."**

Delray was grinding his hips in the wet Speedo a little too close to Uncle's face for his comfort, and the rest of the song blurred by. The part about "shakin' hands with the guvnah" went right past a distracted Uncle.

"Sounds great, guys. Send me an mp3, and I'll play it for Justin. We'll be looking at rushes from Marie's video later tonight."

"Cool." Danny and Delray spoke as one. *All they need's a Curly*, thought Uncle as he walked back around the house. He was going to try Marie's cell but remembered there was no reception in the Bowl. His knees crackled like bamboo as he got in the car and dialed Max Stone.

"How bad can it be? I just birdied the thirteenth. Wasserman's in the creek and Maynard's in the bunker. How are you?"

Uncle crowed about Marie's shoot and the next Delray smash but then quickly got to business. "What's up with this trust thing, Max? I thought we had months or years to file. I mean, Roc's still officially 'missing,' right?"

"According to my research, the element of peril accelerates the presumption of death. He'll be officially missing for quite a while but ... between us, who okayed that stunt? Did Roc do any practice runs? Enquiring minds want to know, and it's just a matter of time before that foam-dome Sparx on MTV gets on your case, Uncle."

"Roc was psyched, Max; he saw an opportunity and jumped, so to speak. As long as the revenue is uninterrupted in the meantime, I can burnish Roc's legacy in the manner it deserves, right?"

"You need to know that Roc's daughter, Emma, has petitioned the court to set up the royalty stream to flow directly to her trust; it would mean you'd have to get paid by *them* on all future Roc-related business. She's represented by Litzenberger, Stasiuk, Horvath, and Bucyk in Boston. They're straight, but slow as the 405 at rush, and they worship paperwork."

"What about funnelling everything through Strange Savage? It's offshore."

"Uhh. I don't recommend that, Uncle, for a multitude of reasons. I think we have to sit down with the daughter, her mother, and the lawyers and work something out. How soon can you fit in a trip to Boston?"

"Let's do it here, offer to cover their expenses, put them up at the Beverly Hills, cabanas, the whole deal."

"Won't work. Bucyk hasn't left his office in a decade, and I think we should be seen as playing ball. Speaking of which, I'm ready to tee off on fourteen, so let me know. Soon."

Uncle leaned back in his seat with a long sigh and dialed Candy.

"Good timing. Pook's office just called, and he can see you at three. Don't overdress." Uncle understood Candy's skepticism about the unusual treatments he received from Mork Pook, but they worked. "The screening room's booked for seven, and Justin says he'll meet you there."

"Cool. Listen, Candy, I need you to do something for me. You know Marty Cockburn, the lawyer in New York who dealt with the bootleg thing in Shanghai for us?" Uncle paused for her reply. "It's pronounced Co-burn, Candy. Anyway, would you fax him a letter transferring the Molo Music royalty stream to Strange Savage? I need it done by the end of the business day in New York, so if you don't mind, would you sign it for me?"

Uncle told the driver to head into Beverly Hills for his appointment. "You copied it perfectly a couple of years ago when I had that sprained wrist, remember? I don't know, use tracing paper or something. Thanks. No, don't worry; I'll let Max know. He'll be all uptight about it, professional jealousy of course."

Thirty-Eight

In flickering candlelight, Uncle was gazing vaguely at the lacquered bonsai trees in the dimly lit office, while being rolled back and forth, naked and covered in almond oil, on the latex-covered forearms of Dr. Mork Pook. Pook, who resembled a muscular penguin, was dressed in a modified karate robe. "You're not built for the lotus, you know," he gently admonished, "and don't tell me this chafing on the knees is just from prayers."

Uncle's body was releasing toxins, or the remains of the oat burger from the Newsroom, and his voice revealed its weariness. "Lots of meetings, Doc, and the knees ... I don't know." He was picturing Marie's most recent waxing of his head but just as quickly banished the image, given his present position. Pook swung his chair around the table and inserted his stubby fingers into the base of Uncle's head, telling him to relax.

"Hmm. Lots of cranial activity as always. Any holidays on the horizon for you?"

Uncle was passing into a semi-conscious state and failed to reply but heard his phone hum through the ocean sound effects and pan flute music the doctor favoured. As soon as it stopped, it started buzzing again until he couldn't ignore it. "Sorry," he mumbled, pulling the phone from his pants, which were hanging on the back of the door. "Uh-huh?" Pook snapped off the plastic sleeves and eased out of the room. "Justin, slow down man, I'm just ... what?"

Uncle could have left the cell in his pants and still heard Savage on the other end of the line. "Treatment? Well, I'm just finishing one actually, why?"

Savage screamed even louder. "No, fuckhead, did you look at the treatment before they started shooting?"

"I think it was in French, man, I don't remember. But this guy won the Palme D'or; he knows what he's doing." Uncle's mind was still sluggish.

"I don't care if he won the Palm Olive, this is a mess." Justin's voice lowered, but he spoke in a staccato burst. "Accounting sent down the budget for today's shoot. It's 820K, and that's not including the director or his people. Rental of the Hollywood Bowl, gown by Gauthier, 3,500 extras, catering from some place called Fauchon in Paris, and the cocksucking Hollywood Bowl orchestra. There isn't a stringed instrument within ten miles of that song, Uncle, or hadn't you noticed?"

Clarity was returning too quickly to Uncle's mind, and it dawned on him what had seemed odd about that morning's shoot.

"Oh, and you'll love this. They've committed to another day's shoot. Today was just for her feet."

The oat burger was turning rebellious as Uncle sat down on Pook's table. He noticed that his phone was soaked in almond oil. "Okay, Justin, chill, man, we'll figure this out."

"Speaking of figures, oh master of the bottom line, the only reason this thing got by accounting is because some dim bulb hadn't noticed that the budget was in Euros, not francs, which multiplies everything by about seven. For her troubles, that member of our faithful staff was walked out of the building and given her severance in fucking Italian lira." Justin finally paused, and a wave of doom washed into his voice. "My father will nail me to the mast of his precious *Lady Suzanne* sailboat when he hears about this. Christ, Uncle, did she drug that skull salve she uses or what?"

Trying to quell the panic in his tone, Uncle assumed the pacifier role. "Listen, let me fix this as best I can. Hold the invoices, blow out tomorrow's shoot, and give me a chance to talk to Marie and her father."

"It's too late, Uncle," Justin replied coldly. "We can't bargain with the Bowl; I'd wipe my ass with those invoices if I could. I already cancelled the shoot, and I'm not going to release that piece of crap. My rep has been trashed badly enough by this fiasco, and like the old man said, 'Don't throw good money after bad.' I gotta send some memos."

"Wait!" Uncle called out desperately to a dead phone. He threw on his clothes and raced to the parking lot. Sitting in the back, trying to even his breath, he became aware that the entire car reeked of almond. Looking down, he noticed the stains seeping through his clothes, and he stared at his phone as it vibrated in his hand.

"*Ma cherie*, where did you go? You missed the best part, when the hairplane threw the rose petals and the musicians did the May Day dance around me. It was exquisite. I am so happy. Uncle?"

"Marie, did your father ever talk to you about the cost of this video?" Uncle's voice was flat.

"A little. He told me that the crew would have to have Perrier Jouet instead of Dom Perignon to keep the budget not so big."

"I see. Marie, this is my responsibility, and I'm going to have to deal with it. But I realize that I've misplaced my trust. Perhaps it will surprise you to know that spending over three quarters of a million dollars filming your feet is not considered reasonable, even by rock and roll standards. And by the way, just for the record, was there any real reason for hiring the Hollywood Bowl Orchestra?"

"Papa said it was just for the vibe of it. They would give a certain elegance to my video, you see."

"Uh-huh. So they weren't actually in the shot? Much like they weren't on the song itself?"

"*Exactement.* I knew you would understand. My father is an *artiste,* and I told him you work with real *artistes.* Is there a problem, *mon amour?*"

"You mean aside from the fact that the label is going to shelve the project, cross-collateralize the budget against anything else I bring them, and that it makes me the laughingstock of the music business? No, otherwise, everything is fine, Marie."

"What does this shelf mean?"

"It means that your career is apparently going to be short-lived, my little *tarte aux pommes,* unless I can bring about a financial miracle by tomorrow morning." Uncle heard the sound of stifled sobbing over his phone. "Look, I'll try to think of something. Why don't you meet me, and we'll have a nice dinner, a bottle of Chassagne, and we'll work through it?"

A long pause followed before Marie replied, "I'm sorry Uncle, I have let you down. I understand. I need to be alone right now."

For the second time in a few minutes, Uncle stared at a disconnected cellphone. Slumping back in his seat, he began rhythmically rubbing his head and humming "Ooo lala."

Knowing he couldn't cope with the office, he told Roscoe to drive, anywhere, and received a quizzical expression and a shrug in return. In fix-it mode, he always needed to keep a clear head; the addition of Marie to the mix saw him veering into foreign territory, one where emotions could derail everything. For the first time since the millennium, he switched off his phone; then, it had been widespread fear of the Korean virus that had threatened all communications systems. He watched the early evening crowd at the Ivy valet parking their Humvees and vintage Jags, everyone fit, rich, and in control. A gallery opening on Melrose spilled onto the street, where the same people in artsier attire smoked and accepted drinks from narrow blondes. The marquee of the Troubadour brought back the memory of the launch for Roc's second record — the euphoria, the buzz of expectation, the sight of Frankie crowd-surfing as his vinyl pants split inconveniently, and the ever-resourceful Candy, in her Angela Davis hair days, sewing him back into them before the encore. He and Roc had always been the calm at the centre of it all, the perfect balance of creativity and cunning. Uncle still believed in Roc, absolutely, but he realized, maybe for the first time, that he doubted himself. Sure, in Hollywood, you live and die by the "bullshit baffles brains" credo, but maybe his time was up, just like Roc had said of himself at the meditation centre that night.

As they drove down the Miracle Mile, Uncle realized that the car, like a homing pigeon, was approaching the office, so he gave in to the pull, reckoning that a change of clothes and the comfort of his inner sanctum might be the tonic for these feelings. Seeing a few of Delray's faithful, a strange mix of middle-aged mall moms and Target teens, maybe the daughters, waiting in front, Uncle slipped in the security door at the back and through the darkened foyer into his office. Extracting a fresh caftan from the closet, he resorted to a can of Lone Star and got comfortable on the floor. He pictured little Venn diagrams on the ceiling, representing his various financial interests, and he couldn't stop his mind migrating to those over which he had signing power, even if they weren't his to access, as he was now actively planning to do. There would always be other financial opportunities, many of which were now in play and sure to pay off; but there was only one Marie. This was the one thing he had to hold on to. He switched his phone back on and dialed her number but didn't leave a message. Then he called Julie.

"Hi, swami, what's shakin'?"

"Hey, Jools, I'm looking for Marie. Have you seen her?"

"Isn't she with you at the screening? That's where she was heading; we were talking about meeting up later at the Sunset. You running late, big boy?"

"You know me. Thanks. Maybe I'll see you later."

Surely Justin had cancelled the screening; it was scheduled to take place at the label. Uncle glanced at his watch and thought that maybe Marie was waiting there, so he lumbered to his feet, ignoring the slicing twinge in his left knee. Walking to the car, he made a reservation for a booth at Melisse and felt better already thanks to the adrenaline of action.

Rush hour was in overtime as Uncle made his way back to the valley. "Marty, you old fox, glad I caught you. How are things in Jersey?" Uncle chuckled at the reply and went on. "Listen, did you get my fax? Yeah, that's right, just as it says. I want to transfer the whole catalogue stream." Changing hands with the phone, he lunged for a Perrier. "You're a suspicious old coot. No, it's just a paper thing having to do with Roc's passing. Hmm … yeah, tell me about it. Max is out of town, and I can't reach him, unless you're too busy.… Okay, great, you're a mensch.… I owe you a case of Chivas. Ciao, Marty."

A few cars remained in the label lot when Roscoe pulled into the visitor's space and let Uncle out. Uncle waved to the security guard and strode confidently toward the screening room past empty desks and quiet offices. As strains of "Ooo Lala" passed through the closed door, he paused and took a deep inhalation of courage then stepped into the darkened room. The first thing he made out was the familiar scent of Obsession perfume, followed by the silhouette of a lone figure in a front row seat that he eventually recognized as the other half of Strange Savage. Making his way down the aisle, he kept expecting Justin to turn and respond to his greeting. As Uncle came face to face with what he anticipated would be a sullen or certainly chilly partner, he stopped to take in an image that he knew would remain — Justin, passed out in his underwear, head lolling to one side, with an empty bottle of Dom Perignon at his feet, his hands bound to the chair by a pair of promotional "Stop Before I Start" handcuffs and his face looking like it had been run over by a Lancôme truck.

Uncle hit the lights, and Justin moaned, "You're my negligée, I'm your matinée."

"Justin?" Uncle bent over the remains of his partner, throwing his inside-out Armani jacket over him. "What the fuck, man?"

"Heyyyy, my brother, *ça va*? That was so cool of you to arrange all this. You redefine partner, Monsieur Strange. And by the way, no sweat about the budget ... worth every *centime*." At this, Justin passed out again with a euphoric expression, and Uncle left quickly, picking up the handcuff key and pocketing it on the way out.

Thirty-Nine

Leaning on the railing of the deck, Roc let his gaze wander over his adopted neighbourhood, the low, tiled roofs turning to silhouettes at dusk, the warm yellow streetlamps, and the jacarandas lining the street, almost in season. He found himself looking forward to the electric purple bloom of the jacaranda trees in an emotional way and pictured himself as he had slowly driven down slanting streets in West Hollywood one late afternoon shortly after arriving in California, caught by their sudden lavender beauty on full display. He strained to make out bits of conversation from the street, invisible to him even though it was so close. A disturbing feeling that had been drifting through his emotional landscape returned, and he thought it might stay longer this time. It was the sense of looking at the world through glass, being part of it, but not able to take part in it. He realized later that even the Marie session, absurd as that whole situation had been, was strangely welcome. Even while watching on the security TV, he'd been actively involved in producing the song by headphone, and it was a buzz. *How pathetic,* he thought, and poured himself another glass of Sancerre. But true, he realized, considering the secret thrill he'd gotten from ordering Chinese take-out the other night.

Uncle kept saying that the Big Sur plans were in the works, but now that the agent had found this perfect property with a teardown on it, the new mantra was "permit problems," and the repeated mention of a "native burial ground" issue or the "unbonded local labour" thing was anxiety-producing. Roc had gotten major creeps when Uncle asked him to sign off on some postdated bank papers. And yes, kicking the fridge and throwing the menu book across the room had probably been a somewhat extreme reaction to the lack of bottled water at three thirty in the morning. And … he'd been organizing his photos of Bobbie into a folder on his laptop.

Roc did what he always did when things like this happened: he picked up his guitar and got lost. When he heard the low roar of an electric guitar from the studio, he was writing furiously into a notebook on his lap. He must have been playing when the system was disarmed, but he was unconcerned, assuming it was Stick, who'd been here every night this week. The only drawback to this otherwise welcome intrusion was it meant the end of writing for the moment, given how loud the younger musician liked to play. The sound was distorted, but he found the chords evocative and soon realized that he had transplanted his idea onto Stick's. As the security screen cycled through the studio, Roc spotted Stick strumming rhythmically, nodding, eyes closed. He imagined someone looking in on his process and felt a bit like a voyeur. Turning away from the screen, he took a sip of wine, and with the warm flush came an overwhelming urge to play music with someone, someone other than himself on tape. He picked up his guitar again and strummed along with Stick, whose playing rose in waves from the floor below.

With a bleat of feedback, the music jerked to a halt, but Roc kept on playing and humming indistinguishable words to himself. When the music didn't start again, he watched the screen until he saw Stick staring at the post-it Roc had attached to the amp earlier that night:

I don't care who influences me ... as long as it's not myself — Pablo Picasso

Stick turned when Roc pushed open the studio door, but if he was surprised, he didn't reveal it.

"Hey."

"Hey yourself. It's Stick now, right?"

"Uh-huh."

"Cool." An exchange of masculine smiles filled the space that followed. "You know that thing you were just playing ..."

"Yeah. It's not anything, really. A few changes. I can kinda hear a half-time groove under it."

"You're in D, right? I was hearing a few broken phrases and then up the octave for the next time through. You wanna play it?"

Stick flicked the standby switch, and the Marshall groaned in reply. The sheer volume made Roc's heart jump. "Sorry, man, I always play this loud. I'll turn it down a notch."

"No, no, it's great. I know how you play. I dig it."

Wordlessly, the two musicians found a common groove and fell into it. Roc sang some lines over the verse section:

> **"Barbed wire stars**
>
> **Snow white pages**
>
> **Travelling light**
>
> **Midnight rages ...**

"I don't know about rages. Sounds a little Elizabethan," Roc smiled.

"No, it's perfect. How about this for the second part:

> **"Wake a dead city**
>
> **Blow the ashes away**
>
> **Everything matters**
>
> **But none of it stays.**

"Sorry about my singing," Stick shrugged. "The phrasing's a little different."

"No worries. I'm thinking longer lines for the chorus. Maybe go to the B minor." Roc half-sung, half-spoke,

"The night's so blue you could drink it.

"This is totally obscure, but how about…

"An aerial photo of an empty street."

"That *is* obscure, but I like it. We need a different chord change here. The A minor is kind of dark."

"Maybe C major."

Roc sang tentatively,

"On a bridge, in a café

Trying to warm up in a doorway."

"You just came up with that?" asked Stick in awe.

Roc laughed. "Not exactly, I was playing along upstairs when I heard what you were doing, and it came to me then."

"The other line I had to go with line two was 'Pale fire/All flame and no heat.' Don't ask me what it means. My girlfriend was reading the Nabokov book *Pale Fire,* and it just sounded cool."

"Good enough for Vladimir … let's see what we've got."

The next hours passed in musician time, trading ideas and riffs. Stick switched to drums for a while, and Roc worked on a second verse lyric. Around five, he realized he'd been staring at the page without a thought in his head for some time. "I'm fading. You want to do this again?"

"Any time."

"Tomorrow? Maybe a little earlier." Roc smiled wearily. "I'll send your dad home by midnight."

As Roc climbed the stairs to his room, Emma watched through the glass from the darkened control room, where she sat motionless, curled up in the engineer's chair with her sweater pulled over her knees.

Forty

Dawn was seeping into West Hollywood, illuminating the tops of the buildings in the city below, and Emma closed her eyes for a moment. When she opened them again, she noticed that the streetlights had been extinguished. She and Stick had ridden silently from the studio to their borrowed home on Blue Jay Way. She stood shivering slightly at the open French doors off the bedroom; he lay in bed, and although she couldn't see his face, she was sure he was awake.

"Did you tell him about me?" Emma posed the question in an almost-whisper without turning around.

"No. I wanted to," Stick answered quietly. "I was kind of freaked by the whole thing. It's not every day you write a song with your girlfriend's dead father. Sorry, I didn't mean that the way it sounded."

"But Richard, you were in there for over three hours." She tried unsuccessfully to keep the protest out of her voice.

"I know. I thought about it a lot, but I didn't know where to start. He just came in and asked about my song idea, and we went from there, and then boom, it was over."

"So, does he live there?" Emma turned and walked back to the bed, looking imploringly at her boyfriend. He pulled her to him and pressed his nose into her neck.

"I guess. We didn't talk about anything but the song. How bizarre is this? I was trying to imagine what was going on in your mind when you realized it was your dad jamming in the studio with me. Fuck! I wrote a song with Roc Molotov tonight, and I can't tell anyone."

Emma's shoulders were shaking, and Stick pulled her close. He pushed her hair away from her face to see she was crying and smiling. "I knew he was still alive. I was sure, even without that thing I spotted on the computer. Oh god, Rich, I'm totally confused. I think I need to talk to my mom."

"Really?" He watched the early morning light catching the shine of her moist blue eyes. "But he's in hiding, right? I mean I don't know why, but he must have a reason. What would your mom do?"

"Oh, probably call the bloody National Guard. Call my aunt who would call a close personal friend at the *Globe*. Then she'd call her lawyer. Okay, that would be a bad idea." She jumped out of the bed and pulled on a sweatshirt, almost twitching with energy,

"My dad's alive, Richard.... I can't believe it.... I mean I do, but ... and you wrote a song with him. I'm totally happy, but what does this all mean?"

Stick watched the reflection of headlights on the ceiling as he lay back on the bed. A theory was forming in his head, but he didn't want to give voice to it yet. He knew whom to call, but his dad reacted badly to being woken up at dawn.

"Listen, speaking of lawyers, this is probably a coincidence, but my allowance check bounced today. I called my mom's lawyer, Mr. Bucyk, and he told me not to worry, but he sounded kind of weird. He's always weird, he's like a hundred and six and probably showers in his brogues, but it was different weird. Said he had to email my mom about some irregularities in the account."

Stick's mind was whirling, but he spoke reassuringly. "Don't worry about it, baby, we've got a freezer full of Amy's pesto pizzas.

I better get some sleep; I've got band practice today, and I'll hit my dad up for some cash. He wants me to do some errands for him."

"I'm sorry. I'll let you sleep. I'm going to sit on the deck, watch the city wake up." She picked up her laptop and leaned over to kiss him. "I'm too jazzed to sleep right now. Richard, I've got to meet him. I've waited eighteen years and travelled three thousand miles and been told it was too late. This is my father, after all."

"Well, he asked me to come back tonight to jam."

Emma stood in the doorway, incredulous. "And when were you planning to mention this, little drummer boy?"

Forty-One

Having given up on Heavenly Blessings as a private haven, Bobbie headed to another of her favourite quiet spots, Lake Hollywood. Parking on Wonderview, she walked over to the north entrance and started jogging into the late afternoon light. Checking out fares to Mobile had just been a diversion, but examining her apartment lease with a view to breaking it had upped the ante. All those reasons she had given Delray for why she lived here still existed, but she felt herself becoming unmoored a little bit more each day. She smiled wryly at the thought that if she went back to Alabama, at least she wouldn't have to deal with the state's number one least wanted peckerwood, now that he'd relocated to Lotusland. Reaching the dam, she paused for water and to admire the vista, another stop on Roc's obscure tour of Hollywood, this one having to do with *Chinatown* and Jack as Jake prowling the reservoir. She preferred the image of the lake from *Valley Girl*, and the first sighting of a young Nic Cage.

By the time she'd completed the circuit, a little over three miles later, Bobbie had worked up an appetite that led her to Miceli's on Cahuenga. Still hungry after her salad, she decided to stop at the 7-Eleven in Toluca Lake before catching up on some work. A lot of her overachiever clients were at their most needy after work, stuck in traffic on the 101 or the 5, scheming, brooding, and horny behind their tinted windows.

Fuck it, thought Roc as he grabbed the hat and glasses he'd worn to the tribute. Eddie must be off on some top secret Uncle mission, and the fridge was empty. He remembered a 7-Eleven a couple of blocks away and figured he wouldn't run into anyone except for the usual mini mall zombies. Lately he'd been feeling restless, and with the delays on the Big Sur house, he'd been getting serious cabin fever. A nervous foray to a convenience store wouldn't solve that, but he did smile at the thought of Uncle freaking when Roc told him, if he did. Okay — a little adjustment of the hat, collar up, shades on and out the door.

The evening was cooler than he'd expected, and Roc found his senses working overtime, as XTC would say. The crunch of his feet on the sidewalk, the smell of the evening jasmine, the hushed tones of a young couple passing by in conversation, the jolt of the neighbour's dog racing to the end of his leash a few feet from Roc — it was all more real life than he'd experienced in weeks, and it felt strange, dangerous, good.

The 7-Eleven looked more upscale than he recalled, but that wasn't saying much. It was also considerably brighter, cartoonishly so. There was an instant teller servicing a nervous-looking suit while his wife waited in the idling BMW, and a couple of young white punks were laughing loudly in the phone booth as one of them ripped the directory off the chain and tossed it into the parking lot. Inside he could see a young girl at the cash, alone and reading. The bell on the door announced his entry, but she didn't look up from the *US* magazine that entranced her. On his own in a 7-Eleven, Roc found himself looking at items he had no interest in, giant cheese balls in industrial size boxes, rows of cleaning products, wrestling magazines, until he located his brand of shakes in the cooler. He extracted a six-pack and was debating popcorn or mixed nuts when a voice said "Excuse me" as its owner squeezed by in the tight aisle. The breath stopped in his chest as he realized that he was eye-to-eye about fifteen inches from Bobbie Jean Burnette. She was wearing a white tracksuit and Angel perfume, chewing gum, and looking more beautiful than any girl should in the glare of fluorescent light. She flushed a deep red, looking at the mango strawberry shake pack and back at Roc.

"Oh, I'm sorry … I … it's just that you look like … I mean …"

With shaking hands, Roc bolted down the aisle, dropped his purchase at the cash and burst through the door into the parking lot, hyperventilating. A couple of cops were just getting out of their cruiser and heading in, and he willed himself to walk at a somewhat normal pace as they checked him out. He couldn't help but brush his hand along Bobbie's car as he looked inside, for what? Turning abruptly into the wrong street, he ended up walking a very long way, lost, before ending up at Eddie's place around an hour later. By then he'd written the whole song in his head.

"Eddie, I need you and Stick, right away." He hung up without waiting for a reply, rushed into the studio and grabbed a blank pad. Roc scribbled for a few minutes then picked up his blonde Telecaster, plugging it in to the Marshall stack against the back wall of the studio.

A few minutes later, Stick walked in. "Hey." Roc walked over to the drums as the young player sat down and tightened his cymbals.

"Here's the riff." He slashed away at a crunchy guitar figure a couple of times. "Straight eight off the top, full thrash then break it down to kick and guitar for the verse. You'll feel the build over the pre-chorus, then hit it hard for the chorus. After that, just follow me."

Stick nodded as they heard Eddie on the talkback. "Rolling, Roc."

Without even a count-in, Roc launched into the giant riff, feet planted directly in front of the bass drum like a street fighter. Stick locked onto him, and the two hammered the opening like a demolition team in synch. Roc pulled away at the last second and swung around to face the microphone in the centre of the room. His eyes were closed, and his voice had a strange, scared tenderness to it.

> "Am I fading from the picture
> Was I ever really here
> Am I falling through the trapdoor
> As you watch me disappear ..."

He slammed an open chord on the guitar at distortion level leading to the next section.

> "From a passing car
> Down some dead end street
> In a half-remembered song
> Sad and incomplete ..."

Hitting the chorus at even greater intensity, Roc spat out the lyric as Stick crashed his ride cymbal and thundered along with Roc's guitar.

> "Maybe it's always been too late
> Maybe I waited for too long
> Maybe we'll never understand
> What went wrong
> Cause I'm here ... but I'm gone ..."

The intensity dropped just enough for the pain of the second verse to show through, then they careened furiously through another chorus. The bridge seemed to elevate, as if there was some hope in the chaos that they'd created.

> "Like an echo like a shadow
> That the lonely night takes in
> Give me a second or a lifetime
> Your breath upon my skin ..."

As the final chorus chord rang out, Roc yanked off the Telecaster and leaned it against the amp, creating a roar of feedback. Stick sat, dripping at his kit, hands hanging by his sides, just staring. Roc turned and mouthed the word "Thanks," and Stick saw the tears running down the singer's face as he left the studio. There was a long silence once Eddie had switched off the Marshalls, and he looked at his son, still sitting at the drums.

"Holy shit. What was that all about? When did you know.... Okay, this is officially a mess."

PART IIII

This is my swan dive

Forty-Two

"I used it all." Justin's tone was terse. "Even after cancelling the second day and refusing to pay Papa, the whole fiasco came in just under seven figures. I kissed some major tuchas in accounting to get the tech costs spread around, but I still had to pay the rest out of Strange Savage. I mean, you just don't see creamed pigeon at craft services on a Weezer shoot, say." The young executive pressed his lips together and stabbed at something on his plate. "Oh, Christ, don't get me started."

Uncle's rectal muscles had little clench left after the last couple of weeks' toll, but Justin could still get an involuntary flinch out of him at the mention of the Marie video. His pragmatic side had accepted Marie's half-hearted version of the screening room incident, and he needed Justin in his camp, if only to share the inevitable fall this mess would provoke. Oddly enough, without a single cleavage shot, never mind one of the singer's face, MTV had been airing "Ooo Lala" to great phones. He guessed that there were more foot fetishists in the eighteen- to twenty-four demographic than previously acknowledged.

Justin shrugged at the waiter's reminder of extra charges for another dry piece of pita and dug into the plastic bowl of shared hummus that sat between them. He looked around nervously, but they were the only customers in the greasy falafel joint on Gower at three in the afternoon. He lowered his voice all the same. "That jerk in royalties got all snaky with me about another advance on *Higher than Heaven*, going on about some transparency shit and my involvement with your company. I think you'll have to get the kid, or her lawyer if she's not old enough, to sign off on it."

Uncle stared pensively at the flecks of baba gannouj on Savage's silk Industria jacket and fought back nausea. His mind travelled again to Eddie's place, where Roc had been holed up in his room, refusing to communicate or work on any new material. As if reading his mind, Justin gestured with a forkful of pickled turnips. "Where the fuck are the rest of the songs for the Roc archive release? And don't give me that 'baking the master tapes to bring out the missing top end' bullshit again. The stuff you played at the meeting was amazing, but people are starting to doubt that there's anything else, and five songs is not enough to match the hype. It could be himself belching into a bullhorn; it doesn't matter, Uncle."

Uncle Strange nodded, trying to look engaged as he shifted uncomfortably in the tiny plastic chair. Justin leaned back and picked up a toothpick from the dispenser on the table. "You saw The Cocktails statement, no doubt — returns up the wazoo, God help us. And that press release about scaling back the tour to 'get back to our roots,' please. When I saw Frankie on *E* going on about wanting to be 'closer to our fans,' all I could think of was paternity suits or crushed soccer moms when Barry lands in the mosh pit."

The flickering fluorescent light above Justin's head was slicing rhythmically into Uncle's brain, and he knew he had to bolt. Pretending to get a call, he dug his cellphone out of his caftan and headed for supposedly better reception in the mini mall parking lot. He nodded as if listening intently and tried not to look at the lamb carcass hanging in the restaurant window. Inside he could see Justin picking through the rest of the lunch, and he looked away to get his bearings. Returning to the table, he tossed down a twenty and shrugged. "Marie. Gotta go. I need to check out the mixes of a couple of new songs. See you at the Delray showcase at the Lingerie." Justin belched and nodded, not looking up.

Uncle walked up to Franklin and called a cab to meet him in front of the Scientology Celebrity Center, one of the few places in Hollywood you could count on never meeting an actual celebrity of any stripe. Trying to work out the numbness in his lower back, he'd escaped the grease pit Justin had suggested for their *tête à tête*, and sweated his way up Gower Street in the afternoon glare. As he waited for the cab, Uncle admired the façade of the imitation Normandy chateau that according to Roc, used to be the Elysée Hotel, onetime home to Bogie and Edward G Robinson. He recalled his brief encounter with the "church" in the eighties, when Dianetics was synonymous with brainwashing. One good thing had come from the "Cold Spark" video shoot that Roc and the boys had done there — Danny had met his girlfriend Gwen by agreeing to a personality test after the shoot. It reminded him that Danny often seemed a heartbeat away from dedicating his life to some guru of the moment, and he hoped that none of his and Gwen's hocus pocus tendencies were rubbing off on Delray.

The cab arrived, and he directed the driver to the office. As the springs in the frayed seat toyed with his sciatic nerve, he knew he was missing Marie terribly, flaming *tarte* that she was. Despite what he had told Justin, he hadn't seen Marie in weeks, and the cold reality included the fact that there wasn't a single bar of music recorded for her upcoming album. Fantasizing about the healing properties of her pout on his aching dome, Uncle left Marie a message inviting her to the Delray show, the one bright spot on the calendar.

Forty-Three

It was in another black frame of mind that Roc woke up and realized that he'd slept until mid-afternoon. Not that it mattered, given that he was existing in a place that increasingly felt separate from the rest of the world and its concerns. Since seeing Bobbie Jean at the 7-Eleven, he'd plunged into an intense period of writing and recording with Stick and Eddie that began nightly around midnight and continued through the Elvis hours until they had nothing left. He ignored Uncle's calls; in fact, he hadn't bothered to recharge his phone. Eddie's attempts to get them in touch had been rejected with some hostility; and Roc irrationally blamed Uncle for this hopeless state of isolation he was in. With Eddie, he'd taken responsibility for blowing his cover with Stick and given strict instructions that the all-night sessions were not to be mentioned to the anxious manager. The music that resulted was aggressive, at times angry, at others mournful, and like nothing he'd written before. With Stick, Roc was creating something new, a sound that neither would have come up with on his own. It had started with "Pale Fire" then "Here But I'm Gone," but he had no sense of where it was going next, and that fit the shapeless nature of his life. For Stick, it was a door that had smashed open in his creative world; but he had no better idea of where it was leading.

He was, after all, collaborating with a man presumed dead. His father's nightly presence meant that Emma had to hear about the sessions when her boyfriend crawled with the dawn into the house on Blue Jay Way. She was asking fewer questions, but he could feel her heart aching, and knew how much she wanted to be there.

Across town, in Santa Monica, Bobbie was in her own dark place. As time passed, she was less and less sure about the phantom she had encountered in the Toluca Lake convenience store. But every time she convinced herself that it was her overactive imagination, she pictured the pack of shakes sitting on the counter as she checked out, and the confusion returned.

She forced herself to get out, do some phone work, but it was getting harder, and a client had caught her crying the other day. Luckily, that had turned him on furiously, and the call had been mercifully brief. She'd called her mama three times that week, and when the phone rang, Bobbie assumed it was her Alabama lifeline. "Hey there sweet pea, how're y'all doin'? Just settin' there, starin' at my picher, I bet."

Delray seemed to have vulnerability radar, and Bobbie found herself perversely glad to hear his damn fool voice. "Oh, hi Delray. I see your video enough these days, so I surely don't need any photos of your hayseed self."

"Well, what you need is a taste of your good old boy in the flesh, sugar plum. Now, before you get all uppity with me, I'm just invitin' you to my show tonight at the Club Lingerie. And no, there won't be any peelers there; it's a rock joint at Sunset and Wilcox. Eight o'clock, your name'll be on the list."

Knowing that this could be a regrettable choice, Bobbie let the need for distraction win. "Well, you know, that would be real nice."

"All right, honey bunny, we can do some real sharing tonight. I've been doin' a hunk of work on myself, and I think you'll find a whole 'nuther Delray."

Marvelling at this bizarre mystic hick routine, Bobbie figured she could just ignore it, like so much else about Delray Jackson, and enjoy a night out. "All right, Mr. High on the Hog, I'll see you later. Knock 'em dead."

Later that evening, inside the velvet rope at the entrance to the club, Chad Sparx and the *Beach Blast* cameraman had set up shop.

"Coolio or what, here we are at the launch of the debut Delray Jackson disc at the Club Lingerie in Hollywood, where inside a wicked horde is grazing and getting totally boxed waiting for their hillbilly hero to show up. You might be asking yourself, like who is this complete Philbin who's jacked the charts with his hit single, 'Cowboy Dude'? Check it out, 'cause *Beach Blast*, as usual, has the dirt. Earlier today I spoke with Hector Castillo, the head valet at the Sunset Lagoon hotel, about a very sketchy encounter he had recently."

Viewers saw a small, impeccably-dressed man with shiny black hair looking uncertainly into the camera. "So, Hector, dude, tell us about what happened last month in the parking garage."

"I was parking a guest's car in the underground when I saw Mr. Molotov talking to another man. This was not so unusual, because Mr. Molotov always liked to park his own car. I must say that he always remembered the valet team at Christmas too."

"Cool. So was this other dude all rattly or what?"

"I could tell that something was wrong. Mr. Molotov was trying to back away from this man. That's when I saw the knife. At first, a piece of meat came from the tip, but then when Mr.

Molotov saw me, the other man passed the blade across Mr. Molotov's shoulder and made him bleed."

"Did you get a look at this ass clown?"

"Oh, sure, I had seen him before and asked him to leave the premises, but he didn't seem to speak English."

"So, Hector, for our viewers who are mondo curious, is this the dork in question?" A promo photo of Delray, identical to the one at the door to the club, flashed on the screen.

"For sure, Mr. Sparx, that's him."

The camera cut back to Chad outside the club, wearing a stupefied expression. "So, there it is, *Beach Blast* faithful, Roc Molotov got slit by one Delray Jackson shortly before he was cashed. It's getting redonculous, folks."

Inside the Club Lingerie, the room was filled to loud capacity by a unique assortment of teenage girls with ID, women who could be their mothers and in some cases were, and shit kickers from another planet eyeballing the talent. Some very unhappy ticketless yahoos were setting up an impromptu tailgate party in the parking lot, until the LAPD suggested otherwise.

The raucous crowd took it up another notch when Dwight Yoakam, in a gleaming white Stetson, screamed a long "Yeeehaw" into the mike at centre stage. "Welcome to the Club Lingerie. We got ourselves a real redneck revival tonight!" This brought a thunderous response from the room, and the stomping that followed almost drowned out the rest of the intro. "If you like your twang on the trashy side, you're in the right place, folks. Featuring a rockin' band some call The Cocktails, but for tonight only, known as 'The Forty Ouncers,' please say howdy to my good friend, Farcry, Alabama's own Delraaayyy Jackson."

Delray took the stage to a rollicking train groove, slapping hands with the front row faithful and yelling "Wee doggie" at the capacity crowd. "Ain't we in hog heaven tonight?" he shouted.

With a wellspring of unwarranted confidence, he instantly owned the room and blasted through the eight songs that he and The Cocktails had rehearsed in the preceding week. Just before the closing number, Delray grinned and started unbuttoning his blue sequined satin shirt. "Man, I'm sweatin' like a whore in church up here." Seemingly on cue, two forty-something frosted blondes jumped on stage to assist in the process. "Well, shitfire, if we ain't got a couple of real lookers here." The "lookers" were swarmed as they climbed down into the crowd, and the souvenir was torn into tiny shreds before security moved in.

Bobbie remained in the shadows at the back of the club, shaking her head in wonder at the silliness going on in front of the stage and avoiding Uncle, who was deep in conference with a young woman she finally recognized as the girl from the photo with Roc. "This here's our last number," a beaming Delray announced as Danny launched into the now well-worn beat of "Cowboy Dude." "Any of y'all that aren't plumb numb can get up and shine your belt buckles on the dance floor." Suddenly Uncle was no longer there, and a morbid fascination drew Bobbie closer to Julie, who was left on her own. At the end of the song, Delray tossed his hat into the crowd and faux-surfed his way offstage, but the crowd wasn't going to let it end there. He was joined by Dwight for a less than stirring version of the country chestnut "Big John," but the finale was impossible to have foreseen. Marie, done up like Brigitte Bardot meets Dolly Parton, sashayed to centre stage and performed a sultry southern take on "Je t'aime," with Delray interjecting the odd "Ah know," to roaring approval from the Lingerie throng.

"Excuse me," Bobbie said to Julie over the din of the club. "I'm Bobbie Jean Burnette. We haven't met, but …"

"Hi, Bobbie, nice to meet you." Julie extended her hand. "I'm Julie."

Bobbie hesitated then plunged ahead. "This is kinda queer, I know, but I'm … I mean, I was … Roc Molotov's girlfriend, and I know that you were … with him just before he …"

Julie's eyes widened, and she grabbed Bobbie's hands. "Oh, I'm so glad to meet you. Yes, I met Roc, but I didn't know him really, or … it's the picture, right?" Bobbie nodded, and Julie continued. "Nothing happened, Bobbie, I swear. Oh god, it was just a crazy night, and I was hanging out with my friend Marie," she gestured toward the stage, "you know the 'Ooo lala' girl?" Again, Bobbie nodded. "And Uncle, who Marie's been seeing, had hired this photographer; he said he wanted Roc to get in the gossip rags looking sexy, so he took these shots of us." Bobbie tried in vain to not see the shot of Julie and Roc in her mind, much less the one of them dancing that had appeared in *Rolling Stone* the week he died.

Bobbie had to shout over the cheering crowd in Lingerie. "You mean y'all weren't … seeing Roc, or …"

Julie cut her off. "No no, I'd only met him that night. I mean, he's a great guy, or he was, but, no …" She paused and looked sympathetically at Bobbie. "He wrote 'Swan Dive' for you, didn't he?"

Bobbie was trying to keep her emotions in check. She knew there was more to this story. Julie continued, "God, what a beautiful song. He must have really loved you, Bobbie. I'm so sorry if that hurt you. I've been called about that damn picture by people I haven't talked to since grade school."

"Well, there was another one, you know," Bobbie said, sensing the truth of what Julie said. "It was sent to me the day before Roc disappeared. It arrived by courier in an envelope with no note, but I'm pretty sure I know the vermin who sent it. I just don't know why." Now it was Julie's turn to listen and nod. "You were in some nightclub, and I thought for sure that … well, you know."

"Bobbie Jean, I swear …" Julie began.

"Don't worry, I believe you, Julie." Bobbie paused, and both women looked toward the stage, where the "Je t'aime" moment was passing into history, and a gleaming bald head emerged from side stage to help Marie exit. His smarmy glow froze into something else as he looked across the heads of the crowd and fixed on Bobbie and Julie conferring by the back wall of the club.

"Hey, Bobbie," said Julie, grabbing her arm, "you want to go to the party at Spaghettini?" She pulled an invitation featuring a drawing of a holster with sunglasses in it from her bag. "I think I can get us both in."

Bobbie pulled an identical one from her jeans pocket and grinned. "No sweat. I hear tell the drinks are free."

Bobbie offered Julie a drive to the restaurant, located just above the Sunset Plaza. "You actually dated Bubba back in Alabama?" Julie asked incredulously.

"I think 'dated' is glorifying things a bit," Bobbie explained as they pulled up to the valet parking. "Delray goes more for the head in the toilet, panties around the ankles type." Julie laughed at this image as Bobbie recounted the senior prom incident. "You gotta realize that, cute as he may be, this good old boy has the I.Q. of a milkshake."

Waiting at the bar at Spaghettini, Bobbie found herself trustingly relating to Julie the 7-Eleven encounter when Delray leaned in from behind them. "You mean like that time Randy saw Elvis at the Piggly Wiggly?" He snorted with amusement as Bobbie and Julie exchanged conspiratorial looks and waved to an approaching group. Marie arrived wearing a chiffon outfit that looked like it was designed by a cake decorator and accompanied by a glowing Uncle and Justin.

Delray greeted them with bear hugs. "Yo, J-man, Stretch, how about your little toot sweet?" He air-kissed Marie and gladhanded his way around the room as they were escorted to a prime table. "Bad news, folks, they couldn't get Krispy Kreme to cater, but strap on the feedbag anyhow." Bobbie found herself seated between Delray and Uncle when the celebrity restaurateur/owner delivered a surfboard-shaped pizza with little pepperoni Stetsons on it. At the urging of a nearby table, Marie and Delray reprised their version of "Je t'aime" to table-banging accompaniment. Constant interruptions marked the meal; one of the hotties from promotion approached with an older woman.

"Hey, Delray, killer show! Would you sign my mom's butt?"

Marie slid her hand under the table to distract a subdued Uncle, whose attention was threatening to wander, while the rest of the table avoided the spectacle. Delray found it necessary to inscribe his full name, along with the recipient's and a lengthy message, to her giggling pleasure. Justin cozied up to a cool Julie but kept giving Marie knowing slit-eyed looks. Numerous Lone Stars into the evening, a somewhat mellowed Delray leaned over to Bobbie. "Hey there, punkin, are you feeling the joy like I am, 'cause this here's turnin' into a bit of an energy vortex for me. We could head back to my hotel and connect a little more deeply."

"Actually, Delray, I think that's about all she wrote for me, so thanks for everything. You got lots of people dyin' to connect with y'all here."

"Ah hell, Bobbie Jean, don't get all skittish on me. I know we had some issues, but that don't mean we can't get neckid and do a little purging of our love toxins together. We could order up a lemon icebox pie and see what happens." Delray leered at her, and Bobbie caught Julie's bemused look.

As Delray clutched her sleeve, she bumped her elbow into his latest Lone Star, sending it flowing onto his lap. He jumped up and teetered dangerously, sending the remains of his pizza onto Justin's shirt. A look of disgust was the record exec's only response while Delray tried to clean it off with his beer-soaked napkin. As Bobbie saw her exit opportunity, Julie slipped her a phone number, and hasty goodnights were exchanged.

Forty-Four

For the first time in weeks, Roc looked at himself and registered surprise. He peeled the post-it from the mirror.

Death is nature's way of saying your table is ready.
— Andy Warhol

He smiled as he noticed that the salt-and-pepper patterns in his hair had migrated to his unshaven face. His eyes resembled tunnels, and was that furrow between them the product of squinting, extreme fatigue, or time? Roc realized that he didn't give a shit as he wandered onto the porch in the late afternoon with his first coffee of the day. He noticed the mockingbird, his mimic friend in the magnolia tree, going through his repertoire. Roc observed that his singing was even better at night, and he felt a kinship there. *Is this what's it's like being old, when your world shrinks and things close at hand take on more and more importance?*

He thought about his mother in Duluth and wished that he could tell her that he wasn't gone. Of course, then a quite lucrative enterprise would dry up for her. He'd seen her again on TV the other night; she'd moved on from limited edition guitar picks and lyric sheets to the real high-end stuff — locks of hair and "one-of-a-kind primary school spelling tests." *No, better dead*, he thought wryly. For some reason he was enjoying holding out on

Uncle, knowing that the manager was increasingly desperate for archival material. This latest work felt too much like something new to be relegated to the "from the vaults" releases, even if that work was guaranteed a huge audience. He dreamt of putting out something under a band name for Stick and himself, but how would that work? He headed back in and picked up a notebook then grinned as he thought about where he could put his latest addition to the post-it exchange,

Ambition is the death of thought. — Wittgenstein

Uncle, never one to let much stand in the way of ambition, was tucked into a table by the window at God's Green Urth, nursing a beverage that smelled like fertilizer, and watching for Emma's arrival. Too embarrassed to use his cell in the tiny café that she had chosen for their meeting, he was forced to surreptitiously ogle three granola mamas, breast-feeding their eager urth urchins at the next table. Emma's Doc Martens looked like gravity boots, holding down her tiny frame as she arrived at the table. As at their last meeting, her eyes seemed to take him into their true blue depths and blink him back out like a speck of dust onto Santa Monica Boulevard.

"Karl." She shook his hand firmly, thwarting his attempt at a more intimate Hollywood hug, and he winced at the sound of his own name.

"Emma," he smiled with all the warmth he could muster. "I see L.A. is treating you well. I don't remember ever seeing freckles on your mother."

Now it was her turn to wince at the mention of the one person she'd been avoiding contact with these last weeks. The waiter recited a list of specials that included vegetables Uncle was sure had been made up on the spot, and Emma ordered a beet and watercress shake. That wasn't going to sweeten her up, Uncle reflected, as he reached into his bag. "I thought you might like an advance copy of the memorial DVD. Quite a show, wasn't it?"

"Wonderful," she nodded, sipping on some water, "in a kind of morbidly cheesy way." Uncle tried to laugh along with her but sensed the tone not going in his direction as she continued. "So, are you going to roll out with a $19.95 list? How are the advance orders?"

"Uh ... maybe half a million," Uncle mumbled.

"That's just domestic, right? And I'm guessing you didn't have to grant any controlled composition rate." Uncle shrugged in mute agreement as Emma hit the calculator on her PalmPilot. "I'm assuming a twelve and a half percent royalty as usual, right?" She hit a few keys then looked up at a stunned Uncle. "Did you build in bumps at each 100k?" Uncle again nodded as Emma brushed a slice of hair away and stared into him. "You know, Karl, if you add that to the seven hundred and fifty K advance you just got on *Higher than Heaven*, subtract your richly deserved twenty-five percent commission, and allow for returns, my attorney should still be emailing me a notice of deposit of around a million and a quarter by Monday ... wouldn't you say?"

Uncle forced himself to take a deep slug of his manure smoothie to buy a moment to think. "Very astute, Emma. If you'd ever like a job, I could certainly use you in business affairs at the new label I'm starting." If it was a joke, it lay there. If he was serious, she let him dangle. "You know, the record business is very complicated. Issues like recouping of costs, earning back of advances, and as you mentioned, the ever-present risk of returns, all factor into the bottom line. You are quite correct that *Higher than Heaven* is a huge sales success story, but the two albums that preceded it were not. And as the good people at Graceland will tell you, while an artist who has passed away can still have considerable earning power, there continue to be substantial outlays required to maintain the revenue stream," he paused to add weight to his conclusion, "for all concerned parties."

Emma nodded, her calm presence masking some inner agitation, but completely disconcerting Uncle, who was used to being the manipulator. He pressed on. "Label reserves aside, the costs of the show itself were considerable, and there was a major donation to the World Wildlife Fund, which I'm sure your father would have wanted. I think to expect funds to be processed that quickly would be a little unrealistic." At this point, his voice carried a certain patronizing tone, but Emma remained unruffled.

"Points taken, Karl." She smiled reassuringly, and he relaxed too soon. "I've been assured, however, that you would have made certain that the box set, as well as the concert CD and DVD, wouldn't have been cross-collateralized, and if I recall correctly, the account was less than six figures in the red anyhow, a drop in the bucket at this point. I'm guessing the concert paid for itself, to say nothing of the piece of the ad revenue from the MTV special I'm hoping you negotiated for Strange ... Savage." She separated the last two words to give them a specimen-like ring. Uncle knew that any thoughts of Emma agreeing to sign off on an advance were long gone; he was thinking of how he could escape with his manhood intact. But it was too late. "Mr. Stasiuk said he needed to speak with you concerning some irregularities in the merch agreement. Shall I have him call you at the office today?"

Uncle clenched his jaw tightly and forced out the words. "I'm sure your father would be very proud of you, taking care of his legacy so attentively."

"Here, let me get that," said Emma, picking up the bill. "Nice of you to think about the pandas." Uncle creaked as he got up. "It's his future I'm more concerned with, Karl. If you keep your hands on the wheel and out of the till, it all should be fine. Stay in touch."

Emma breezed out the door of the café and let out a breath she felt she'd been holding in for the last thirty minutes. Stick handed her a helmet as she smiled and climbed behind him on the bike, and they sped off down Santa Monica Boulevard, heading west.

Uncle paged Roscoe and waited in the sun, squinting, till the car pulled up in front of the café. It had taken his knees so much time to straighten once he'd gotten up that he hadn't witnessed Emma's departure with Stick. With an organic war starting in his stomach to match the hostilities being played out in his head, he also turned west. A call to Eddie resulted in a non-committal reply to his anxious request to speak with Roc or to receive any shred of news about material for the *Echoes* release. It was only a matter of hours or minutes before Justin would call, wanting an update on Uncle's mission to have Emma sign off on another advance. Seeing Marie last night, first onstage with Delray then later at her apartment, had cheered him considerably; the twinge of guilt was minor as he flicked on the newest surveillance gadget attached to his phone, and the sounds of Marie's morning made their way into his headset. He'd already heard her arguing with her father in French on her own phone, in which he had implanted the device. Now, she was singing along in the shower with her beloved Serge Gainsbourg CD. The agony of hearing it was mitigated only by Uncle's fertile imagination. He directed Roscoe to a quiet Santa Monica street and asked him to pull over and raise the privacy window. Uncle switched off the Marie link and rested his head on the seat while performing some Mork Pook-prescribed tuina self-massage on his aching knees, only somewhat resembling an overturned cockroach struggling to right itself. Abruptly straightening, he leaned over to the driver's window. "Hey Roscoe, would you follow that silver Toyota; stay a couple of cars back and then pull up when I signal. Thanks, man." Uncle extracted the Hot Wheels card and dialed the number.

Bobbie figured she could get in at least one call before hitting the Coffee Bean on Montana, and switched on her phone. She might have waited until she was fortified with caffeine and sugar if she'd known who it would be. "Well, if it isn't my bald eagle. Do your manly tail feathers need a little affection today?"

The half-whispered voice chilled her. "Actually, my talons need some sharpening today. I've got my prey in sight."

"Why don't you close your eagle eyes and relax. Let me stroke your tail a bit." This had worked on his first call, and Bobbie didn't want to spend any more time than she had to with her weirdest client.

"Why don't you join me in my nest today? I don't feel like flying solo."

"Now you know that's against the rules, mister. Why don't you put your wings on glide, and we'll have a nice flight, all right?"

"Are you wearing that cute little denim vest you had on last night, you sweet thing?"

Bobbie had to swallow and catch her breath. "Now, I'm not sure how you know what I had on last night, but I think we'd better end our little phone fun for good right now. I never meet my clients, and I'm not about to start with you."

He wanted to continue the game for a while as they pulled off of Ocean Avenue onto Montana. "Not till I get a little closer look at you, honey. Did you know that an eagle can spot a little bunny rabbit trying to escape from almost a mile away?"

Bobbie gripped the wheel tighter and felt her throat getting dry; she searched for a place to park near 15th Street and a chance to catch her breath. Her caller made a low moaning sound over the phone, and she wondered why she didn't just hang up. Of course he'd probably just call back, and it would start all over again. "There you go, you must feel better now you're not moving." She put her car in park and tried not to panic. "And you don't have to worry about meeting me. We've already met; we just have to get to know each other better, Bobbie, that's all."

Snapping her phone shut, Bobbie jumped out of her car as if it was about to blow up. A midnight blue town car pulled up beside her, close enough that she had to lean her back into her mirror, and the window eased down. "Some say that eagles and vultures are related," said Uncle, rubbing his head slowly and smiling, "but I don't believe that, do you?" Bobbie just stared at this seemingly deranged man as the window went up again and the town car pulled away.

At the corner of Montana and 24th, Uncle had Roscoe pull over so he could lean out the open door and vomit. Waving his concerned driver off, he closed the door and fell back into the seat. Terrifying Bobbie hadn't been on his agenda when he had first called her phone sex service, but it had become necessary when Delray had passed on her story about seeing Roc at the 7-Eleven. The manager and his newest star had chuckled over a few Jim Morrison and Syd Barrett anecdotes, but Uncle knew there was more to it, and he was afraid that it could mean the beginning of the great unraveling. Or had that already begun? He didn't know anymore, and didn't want to think about it, so he switched on his Marie surveillance to kill time until they met later that afternoon for their coastal getaway.

His stomach was beginning to right itself as he pulled on his headset, leaned back, and closed his eyes. At least she was speaking English. Sort of. "... and you are believing that he is working at this 7-Eleven?"

Next came Julie's laugh and then, "No no no. But that's where she says she saw him. I mean she was his chick, and she should know, right?"

"So, should I advise this to Uncle, do you think?"

Julie turned serious. "No way. Listen, Bobbie's really cool and I really feel for her, you know. I just thought it was so weird. And Uncle never said anything to you about any of this?"

"Not even." Marie paused. "Maybe Roc could be writing me another song then, eh?"

Uncle leaned forward in his seat, turning up the volume as the girls' conversation faded in and out. "Ooo lala, *c'est moi et toi*." Julie laughed at her own singing, which to Uncle didn't sound any worse than his beloved's vocals. "Listen, honey, you can get J-Lo's people or Britney's or whoever at this point. Stick with the ones that are still breathing."

Marie giggled, but her reply was serious. "But is the Roc Molotov still alive or still dead?"

"Good question. Hey, you want to go for lunch at the Skybar? My friend Alan, who was the forklift driver in the first *Austin Powers*, is working and he'll get us a great table."

"But if he is not dead...." Marie let her thought hang.

"Alan? Oh, he is extremely vital. One time on the roof of ..."

"Non, I mean Roc. If he goes to the 7-Eleven and one of those pappapasties see him ... it would become terrible for Uncle."

The sound of running water obscured Julie's reply, but Marie's next words were crystal clear. "Maybe it could be better if he was really dead."

"Marie!" Julie managed to laugh and sound completely outraged at the same time. "What do you want to do? Call Tony Soprano? My friend Jason played a hit man in *Jackie Brown*, but that's as close as I get to all that."

"If he is already dead, who might know?" There was a teasing quality in Marie's voice that Uncle recognized as masking a very serious notion. As the girls left the apartment and Marie's phone was dropped into her bag, Uncle leaned back again and closed his eyes. The truly terrifying realization was that the idea she had expressed wasn't terrifying to him at all.

Forty-Five

"You're sure this is the right time?" Emma shouted into Stick's helmet as they rolled along Ventura Boulevard, past a crowd of valley chicks and their nearly hysterical mothers outside of Tower Records, which featured a sign reading, DELRAY TODAY. He put his hand over hers where it held onto his jacket, and gave it a gentle squeeze. At the light, he turned back to look at her.

"There is no right time, Emma. But I think he's going to be cool." He paused and added emphatically. "I *know* he's going to be cool."

"What did you tell him?" Her words were lost in the rev of the engine as they pulled away from the light. Once they reached the alley beside the studio in Toluca Lake, Emma hesitated getting off the bike as she removed her helmet and shook out her hair. "You said your girlfriend wants to meet him? Oh God, Richard." She checked herself in the bike's mirror.

"Sorry. But you wanted to surprise him. It was the best I could come up with. It's not like a fan thing or anything; he knows you dig the music, and I had to say that you were there that first night."

In the studio, Roc had his back to them, hunched over an acoustic guitar, tuning. "Hey," he called out in reply to Stick's greeting. "I've got this cool two-chord vamp thing, kinda reminds me of some of the stuff your band is into." He turned to face Stick and saw Emma at his side, holding his hand, quiet and vulnerable. A long, speechless moment followed as she and Roc locked gazes.

"Tabby." His voice, soft, sounded like he was making an observation to himself.

After a shorter pause, she barely whispered her reply. "Emma."

"Emma, yeah." He swallowed and stared at her, starting to smile. "Emma ... it's really good to meet you. I mean, I know you, but ..." No more words came as Roc gently put the guitar on its stand and walked over to embrace his daughter for the first time. Stick slipped silently out the studio door.

"Dad ... I missed not knowing you. I was going to come to California to find you and then ... I'm just glad I'm not too late."

"You look so much like your mother, it's incredible. How is she?"

"The same. Obsessed, intense, relentless, and totally loving."

Roc laughed at the description of the woman he had once fallen in love with. "Did you get any of that along with the blue eyes?"

"Maybe." Emma smiled and wiped her sleeve across her eyes.

"So many times I wanted to meet you, but Tabatha had it all worked out, and I just went along with her wishes. I hope you know that I loved you anyway."

Emma nodded. "Yeah, I guess in my way I did. I blamed her big time when she finally told me that James wasn't my dad. I was also incredibly relieved; he's such a geek. I mean he's nice but much more acceptable as a stepdad, you know."

"Hey, you want a drink? All mod cons here at Eddie's joint. So you and Ed's son are happening? Small world getting smaller. That's cool; he's a great kid. Wonderful musician too."

"I met him at a Maureen's Ankle gig, and he told me his dad had worked with you. It couldn't have been any weirder."

"No kidding." Roc awkwardly put his arm around Emma's shoulders as they walked to the kitchen. "So, what were you doing in L.A. anyway? I get the feeling we've got a lot to talk about." He smiled at the post-it on the fridge door. "More of Rich's handiwork?"

What can be explained is not poetry - Carl Sandburg

Emma giggled, and it broke his heart a little bit to think about the eighteen years he'd missed. She brushed her hair out of those Chagall-blue eyes, and they sparkled at him. "I came out here to find you."

Two hours later, they were on the patio, laughing about the cellphone call during the tribute.

"Hey, can I come up?" Stick had never seen Roc's room.

"Sure, but I didn't clean up for you." Stick joined the father and daughter reunion and shared the good feelings in the air. "Emma says I have to call you Richard. That cool with you?"

Stick just laughed.

"Dad ... I can't believe I'm using that word ... can we be serious for a moment?" He shrugged in response. "Do you have copies of any of your original agreements with Karl?"

Roc smiled and gestured toward his tiny room. "Not handy, why?"

As she pulled out her PalmPilot, Stick got up. "Need anything at the store?"

The two young women in nearly matching sweatsuits leaned on the railing in Palisades Park overlooking the Pacific Ocean, the Gold Coast, and to the south, the Ferris wheel that dominated the Santa Monica pier. Both had their hair tied back and were sipping on a water bottle. Julie gripped her sneaker and stretched out her leg. "This was a great idea; I'm so glad you called me."

"Well, I have to do this. We Burnette women tend to acquire a bit of a caboose."

Julie laughed. "We could be sisters, you know."

"Well, sure, why not?" Bobbie replied. "You be the cool one, and I'll be the one that says things like 'aw shucks' and 'give 'em what for,' okay?"

Julie laughed and tried out her best southern belle. "Hey, sugar, I've been to a few tractor pulls in my time, and the Marshall Tucker Band is all right with me, y'all."

"And I'm so totally all about that," Bobbie giggled in bad Valley speak. "Or not." Looking in the direction of the pier, she said, "I used to come here about every day when I first got to town and didn't know a soul."

"My dad used to bring me here before he split. I remember being carried on his shoulders through the crowd. The old wooden carousel he took me on is still running you know. Now it just seems messed up down there and makes me nervous."

"Yeah, I heard someone got himself shot on the pier last year." Bobbie nodded seriously.

"Someone gets shot just about everywhere in this town," Julie added ruefully.

They started walking north toward Arizona Avenue, where Julie's BMW was parked. A kid in a pink helmet wearing a hellbent expression flew by on a little pink bike with training wheels; a panting dad ran just behind. Under an ancient tree, a group of Goths smoked in the shade. A wheezing geezer with a walker shook her head disapprovingly in their direction as she laboured along the path in a wool suit.

"Listen, Julie, I called you 'cause I need some serious sorting out, and after our conversation at the Delray thing, you just seemed to me like a real understanding person." Bobbie hesitated, but Julie smiled encouragingly, so she continued. "If there is any chance that Roc is still alive, and I am truly starting to entertain that thought, I need to know." She gathered her emotions in and went on. "Because every day without him is miserable, and I'm afraid to believe the thing that I want most to be true."

Julie stopped and hugged Bobbie, who continued, "Now I didn't want to lose it here with y'all, but I feel like you understand; and you're very sweet to put up with the likes of me, carrying on like this."

Julie placed her hands on Bobbie's shoulders and spoke quietly and calmly. "Bobbie Jean, I think it's totally possible that Roc is alive." As Bobbie sighed deeply and closed her eyes, Julie said, "But I'm very worried about what's going to happen." She gestured to a park bench, and they sat down. Bobbie splashed some of her water on her face and tried to smile as Julie related her conversation with Marie. "I'm not certain she was serious. Maybe it's a cultural thing; I don't really know Marie that well. We went to school together then met again at a gala opening party for a new rehab place in Bel Air and had a few drinks and started hanging out, you know. But this Uncle character, I don't know about him at all. Maybe you know him better; she plays him like a violin, and that's what makes me nervous. Marie's a laugh but is totally without talent, in case you hadn't noticed. I mean she couldn't carry a tune in a Humvee, but he bought into her whole singer fantasy, and she's going to stop at nothing to keep that fantasy alive. I'm sorry Bobbie, tell me I'm crazy."

A tense expression settled on Bobbie's normally gentle face, and she slowly shook her head. "I wouldn't put anything past that weasel. Wait till I tell you what he pulled with me. The photograph was just the appetizer." Bobbie described her encounter with the evil eagle the previous day.

Julie sat silently in amazement and tried to suppress a smile. "You mean your gig is having sex with guys on your car phone? Wow! How do you get paid?"

Bobbie smiled back, a little wearily. "Oh, yeah, I guess that part is a mite bizarre, isn't it? You see, I started it with one wrong number the week I couldn't make the rent, just after I got here; and it was easy and, strange to tell, kind of a kick. I guess we're all weirdos at heart."

"Oh, don't get me started," Julie laughed. "So, Uncle just pulled up beside you on Montana, rolled down his window, and leered at you. He didn't even say anything?"

"Yep, just looking as pleased as can be with his slimy old self. Oh, he might have said something about vultures, but I was just thinking about escaping before something really awful happened. You can imagine."

"No shit. What a bastard. So, it sounds to me like he's trying to scare you off, in case you were getting any thoughts of trying to find Roc."

Bobbie mulled over the thought. "Could be, Julie. I don't know. I'm confused. I keep wondering why Roc would want to pretend to be dead." She pushed away the memory of the phone screw-up.

A first-time blader rolled off the path in front of them and crashed into a tree. "Ouch! Well, let's find out. What's that engineer's name?"

"You mean Eddie, real nice fella with a pot belly, thinks he's a DJ?"

"Yeah, him. If anyone knows, he does. Let's call him." Julie took her cellphone out of the pant leg pocket of her sweat suit.

"What if Uncle answers?" Bobbie asked apprehensively. "I couldn't deal with the likes of him."

"Don't worry. He and Marie are away on their reunion-in-Montecito weekend. She'd been giving him shade until the Delray show, and he'll be very preoccupied." Julie raised an eyebrow suggestively, which made Bobbie smile. "They're probably up to their necks in a tub of oil, drinking Mai Tais as we speak."

"Yech," said Bobbie as Julie dialed information.

"You ready, doll?" Julie handed her the phone.

"No. But what the hay." The operator responded, and Bobbie made her request. As she waited for the connection, she said to Julie, "They pay by credit card, by the way."

"Let me know if you want to franchise." Julie grinned as someone answered at the studio.

Marie returned naked from greeting the room service kid who had arrived with two Mai Tais and a giant plate of fries.

"What do you donate him here? In France, the tip is inside the bill."

"Oh, I'm sure it was an educational experience for him. Don't worry, my love." Uncle lifted a drink to toast nothing in particular as Marie eased back into the tub, causing a wave of pink bubbles to cascade over the edge. "By the way, what is the difference between fries and *pommes frites*, anyway? Are they the same? It sounds so much better to say, *oui*, I'll have *frites* with my ratatouille." His pronunciation sounded like he was working up a furball.

"Oh, you silly Uncle," she tittered, accepting his offer of a miniature sword with a maraschino cherry and a slice of pineapple, and offering a little trout pout in gratitude.

"Did you realize, my little *coquette*, that Sir Laurence Olivier and Vivien Leigh were married here at the San Ysidro Ranch in a midnight full moon ceremony?" Uncle purred.

"*Mais oui*, but did she not go off her bonkers a little later?" Marie deflected the direction of the conversation.

Not to be deterred, Uncle pressed on in romance mode. "And JFK and Jackie O honeymooned here?"

"So many secrets he had from her, *non*?" Marie dipped a fry in Uncle's drink. "Not true love, I am thinking."

Uncle could see where this was heading, even in his blurry state. He looked across the rolling Montecito hillside of the ranch and thought about the little jewel box burning a hole in his overnight bag. "Surely, a *soupçon* of mystery is a good thing. You know how I love to surprise you, my little *bonbon*." He eased around the steaming tub to get closer to her.

"But some secrets grow large, and maybe they will keep us apart." She floated the bowl of fries between them purposefully. "But I'm certain you could make my uncertain go away," she smiled girlishly, "if you want to." Negotiating through the bubbles until she was behind a confused Uncle, Marie began to massage his smooth head with the contents of a nearby bottle of Ultraglide. He slowly sank in the tub until he rested against her chest, as she made circular motions over his bobbing head. "Hmmm, I look in my crystal ball, and I see that if someone were to go away, it would allow you and me to become so close, maybe forever close."

"Mmmm ..." Uncle drifted into a numb ecstasy.

Forty-Six

With Roc and Stick immersed in the search for the perfect bass drum sound, Emma picked up the phone. "Swirling Sound. No, Eddie's not in, can I take a message for you?" Wondering if Eddie had a new southern girlfriend, she left the control room to find a pen but was stopped cold when the caller identified herself. Emma realized that this must be the mysterious muse for so many of her dad's recent songs. Bobbie, for her part, was equally taken aback to discover the identity of the young woman with the distinctive New England delivery. This must be the daughter Roc never knew.

"Bobbie, I can't talk right now. Can we meet up later, somewhere private? I'm new to California; are you on the west side? How about your favourite beach? Okay. I'm coming from the Valley, so give me a couple of hours to get organized and get directions, say five?"

Emma returned to the control room, and Stick looked up from the console. "Another of my dad's platinum clients?"

"No, just a tantalizing offer of a new long distance plan. She was nice, so we talked for a while." Emma shrugged.

Stick shot her a skeptical look and went back to work. Roc turned, smiling, and just stared at her for a moment as she came and sat between them. "How about if we take a break? It's such a beautiful day. If we had one like this at home, they'd declare a statewide holiday."

"Sure," said Roc. "I've got the L.A. To Go menu book, and we can sit on my porch and feed the leftovers to the squirrels."

Emma wasn't certain he was being serious but realized that he was used to living in a very small world. "No, I mean, let's go out. No one will recognize you with your beard and everything. We'll get take out and have a picnic, I don't know, something." She knew this sounded naïve.

"I'd love to, but … I don't have that option right now, sweetie. I'm sorry. I made my bed on this one, and believe me I've had lots of time to have second thoughts, but this is just how it is right now."

Emma knew she only had one chance to make this happen and took her best shot. "Dad, I need you to be alive. Here and now. I've waited a long time to be with you." She could see her father softening, but he was unconvinced. "Listen, Rich has been teaching me how to drive the bike; we'll just go for a cruise. Is that cool, Richard?"

"Uh, sure. I've got to work on this track anyway. Hey man, if my dad shows up, I'll tell him you're snoozing or writing upstairs and want privacy."

Emma could see her dad struggling, but knew she was tapping into his deeper desires. "You can leave your helmet on for total anonymity, if you like." She smiled teasingly and took his hand.

"Yeah, okay. Let me take a nervous pee. Can you really drive that thing?"

The roar of the ocean was the perfect antidote to the cacophony of thoughts playing in Bobbie's head as she walked down the stairs to El Matador beach. Mix in some bittersweet memories, and she had a lot to sort through. She'd left herself extra time to revisit her favourite place in California and was glad that with the late afternoon cooling off, she didn't have to share it with many other people. A picnicking family was trudging past as she came down, and she recognized that post-beach daze on the kids' faces as they hauled backpacks and sand toys up the stairs. Kicking off her sneakers and tying them together over her shoulder, Bobbie headed straight for the surf and that welcome wash of sound. A wave swirled around her feet. *Roc's daughter, Emma — she'll know if he's alive, won't she?* A seagull screamed just overhead. The Marie tale was chilling, but it too seemed far-fetched. The first time Bobbie had come here with Roc — that night — the first time they'd made love. *Oh God, please let that happen again.* Bobbie shivered, pulled a sweatshirt out of her bag and retreated from the water's edge to walk over to one of the giant rocks that distinguished El Matador from all the other beaches on this coast. She climbed up the side and sat with her legs pulled up to her body, lifting her face to the ocean spray, feeling the cool breeze cut beneath the skin, rocking gently.

As she wove through the traffic on Ventura Boulevard, Emma's steely confidence unnerved Roc, but he'd given himself up to the moment, and his daily obsessions with songwriting, loneliness, and defying Uncle floated away into the Valley haze. She sped confidently through Sherman Oaks, Encino, and Woodland Hills and paused only once to navigate the transition from Ventura Boulevard to Calabasas Road. He offered to switch places, even though it had been awhile since he'd driven a motorcycle. *But you don't forget, do you? Or is that bicycles?* Emma seemed to have a destination in mind, although she was being mysterious about it, and Roc smiled when she took the Las Virgenes turn-off and began the descent to the Pacific down the dramatic Malibu Canyon Road. The vibration of the bike and the shimmer of the ocean had a meditative effect on Roc as they rolled along the PCH in the late afternoon sun. It took him a moment once the bike stopped in the tiny parking area to realize that she'd chosen his favourite beach.

"This is it, right?" Emma smiled. "El Matador, the one in your song 'Underwater Smile'? 'All the sunburned saints of El Matador,' right?"

He pried off the helmet, thinking that Ed's kid had a very small head. "Yeah, this is it. Wait till you see it." Roc inhaled the salt air deeply. They walked to a path leading to a long wooden staircase and started down. Partway down it opened to an unforgettable vista, and Emma stopped to drink it in.

"Those rocks near the shore look like the spine of a dinosaur poking through the surface." She knew she sounded like a ten-year-old. "I can see why this place is so inspiring. I don't think I care if I ever see Boston Common again."

Roc took her hand at the steepest part of the path, and maybe for a minute she *was* a ten-year-old to him. As they came closer to the ocean, Emma paused once more and felt the butterflies again. "If I've done something stupid today, Dad, please forgive me. I love you."

Roc looked at her with tenderness. "Forgive you? I'm so grateful to you for giving me a reason to be alive and not buried in that museum to myself at Eddie's. And except for that one tricky turn in Malibu Canyon, you really *can* drive a motorbike." He smiled at his daughter. "I love you too, Emma."

He looked toward the shore and beyond to the skyline, then the familiar rock formation at the foot of the stairs. The figure clutching itself on the top of the rock looked familiar too, even though he could just make out the silhouette in the slanting afternoon light. *Must be cold up there,* he thought. She seemed to read his mind, as he stepped off the last stair onto the beach, and turned to look back at them. She kept looking, and Roc was pulled toward her like the tide that rolled back from the base of the rock. Emma held back, waiting at the edge of the beach as Roc approached the woman on the rock. He held out his hand and helped her down, and they melted into one figure, unmoving as the water rolled over their feet, in and out. Emma sat down and breathed in the Pacific Ocean for the first time, watching the gulls circling overhead. She squinted, not sure of what she was seeing and then realized it was the dolphins, diving and playing just off the shore.

Forty-Seven

"Seventeen minutes on the left hand side of eight bells here at K-Ed, the rock of the valley, with another instant classic-classic-classic." Eddie's disc jockey intro gave way to the music coming from the control room.

Roc, Bobbie, Emma, and Stick sat in a circle on one of the blankets used for dampening the bass drum, amid take out containers, plates, and drinks. Stick played chopsticks on his knee as one of Roc and Stick's newest songs played back over the big studio speakers mounted above the window to the control room. Emma bounced along to the music, aglow with nervous energy. Roc and Bobbie sat close together, exchanging knowing looks now and then, occasionally whispering in each other's ear.

As the song crescendoed, Roc and Stick toasted with glasses of red wine while Emma and Bobbie talked. "She named me after Emma Goldman, a true fighter, my mom always said. 'If voting changed anything, they'd make it illegal,' that's pure Emma."

"What is it with you two and the quotes?" Roc asked Emma and Stick in amusement before being distracted by the music. "Oh ... listen, I love that coda," he said to his co-writer. "I think it's my favourite part of the song, even if you only hear it once at the end."

"Yeah, totally cool," replied Stick, nodding as the girls resumed their conversation.

"Well, my dad wanted to call me Ambrosia, but my mom vetoed that, said it sounded like a stripper."

"I like Bobbie Jean," said Emma. "It suits you. Very sweet, southern, strong." She picked up a take-out box, peered inside, and curled up her nose before putting it back down.

"Thanks. Of course, the boys at school called me Robert if I got tough with 'em. My mom's favourite singer was Bobbie Gentry, do you know her?"

"'It was the third of June, another sleepy dusty delta day,'" sang Roc, who'd been listening in.

"Yup, that's my birthday, so Mama said it had to be." Bobbie put her hand on Roc's shoulder. "I've missed hearing you sing, you know."

The voice over the speakers drowned them out, booming with reverb. "I'm gonna rock my way right outta here, kids. Back at you tomorrow. And if you've been listening in your car, thanks for the ride!"

The group picnicking on the studio floor groaned in unison at Eddie's sign-off. As the music subsided, Emma cleared her throat authoritatively. "I want to officially welcome you all to the first meeting of the Roc Molotov comeback committee," she continued through the laughter, "and I'll keep my opening remarks as brief as possible." Roc buried his head in his hands. "Should any of today's measures come to a vote, I remind you that the late Mr. Molotov will have to abstain." Roc peered through his fingers, amused at his daughter's assertiveness. "The charter calls for us to use all means possible to resurrect …"

"Uh, poor choice of words," Stick interjected to laughter.

"Okay, *restore* the career of the artist to his rightful place, among the living, with all the rights that this affords."

"Hear, hear!" Eddie stood at the studio door, smiling.

"Okay, okay, I know where this is going, and I appreciate it, and don't think I haven't thought about all of this," Roc jumped in. "You're welcome to question what led me to be holed up in a tiny room above a studio in Toluca Lake with a guitar and a dozen pairs of black jeans, but I have to take responsibility for my own choices."

"But Roc, whose idea *was* this whole thing?" Bobbie asked.

"Uncle!" said Stick, Eddie, and Emma in unison.

"But I agreed," Roc pointed out, "and the legal issues with me becoming undead would kill me." The laughter was subdued in response to his joke. "I don't plan to be here forever," he said, indicating the studio. "I'd love to perform again, but I gave that up willingly. It doesn't mean I can't have a life." He took Bobbie's hand.

"You can have it all, Dad; that's why God invented lawyers." Emma jumped in. "We just need to find the right time and place to make it happen." There was group agreement, and they all turned to look at Roc for his response.

"I'll think about it," he smiled. "But, like it or not, Uncle will have to be involved in this," he continued over groaning. "This has been an incredible day. Thanks to all of you." He stood up and helped Bobbie to her feet. "There's someone I've got to spend some time with."

As they left the studio, Emma leaned on Stick's shoulder and sighed. "The most amazing day of my life, that's for sure."

"More amazing than your first Maureen's Ankle show?" he asked with mock seriousness.

She ignored him. "You should have seen them on the beach. I cried my eyes out just watching."

"Yeah, I can imagine," said Stick, then assuming a daytime TV announcer voice, "Hallmark presents … a rock 'n roll reunion." Emma rolled her eyes as he went on. "I'm seeing slowmo, I'm hearing maybe a solo cello, or ... no, oboe, like in 'Peter and the Wolf,' what do you think, Dad?"

Eddie shook his head, turned on the overhead lights, and started picking up the takeout boxes on the studio floor. Emma punched her boyfriend on the shoulder before jumping on top of him and kissing him.

"I just love your new songs, Roc." Bobbie sat on the bed with the blankets pulled around her while Roc stood on the porch listening to the sounds of the night.

"Hey, I thought you were asleep." He came back into the room and found a spot at the end of the small bed. "Thanks. Yeah, working with Rich has been really cool. It's opened me up creatively, I think."

"But you're there in all those songs. Is anyone ever going to hear them?"

"I don't know what to say about that. I'm just enjoying creating them right now. I guess I'll think about it later, or just give them to Uncle to include on the archives CD."

Bobbie pulled the blankets a little tighter and nodded, keeping to herself any thoughts that would spoil this night she had thought would never happen.

"There is one other song that we didn't play tonight in the studio. It's not mixed yet, but I think it's one of the best of the lot." Roc stroked Bobbie's leg through the bedding. "You know the night when I saw you at the 7-Eleven?" She arched a brow. "I was pretty freaked out that night. I mean, it was my first time out of this building in weeks, and that was strange enough, but then ... well, I got lost on my way back here, and I just wandered the streets in the neighbourhood, hoping to see something familiar, amped up about being out, but like a scared kid, kinda panicky, and I started getting this song idea while I was walking around. By the time I finally recognized Eddie's street, I'd pretty much written the whole thing in my head, so I called Rich and Ed, and we cut it in one pass as soon as they got here." He got up and picked up his guitar, then sat back down on the end of the bed. "We still have to work on it; I needed a little distance before digging back into the track. Anyway, do you want to hear it?"

Bobbie just nodded sleepily as Roc started strumming the opening chords. He sang,

> **"Am I fading from the picture**
> **Was I ever really here**
> **Am I falling through the trapdoor**
> **As you watch me disappear ..."**

Bobbie felt a shiver race down her arms and she huddled further into the blankets. Roc closed his eyes and continued with a much softer version of "Here But I'm Gone" than the one he had recorded the night it was written.

Bobbie leaned across the guitar and kissed him at the end of the song. "By the way, I almost keeled over that night at the 7-Eleven, but that's all right." She smiled indulgently, "It's amazing, honey. I love it. It's not like anything I've heard you do before."

"Thanks. Yeah, I'm not sure where it came from."

"'I'm here but I'm gone,'" Bobbie quoted. "I reckon it sounds like someone who feels cut off from what he loves. 'Am I fading from the picture. Was I ever really here.' That's the lyric, right?"

Roc nodded, looking down at his guitar, thinking about the meaning behind what he'd written. Bobbie spoke softly. "You're here now, aren't you?"

"I want to be," he said, looking up at her. "I really want to be."

Forty-Eight

Uncle awoke in his cabin at the San Ysidro Ranch with a raging case of the night terrors, having dreamt of murdering his best friend in the world. Images of Marie in her little red shoes stringing exposed wire across the empty stage of the Hollywood Bowl and Uncle himself methodically squirting Ultraglide on the wire gave way to a scene in which Roc stood silently at centre stage while Uncle ignited the whole sticky mess.

Shaking and damp, he got up and listened to Marie breathing softly, noticing that she pouted, even in her sleep. He shook off the nightmare but couldn't rid himself of the idea that Marie was actually suggesting a real life version of the dream. Quietly sliding the door shut, he stepped into the cool night air and gazed up at the Montecito hills silhouetted by the moonlight. He needed clarity, maybe more than ever before, to get through the various minefields that lay ahead. Wasn't he working in these people's best interests as well as his own? Justin, the ultimate label weasel, spoiled industry brat, expecting Uncle to carry him. The Cocktails, a train wreck in the making if there ever was one. He glanced back through the glass door at Marie — this time, he'd really let his libido take the wheel. It was worth it, wasn't it? And Roc — who would have expected him to dry up, with all the creative freedom in the world to do what he loved best? Or was he holding out, as Uncle suspected? And that fucking precocious little twat of a daughter, like he needed her in the mix. Thank God for the pride of Farcry, the hillbilly with a hit.

Later, Uncle tried to stay focused on Marie's miniskirt as it travelled north, while she raced through a red light in downtown Montecito, singing along loudly with Serge Gainsbourg. Once they were out of the hills and they pulled onto the 101, he checked his messages and tried to disguise his surprise at hearing one from Roc.

"So, I am desiring the crab cakes from the Ivy, maybe some mimosa to erase my head. What do you say, my big boy, Beverly Hills or By the Shore?" Marie conducted the orchestra on the CD, raising her hand through the convertible opening in her Citroën's roof.

"If only I could, my love, but the music business requires my attention." The only advantage to disappointing Marie was the turn-on he got from her bruised puppy expression. "But this just means the joy of anticipating seeing you later, *ma petite*." He was tuning up for a day of placating and manipulating. When she dropped him at the office a heart pounding fifty-three minutes later, she turned her cheek to him for the briefest of air kisses before screeching into the eastbound traffic on Wilshire.

The camera followed Uncle's arrival as he stepped out of Marie's car into the *Beach Blast* microphone. "Uncle, dude, was that Marie Ladurée? Righteous."

"Hey, Chad, what's up?" Uncle immediately had his guard up, given *Beach Blast*'s ongoing Roc reports.

"Ooo lala! Wicked vid, man."

Uncle relaxed slightly. "Yeah, thanks. I know you guys have been calling about having Marie on *Beach Blast*, and we're all over that."

"Cool. The Delray duet was epic. Any thoughts of releasing that?"

Uncle was restlessly moving toward the door of his office. "Stay tuned, Herr Sparx. Listen, I gotta ..."

Chad assumed an ultra-concerned expression. "That was so weird about Delray attacking Roc just before he cacked."

Uncle paused. His gaze bored into the interviewer's eyes. "Mistaken identity, Chad. Happens all the time. A dark parking garage, a brief encounter ... memory's a funny thing." Uncle's tone suggested a conclusion to the matter. "And in light of the loss of Roc, a truly superfluous pursuit." Uncle winked at the camera. "Good catching up with you, brother."

Chad nodded, giving Uncle his trademark spacey grin and rubbing his fingers together. "So I guess you'll have a boatload of copyrights on that Roc box set, right, Uncle?"

The camera didn't catch the tiny shudder that Uncle experienced on his way through the door. Inside, Candy stopped him with a finger in the air and a nod in the direction of his office. Sitar music wafted out.

"Sorry. I couldn't stop them. At least they brought their own pillows." Candy smiled and handed Uncle a three-inch stack of phone messages, the pink ones on top signifying priority. He noticed the name on the first one. "Max is pissed that you're using Cockburn, who called him asking for copies of the Roc publishing deals. He says he won't send them until he speaks to you, so ... I faxed them an hour ago." Uncle nodded appreciatively. "And I think Justin has you on speed dial, but I consolidated the forty-odd calls into one message." Looking in the direction of the office, she added, "Let me know if you want me to run out for incense."

Uncle entered his office warily and was immediately group-hugged by Delray, Danny, and Gwen, wearing matching lime green djellabas. "Welcome to our joy," a dreamy and very pregnant Gwen offered as Uncle almost bounced off her belly. "We've moved into the ashram in Topanga Canyon; they've got a birthing pool that our doula says reduces cellular blockage." Uncle just stared at them then switched off the Indian music.

"Rrright," he said, "not too early for a Lone Star, is it, big boy?" He grinned at Delray, who had been uncharacteristically silent thus far.

"Hey, thanks Uncle, but I don't like to dull my growth edge before noon." Delray flashed a peace sign, grinning moronically.

"So, Danny, how are the rehearsals going? You guys were great at the Lingerie last week." Uncle tried to shift into work mode, at odds with the prevailing grooviness.

As the three visitors sat down on their prayer pillows, Danny patted an empty one, indicating that Uncle should join them, a gesture he chose to ignore. "That's what I came to talk to you about. I'm leaving The Cocktails, and as a spiritual man yourself, I'm sure you'll understand why."

Gwen interrupted. "Terra Firma, or Danny as you have known him, has to follow his beacon, honour his mission."

Danny continued, "We've got some issues, Uncle, and I don't think that Frankie and Barry can overcome their personal toxic obstacles; but I'm going to offer a special prayer to choicefulness tonight." Uncle nodded uncomprehendingly. "First, though, we're going to fill the birthing pool with Kabbalah water." He smiled so sweetly that Uncle didn't have the heart to tell him to fuck himself.

"Hey, you two love doves, do you mind if I have a word with my man here?" he said, indicating Delray. "You're welcome to use the phone in the other office if you want to page your doula or something."

They nodded obligingly like a pair of matching plastic spaniels in the back window of a car. Uncle escorted them to the door and closed it before addressing Delray. "So, my brother, are you going to be purging your toxins in Topanga like Numb and Number, or could I interest you in a malted beverage?"

Delray glanced in the direction of the door and shrugged. "What the hell, don't mind if I do."

Uncle pulled a Lone Star from the fridge for Delray and one for himself, to take the edge off a day that had started badly. "Here you go, stud. So, Danny and the boys have issues, do they? Listen, Delray, you're no pussy-boy, so I hope you're not buying into this crap; it's guru *du jour* with those two, you know."

"Hells bells, Uncle, they're makin' me the godfather, and I feel like I need to step up. Besides, you should get a load of those hippie chicks in them see-through blouses at the outdoor prayer sessions." Now he was talking Uncle's language. "I'm not sure about them pit bushes, but you don't have to fondle them, do you?"

"No, I don't think that's required. So, you'll be at the ashram if I need to reach you?"

"Damn straight. Tonight we're going to work on drawing the light and eliminating the chaos. Cool, huh?" Delray continued in a conspiratorial tone, "The only thing that gets me kinda skittish is when Gwen, or Stella Luna as she's taken to callin' herself, talks about her transparency aspirations. I mean, she's got a bun in the oven for godsake, even if she is built like a brick shithouse."

"Listen, I've got to get to work. Would you mind telling Terra Firma and Stella Luna that we can do some more sharing at another time?"

"All right," said Delray, draining his Lone Star. "Dang, I needed that. Well, trust your journey, boss."

Forty-Nine

Uncle trusted his journey, but not his girlfriend. As he made his way to the studio via Laurel Canyon, he flipped through some papers and listened in on Marie's lunch at the Ivy with Julie. Some actor friend of Julie's had sent over a bottle of champagne, and he heard the girls giggling and dissing the donor as the cork was popped. Uncle emailed Justin and Max Stone to avoid actual conversations. Marie's lunch babble got cut off around Lookout, which was all right, because he wanted to focus his energy entirely on Roc Molotov.

In his message, Roc had said he had some things to play and things to discuss. Fair enough. As long as Roc didn't want to go on any more field trips, Uncle could handle any topic that came up. It was the new music that he needed desperately, no matter what it sounded like. Uncle toyed with the idea of trying to slip the publishing reassignment contract past Roc, figuring that Cockburn would be cool with backdating it, thus resolving some sticky issues with the pesky teen.

As he pulled up, he noticed a motorcycle in the alley beside the studio and wondered if Eddie was having another midlife crisis. Alerted by the disarming of the security system, Roc came down to meet Uncle, and they embraced warmly. Roc noticed the smell of beer on Uncle and chose to ignore it; Uncle caught a whiff of some designer perfume on Roc but hid his puzzlement with faux warmth. "How are you, my brother? I was very happy to get your call. Can't wait to hear the new songs."

Roc was loose but reserved, Uncle could see. "C'mon in the control room. You want a drink?"

"Maybe an ice tea, it's early." Uncle grinned. "Hey, listen, just before we get going, I wanted to show you these." He extracted an envelope from his bag. "The fan club's taken it upon themselves to offer some ideas for a monument. What do you think?"

Roc found himself looking at an artist's rendering of a tombstone in the shape of the headstock of a guitar, with the words ROC IN PEACE etched across the top. "Way cooler than Jim Morrison's at Père Lachaise, wouldn't you say?" Uncle leaned over Roc's shoulder to share the viewpoint. "You know, with the beard and hair, you're starting to give me a bit of a late period Jimbo vibe," he went on jovially, "minus the breadbasket, of course." He chortled, to silence from Roc, realizing that this might not have been the best opening. "Anyway, this can wait."

"I'm not dead." Roc spoke without emotion.

"Of course you're not," replied Uncle, trying to rescue the mood, "but the fans need somewhere to gather to share their grief." He realized he was sounding like Gwen for a moment.

Concealing his disgust, Roc hit play, filling the room with the opening to "Pale Fire." Uncle sat perfectly still in the big studio chair, knowing that he was hearing the work of an artist at his very best. As the half dozen songs played, his excitement grew as he realized that this was all he needed to complete the first *Echoes* release. He also felt a huge measure of pure relief, since this also represented the ticket to an ass-saving advance. He turned to Roc after the last song faded out. "Fucking amazing. This is the best work you have ever done. You know that, don't you?"

Roc smiled. In spite of all Uncle's inappropriateness, he knew Roc best, and his praise still carried some weight. "Thanks. Yeah, I know. I'm not sure where it all came from, but I'm just glad it came at all."

"I have to be honest, my good man, I was a bit worried. It's not like you to be so remote." With his hands outstretched and stubbled head glowing, it struck Roc that Uncle resembled a saguaro cactus. "Listen, good news, I think the agent has neutralized the native burial ground issue on the Big Sur property, so we can start inspections. They're saying there could be a flood insurance question that needs …"

Roc held up his hand at the whiff of bullshit that had entered the conversation. "Uncle, before you go any further, I've got something to tell you. I've engaged a new financial advisor who's going to be overseeing all aspects personal and professional." Uncle froze, expressionless, as Roc continued. "Not to step on the management side, of course, but you'll need to provide full access to all the books, et cetera." Gently putting his hand on Uncle's back, he guided the big man out of the studio. "C'mon, let's continue this upstairs."

With his knees creaking like a rickshaw, Uncle laboured up the stairs after his friend. Roc called out from the porch with good humour, "Come into my office. I understand you two have met."

"Emma." Uncle offered a funereal smile. "Nice to see you again." He struggled to keep his composure, pushing back for the moment the flood of questions rolling into his head.

"Karl." Emma nodded coolly.

"Uncle, Emma's going to look after the business side of my career from now on. She'll work closely with her mother's lawyers in Boston, and she's engaged Wasserman out here on the financial management side. I'm sure this is not a happy situation for you, but we've discussed it, and it's with her best interests in mind that I feel I need to make the change."

Uncle tried to steady the ground beneath him and stalled. "Mind if I sit down?" He eased into a deckchair and nodded rhythmically, looking back and forth between Roc and his daughter. He attempted to inject some levity as Emma and Roc sat down. "Well, first of all, I'm delighted that you two were able to meet ... here in the afterlife, but don't you think you're a little late, if you'll pardon the term, to be renegotiating our business relationship, my brother?" In his swirl of thoughts, Uncle was trying to figure out how the two could have met. "Of course, Emma's interests overlap with ours, but I still feel better qualified to guide the good ship Molotov through the rapids of the music business. I mean, thanks to good planning, right now you're in the best shape of your career, Roc. And if you keep making music like what you just played me, this ride could go on indefinitely, right?"

Roc broke the brief silence that followed. "Uncle, let me cut to the chase. Emma has brought to my attention some pretty alarming discrepancies, to put it in the mildest of possible terms, in your accounting practices. As you know, this is not my area of expertise; I always trusted you to do what you do best while you offered me the same respect." He noticed that Uncle's eye was twitching as he nervously rubbed his head in circles. "And I still trust you. I just think that maybe you've gotten overloaded of late with new projects, and your joint venture with Justin Savage, and ... I feel it's for the best." Uncle nodded, but Roc could see that it wasn't in agreement. "Hey, can I get you something? I'm going to run down to the kitchen."

"Yeah, sure, man, anything. Thanks," Uncle said huskily. As Roc bounced down the stairs, Uncle turned his gaze to meet that of his rival for Roc's trust. For a long moment, neither spoke.

"You know, I'm sure it must have been very emotional for you two to meet for the first time." Uncle measured his words. "Roc has been very protective of you all these years, Emma. And he relied on *me* to set up your trust fund and to look after your financial security with total discretion during that time. I only hope that you, perhaps unwittingly, haven't exploited your father at an emotional time in his life." He lifted his palms in a conciliatory gesture. "These ... little problems, that you have quite correctly focused on, are typical of a business that I've spent my adult life operating in. I can assure you that any accounting irregularities can be easily rectified." His tone turned honeyed. "Emma, your dad needs you for so many reasons right now. Just be a daughter to him. Let me handle the stuff I know best. I mean, if it ain't broke ..."

In the kitchen, Bobbie whispered unnecessarily, "How's it going?"

"Too soon to tell," Roc replied.

"I know he's your friend, man, but there's a bit of a vulture vibe," Stick added nervously. "Should we have used a weapons detector?"

Roc smiled. "I think she can handle him."

Bobbie curled up her nose. "You couldn't pay me enough to share air with the likes of that reprobate."

"Nice word, honey." Roc hauled snacks out of the fridge and placed them on a tray as Bobbie threw on some napkins.

"If I knew which one was his, I'd have half a mind to ..."

"Okay, I gotta go. Stick, do you know where the opener is?"

Back up on the deck, Emma's tone seemed at once to mingle pathos, disgust, and amusement. "Cut the crap, Karl. Just because you've swabbed the decks doesn't mean 'the good ship Molotov,' as you call it, isn't leaking badly." She shook her head and met his indignant expression evenly. "I don't think you're a crook, but I think you're in some kind of mess, and, expert exploiter that you are, you're done here. The quid pro quo is this — your agreement in exchange for delivery of the new material."

His mouth tasting like sand, Uncle waited impatiently for Roc to return.

"And financially, it's not a question of 'overlap.' As my father's sole heir, his interests *are* my interests." Emma could hear her father starting up the stairs, and she leaned toward Uncle, who was sweating heavily. "Besides, Karl, you're going to have your hands full with his comeback."

Fifty

Uncle's head throbbed in time to the drilling on Laurel Canyon, which was down to one lane, his car, of course, being the first one stopped as the traffic flow changed direction. The guy in the hardhat and yellow vest looked like Frankie Cocktail, for god's sake. Uncle wondered what would become of those lugs if he didn't rescue himself first then pull them into the lifeboat. Emma had demanded nothing short of a full-fledged concert featuring Roc and the boys. They'd been dumped off the Knack reunion tour; availability wasn't an issue. But Roc, what was to be done here? His friend was in a new place creatively, spiritually, whatever. It was as if the presence of these women had both reawakened him and rendered him oblivious to the fact that he was supposed to be dead. Even as Emma had tossed off revenue projections from the concert like a veteran Hollywood business manager, Uncle had visions of fraud charges and his reputation in tatters. And how would a duped public respond to Roc's return? He knew the label, with their inbred short-term thinking, would love it; and Justin ... with the moral compass of a Washington lobbyist, having learned the business at the knee of his father, Doc Savage, the payola king, could justify anything. Roscoe had gotten out of the car and was having a smoke with the road crew, who seemed to have gone on a break, forgetting the row of cars that stretched back to Ventura Boulevard and beyond. At least the drilling had stopped. To relax, Uncle turned on K-Mozart radio and began to shave his head while the car was still.

Once they hit Sunset, his cell was working again, but before he had a chance to make the first call, the phone vibrated and Marty Cockburn squawked into his ear.

"Okay, I'm looking at a fax from Stasiuk, and it's nasty, Uncle Strange. They're threatening to hold all Roc-related revenue in an escrow account, which I'm confident they could swing long enough to draw blood, unless … hang on, it continues on page two…. I must be missing something … unless you agree to Emma's concert proposal by the fifteenth blah blah blah. I'm sorry, Uncle, I've got to call them; this doesn't make a damn bit of sense to me. I mean, what the …"

Uncle cut him off. "She wants a concert with The Cocktails in L.A. … a comeback show … with Roc." He could hear all the assertiveness drain from his voice.

"I don't get it. The guy's dead."

"Well, she thinks he's alive."

"I see. And is he?"

Uncle paused, starting to reply, then paused again. "Marty, we've got lawyer-client privilege here, right?"

"Uh-huh."

"Let's say he is. What kind of issues do you see coming up?"

"Issues!" The attorney's voice distorted badly, and Uncle held the phone at arm's length. "Let's see. Assuming no life insurance claims, debt problems, and no fake ID and living in Sarasota scenario, I think Roc would be in the clear." Uncle tried to jump in, but Marty steamrolled over him. "But for you, braniac, it's not so good. And unless you envision incarceration as a nice respite from life's nagging little difficulties, Uncle Strange, you might want to consider faking your *own* death, assuming that's what we're talking about here."

"I didn't say that, Marty," Uncle said softly, trying to lower the intensity of the conversation.

Marty snorted into the phone. "I'm thinking ten to fifteen for fraud with time off for keeping your caftan clean. Uncle, listen. Deep breath time here, my friend. I know Stasiuk's partner, Horvath. I dealt with him on that Aerosmith thing. Remember when Joe *borrowed* Ahmet's yacht and sailed it to St. Barth's? I'm sure …"

"Forget it, Marty. This girl's crazy tough. And she fucking hates me."

"So what, she can start her own local chapter of the club. Where's your fight here, Uncle? Listen, we'll move first. Sue her ass, make her prove who she is. Meanwhile, my wife's bookie's brother is a judge in Jersey. They'll have to fight us on jurisdiction. You can make your money moves while it's being sorted out. C'mon!"

Uncle, slumped in his seat, had stopped listening. "Marty, I've got to call you back." As Roscoe pulled into the parking lot of Les Deux, Uncle was rubbing his head in circles when he spotted Marie's car. Finding a wayward tuft, his hand shook as he took a swipe with the razor, resulting in a stream of blood running down beside his ear. As he dabbed himself with a Kleenex, Uncle used all his compartmentalizing skills to file away the Emma dilemma and focus on sweeping Marie off her little red stilettos. He popped open the velvet jewellery box one more time and examined the colossal bauble inside. Marie's reference to a "celebration" reassured him that she knew where tonight was heading.

Accustoming himself to the shadowy interior of Les Deux, Uncle was escorted by the owner, Michelle, to a quiet table behind an Oriental screen. Marie had her back to him, her bare shoulders an intoxicating invitation. Putting his hands over her eyes, he kissed Marie's neck and whispered in his worst French accent, "Who ees eet?"

"François?" she cooed suggestively. Seeing Uncle's surprised reaction, she pouted theatrically. "Oh, a little funny for my big man is too much?"

Uncle recovered quickly and slipped into the banquette beside her. She pressed into him, revealing the satiny minimalism of her dress. His woes became distant.

"You are liking?" She raised an eyebrow.

"I can resist everything except temptation," he grinned.

"Ah, so it's Monsieur Wilde tonight." Marie signalled the waiter and whispered in his ear. She was applying a lip massage to Uncle's lolling dome when the server returned with a bottle of absinthe and two tall glasses with spoons containing sugar cubes. Marie waved him away and seductively poured ice water over the sugar, watching intently as their drinks slowly turned a milky green colour.

As they clinked glasses, a stout, overdressed troubadour with coke bottle glasses approached their table carrying a guitar and launched into a foggy version of "La Mer." Marie's head bobbed in time, and a befuddled Uncle sipped his cloudy cocktail. The singer concluded his performance with a low bow and a smile revealing dodgy dental work as Marie handed him a bill.

Oysters on the half shell, followed by little goat cheese pastry items and something flaming led to more absinthe, chocolate, and eventually, Marie feeding Uncle figs with his eyes closed.

"I have something for you," he slurred, heavy-lidded, grinning stupidly.

"Ah, but first, *moi*." Marie signalled to the waiter, who arrived with a long florist's box. Uncle fingered the ring container in his pocket as the waiter laid the box on the table with a thunk after clearing the dinner debris. Marie, seemingly unaffected by the evening's consumption, opened the gift like a quiz show presenter, revealing a crowd of long-stemmed roses. Uncle cradled her buttocks and smiled thickly.

"You must look inside," she said, lifting his hand from the banquette to the bouquet. A puzzled Uncle felt something cold and hard beneath the flowers and parted them to reveal a semi-automatic rifle, gleaming in the greenery. He pulled his hand away as if a thorn had punctured it.

"A Mas 49-56, *mon amour*. It usually comes with a bayonet and a grenade launcher, but ... the French are so thoughtful, *non*?" Uncle felt his stomach rising inside him and the room pulling him into its spin. He rose on wobbly legs and excused himself. Lying on the floor of the washroom cubicle, blotting his face with a fistful of damp paper towel, he tried to regulate his breathing and rehearse a hasty departure line.

Minutes later, Uncle grabbed the sides of parked cars for support as he wove through the lot towards Roscoe's limo. From his vantage point in the back seat of the darkened car, he watched Marie's Citroën peel out of the lot onto La Grange. He handed his credit card to Roscoe and gestured in the general direction of Les Deux. While waiting, Uncle downed a couple of Evians and a handful of Advil and flicked on the TV. He dimly noticed the tribute concert video of "My Next Life" as Roscoe slipped into the front seat. A slow smile of sweet relief crossed Uncle's face as he watched the familiar images on the small screen; he felt that clamp of tension release a degree or two. Noting Uncle's expression in the mirror, the driver discreetly lowered the window a couple of inches, assuming a major digestive impasse had been resolved.

Fifty-One

Uncle woke in the fetal position, head on the prayer pillow on the floor of his office as the first rays of light found their way between the slats of the blinds. With a remarkable feeling of lucid calm, he studied the patterns on the kilim covering his office floor, thinking that, by all rights, he should be in a serious abyss of romantic and business desperation. He'd spent the late hours of last night on the phone with some techno wonks he knew in Moscow. The image of Roc on the screen from the tribute concert easily transformed into the notion of a 3D version onstage, and as his contacts overseas assured him, a brilliant and groundbreaking concert could be staged within weeks. He joined the early morning joggers on his way to Starbucks in Westwood and marvelled at the clarity the Santa Ana winds afforded the neighbourhood, making a mental note to check out the new Magritte exhibit at the Armand Hammer museum.

Back at the office, he greeted Candy with a Tazo chai tea and a warm smile. His day wasn't ruined when he took the first call from Justin Savage. "I've got what I think is one of my most brilliant notions ever, but before getting to that, I need to discuss moving up the box set release. I know Blade will be resistant, just because, but we'll figure something out; he still lusts after that Korean caviar that no one can get, doesn't he? Listen, I control forty-seven copyrights on that box, and a firm street date of a few weeks from now will bring a worthy advance, especially if it's coupled with ... the Roc Molotov comeback concert."

Uncle turned down the volume on his headset and let Justin spin, enjoying the moment. A cursory explanation of his idea had Savage salivating to multiplatform visions of simultaneous satellite and internet concert events. Justin rang off after requesting one Cocktails song to open.

Candy came in with tracking info from NY and other news. "Okay, so CMT is all set for the 'Alabama Welcomes Delray Home' special. They've got a tractor parade with you-know-which hambone up front, a wave machine in Bear Creek Lake, and a riverboat that brings homeboy to the stage on the beach. The promoter is somewhat curious as to why Delray needs an aromatherapy room backstage, with, as he put it, 'a few of them little Buddha dudes.'" Uncle nodded distractedly without looking up from some stage sketches on his computer.

Candy paused until he returned her gaze. "And Cover Girl is interested in using Marie as their 'it' girl for the new Mademoiselle Allure line."

"Great," he replied evenly, surprising himself at how he had effectively relegated Marie to client status. "Have them send over a proposal and tell them we're definitely interested."

"Okay," said Candy. "Do you want me to take a message from Julie? She's on two."

"No, I'll grab it," said Uncle casually as he watched Candy take her sweet time gathering her tracking reports and leaving his office. "Hey, Jools."

"Hey, handsome, how's tricks?"

Uncle felt a small stirring but pushed through it. "All's well. How'd the Miramax audition go?"

"The usual. They went with the blonde," Julie said resignedly. "Hey, is everything okay with you and Marie? She wonders if something went wrong last night."

"Everything's cool," Uncle replied, "except she gave me a gun ... now, I know squat about weaponry. I mean, I had a brief samurai phase, but the sword collection was purely decorative. A little weird, no?"

"Yeah. I thought you were getting an invisibility cloak. I'll tell her it's all good. She and I are going to Kate Mantilini later. Maybe we'll see you."

Uncle realized that his only distracted thought concerned Julie's choice of wardrobe for the Veronica Lodge biopic audition. This was good. Progress. He didn't return Marie's call.

After a brief stop at a spyware shop, he arrived at Eddie's for the meeting. A makeshift boardroom table had been set up in the studio. Emma was hunched over a laptop with Stick leaning over her shoulder. Roc and Bobbie were sharing a chair and holding hands. Only Eddie greeted Uncle beyond a nod or a "hey," and he was shown a chair with a ragged corduroy pillow alone on the other side of the table.

"Okay, I've been ruminating on this comeback concert idea, and I think I've found a way to make it work without landing any of us in jail." Uncle shot Roc an ironic look. "I found a company in Moscow called Hololeg who've been developing software for a decade or so that couples animated graphic displays with real time musical performance." Correctly reading the wave of skepticism making its way around the table, he held up his hands in the all-too-familiar prayer pose. "Stay with me, good people. The deal is basically this. They store pre-recorded video clips and play back from QuickTime files. They did a major virtual opera performance with the Moscow Symphony featuring some wacked-out Brazilian diva who's afraid to fly. It was so huge, they wanted to do more, but she refused, so they animated her, and now she can do her whole show, including relating to the audience. The mixer can trigger responses from the board using an LPC program."

Emma spoke first. "What's that?"

Uncle was ready. "Linear Predictive Coding. Check it out." He handed her a disc, and she slipped into her laptop. The screen revealed a symphony orchestra performing Shostakovich's *Lady Macbeth*. Moments later a garishly dressed singer appeared out of thin air and began her aria. The group in the room watched in amazement as she reached a musical climax, seeming to respond to the fervour of the crowd with wild arm motions and bows, until she disappeared as quickly as she had appeared on stage minutes earlier.

"Very entertaining, Karl," Emma said coolly, "but we had something a little more flesh and blood in mind."

"No go," said Uncle. "The legal implications of a born-again Roc Molotov I am not prepared to live with." In the silence that followed, he continued. "The band can rehearse with tracks and a stage plot that allows for Roc's image to be projected. Roc can shoot his performance right here on blue screen. His reactions to the crowd can be triggered from the drums."

"You think Danny can handle this, Uncle?" Eddie asked.

"If I can talk him out of retirement," Uncle replied wearily.

Emma was on the verge of shutting Uncle's idea down when Roc spoke quietly. "Rich can do it. I'll rehearse him here, and he can help me with the set list."

Stick lit up. "Cool! I'll start learning the tunes tonight."

"And he'll look great in the Ringo wig," Roc added with a smile.

Everyone except Emma laughed, easing the tension. Uncle took what seemed like his first breath in a while. "I was thinking of The El Ray Theater. They can handle the gear side of this, the lighting's great, and the room is the perfect size for the projection tech."

Stick and Roc began consulting on the show sequence, and Bobbie seemed to be consoling Emma, whose doubts were written all over her face.

"I'm sure you guys have got lots to talk about. Hey, Ed, have you got something cold and wet?" Uncle had his arm over Eddie's shoulder.

"Sure, let's see what's on tap." Eddie headed for the studio door with Uncle close behind.

Fifty-Two

"Are you sure you want to go through with this, honey?" Bobbie put her hand on Roc's shoulder as he leaned into the mirror, squinting as he carefully applied black eyeliner. A bottle of Midnight Velvet sat on the washstand.

"Uh-huh."

"It's just that I feel Emma and I persuaded you."

"You did." Roc grinned at her in the mirror. "But I need to do this. You two conspirators just realized it before I did. We can't live in a little room above a recording studio in Toluca Lake, ordering in Thai food forever." Roc put down the eyeliner and turned to Bobbie. She fought back a grin at his one naked eye and one blackened. "What? Oh, right." Roc grimaced at his reflection. "I know I look ridiculous. But this will be the last time I do this. I'm saying a real goodbye to that part of my life. Listen, Bobbie, you … you, Emma, and Stick brought me back to life these last couple of weeks. I might as well have been dead. Sure, I was writing music again, but I realized that I didn't give a shit if anyone ever heard it."

Bobbie held out a blush brush, and Roc recoiled. "Sorry, baby, you look a mite pale is all."

"That's my look. Every day is Hallowe'en. Am I scaring you?"

"Not unless you start borrowing my mascara without asking." Bobbie kissed him on his neck, careful not to smudge Roc's handiwork. "I love you."

He paused and softened. "I love you too. Bobbie, I'm going to do this show, say goodbye to the boys … on stage, playing our hearts out like we used to, and I'm going to totally enjoy giving Uncle the surprise of his life."

"Hey, Rocco," Eddie called up the stairs, "can I come up?"

"Sure," said Roc. "I've got to review the plan. I've got early onset stage fright."

"He always says that," Eddie smiled as he entered, "and then does a killer show. So, Molo, my man, the 'Tails are rockin'. They know the set cold, just as you sequenced it, and they've been rehearsing with the hologram all week." He shuffled his papers until he found the stage plot and showed it to Roc. "They love the new tunes, especially 'Here But I'm Gone.' So, virtual Roc will do the opening three numbers. It's amazing; he can adapt to tempo changes or even a wrong key, God forbid. Stick triggers the Molo holo, as we've been calling it."

Roc closed his eyes and shook his head, smiling. "Eddie, where would be without you?"

"Focus, focus, old buddy. During the pyro at the start of 'Swan Dive,' Stick will kill the hologram, and you take his place." He gestured at a spot on the stage diagram. "If you land off-axis, just look down and follow the luminous tape. In the light it might be a little hard to find your mark. But hey, you've done this before, right?"

"Right now, I'm not certain," Roc replied, turning serious. "And what happens when people notice?"

"Honestly," said Eddie, arching his brows, "I'm not sure they will; that's the brilliance of this thing. I mean, yeah, the evil genius could probably tell, but you know him. After the opening minute or so, he'll be schmoozing, checking gate receipts, doing mental cup size estimates ... sorry." Eddie looked sheepishly at Bobbie. "The boys will notice right away, unless they're as brain dead as Danny slash Moonshadow or whatever he's called now. But that should be fun. The audience has bought into the whole virtual performance idea, and they won't suspect until your big leap of faith, right, Rocco?" Eddie grinned conspiratorially.

Roc nodded intently. "Yeah, I *am* a little nervous about that, the more I think about it. It's not going to be like the usual mosh pit scene where they're expecting a flying body from the stage."

Eddie put his arm on Roc's shoulder. "Hey, compared to your Malibu theatrics, this'll be child's play, no?"

"Don't remind me."

Uncle sat very still at his desk, headset on, nodding thoughtfully and examining the dust patterns the sunlight made as it streamed through his office window. From talk of details of the show onwards, he had paid very close attention to Roc and Eddie's conversation. He switched off the studio surveillance audio and hit talkback. "Candy, get me Rodney at KROQ."

"Uncle, are you still not taking calls? Since we announced this show this morning, my life has been threatened a half dozen times thanks to your no comps policy. Listen, baby, I'm bringing in your messages, and you deal with it, okay?"

Uncle laughed at Candy's exasperation as she burst in with a neat but towering stack of messages. The top one was from Marie, and he decided to ignore the little heart that Candy had drawn over the "I" in Marie. "I've had it with Weasel Boy Savage. He's gone from whining to screaming to threatening and back to begging again. What do you want me to tell him?"

"Usual El Rey treatment. VIP lounge for the label and reserved seats in the balcony. Absolutely no backstage, okay?" Uncle threw Candy a serious look.

"Fine," she replied patronizingly, "but what about your little hood ornament?" Uncle was too amused to register the vanishing of all pretense of respect from his long-time employee. "She claims that the last time she was at the El Rey, the security took her to a special room and frisked her for about fifteen minutes." Uncle held his hands up in defeat as Candy continued. "Or at least until she stopped giggling."

"Okay, okay, but she's the only backstage, and I'll take her pass. Now will you get me Rodney ... please?"

Candy dropped the message stack on the desk with a thump and strutted back to her desk.

"Hey, Rodney, dude." Uncle perched on his prayer pillow, headset on, sipping an iced cappuccino. "Yeah, it's going to be cooler than cool." He listened then replied in his most honeyed tones, "I can't tell you much, but the technology's been around for awhile. Listen, Rodney, I need a favour. A special announcement today at three o'clock today. A KROQ exclusive.

"I've got a very cool idea for the first five hundred fans coming to the show. Remember the 'Roc-a-like' contest on the 'Reflectors' release? Right. Yeah, the nun in the wig still makes me laugh. Check this out."

Fifty-Three

Uncle had agreed readily to Roc's demand that he be able to witness the show from backstage with Bobbie, in return for the understanding that they wouldn't arrive until after it began. For Uncle's plan to work, it was essential that they not see the crowd, so he rented a stretch with windows tinted hearse-black. This suited the singer perfectly, and he sank deep into the leather seat in hooded sweatshirt and shades, looking like a nervous Eminem. Eddie, a bit stressed at having to play confidante to both sides, waved them agitatedly toward the emergency exit in the alley behind the El Rey Theater, where he looped backstage laminates over their heads. Hood up, Roc clutched Bobbie's arm like a child as they slipped into the building.

Once inside, the familiarity of it all hit him: the shadowy backstage area, techs smoking, huddled over their personal pieces of gear, and the muffled thump of Stick's bass drum driving the band through the opening song. Weirdest of all, though, was the wave of approval from the crowd to the climax of the song. Roc stopped, transfixed by the sound of his own voice. Eddie caught his expression and mouthed the words "Good singer." Maglite in hand, he guided the couple through a gauntlet of dangling ropes, equipment cases, and coiled cables. They were ignored by various crew members, focused on the activity on stage.

The final ringing chord of "Cold Spark" was greeted by thunderous applause, and Bobbie squeezed Roc's arm excitedly. Eddie's stage whisper drew the three heads together. "Okay, Rocco, up this ladder about twenty feet and then hard left on the catwalk. Hold the railing till you get to the crow's nest at the end. I had the spotlight hauled out during sound check. The water bottle is yours." He turned to Bobbie. "You're coming with me, right, Bobbie?"

"I'll stay with Roc if he needs me. Is there room up there? What do you think, baby?"

"It's all right, I'm cool." Roc shook his head and pushed back his hood. "Go with Ed. At least one of us should see the show." She fussed with his hair as he smiled nervously then hugged her quickly.

"I'll hold the beam on your way up." Eddie pointed the flashlight at the bottom rung. The sound of Stick counting in the next song and the ringing guitar at the start almost drowned out his next words. "Then you're on your own, okay? Remember, 'Swan Dive' is song number four, and the flash pots at the end of the intro is your signal to drop down, all right?"

Roc nodded and scrambled wordlessly up the metal ladder as Bobbie watched nervously until Eddie flicked off the beam once he was out of sight. Eddie leaned into Bobbie's ear to cut through the music. "Okay, let's go; Emma's got seats for us in the balcony."

Bobbie hung onto his arm as they wound through the backstage area. "What about Uncle? Won't he wonder why I'm with you all?" She glanced through the curtains as they passed the glowing monitor board sidestage, stopping to take in Stick's intense concentration as the band pounded through 'Flare-Up,' one of the earliest hits.

"Don't worry about the swami. He'll be prowling, schmoozing, and on Marie patrol big time. Let's go." They both stopped cold when they spotted the projected Roc throwing his hair back wildly and seeming to share the microphone with Frankie on the chorus. Bobbie instantly understood why the audience was responding so feverishly to this transparent fantasy. It was mesmerizing, and she was completely thrilled by the sight of a three-dimensional projection of the man she had been sleeping with last night. She caught Eddie's expression of wonderment before he looked away and led her through a fire door into a hallway past merchandise and concession stands to a stairway leading to the balcony.

A young fan, dressed to resemble early period Roc, burst through the doors from the theatre into the hall and rushed to a nearby restroom as the roar from within crested briefly. Bobbie started and whispered to Eddie, "Hell's bells, did you get a load of that?"

Eddie nodded. "Dedicated. Obsessed. Their fans have always been full-on."

"My lord. What are they gonna do when the real Roc shows up?"

"C'mon, Bobbie," Eddie indicated a door straight ahead, "we'll find out soon enough. 'Swan Dive' is after the next song."

They found their seats just as the crowd rose as one to cheer the end of the song. Emma hugged Bobbie tightly, but whatever they said was drowned out by the crowd, stomping and whistling as the holographic Roc acknowledged the response, stalking the front of the stage and coming within inches of touching the hands of the fans pressed in front. Bobbie found herself completely swept up in the moment, transfixed by the illusion, as she and Emma stood clapping along rhythmically to the intro to "Sky Train."

Bobbie watched the holographic Roc, confident and commanding, one moment with his hair hanging over the neck of his virtual guitar, and the next racing to the mic just in time for the opening line of the song. Uncle was, as Eddie predicted, too distracted to appreciate the technological marvel unfolding on stage. He scanned the crowd, a stomping, fist-pumping army on the floor, looking for Marie. Wearing an uncharacteristically demure, billowing black dress, she'd arrived late and had melted into the throng as soon as Uncle had spotted her. Their late afternoon boozy *tête a tête* had whetted Uncle's appetite for aftershow activity, and Marie had seemed so dazzled as he told her more than he intended about the evening ahead. Refusing to go with him to the gig was just another of Marie's endless coquettish whims.

Uncle hastily checked the gate receipts and made sure the merch tables were well stocked. The big mover turned out to be a special one-off t-shirt done especially for the night. It featured a ghostly Roc bathed in a single bright white spotlight, the band in silhouette behind him, guitars fanned out like wings from his narrow frame. Highest quality collectible cheese, he figured. His only regret was the reduced mark-up necessitated by having the t-shirts made in the U.S. on short notice.

Through it all, he shot glances at the stage, not knowing when Roc was going to pull his surprise switch. He figured it would be for the encore, when he'd have maximum time to get to the stage. Tempted as he was, the manager stayed in the front of the house, avoiding the backstage and any possibility of causing wrinkles in Roc's scheme. A pang of nostalgia hit him as he watched the boys, as of old, cavorting on stage; he was reminded yet again of the timeless vitality of so many of the songs. "Sky Train" had peaked during the Japan/Philippines tour, when Danny had been hospitalized from drinking a gallon of hundred-year-old sake. The ex-emperor's granddaughter had been most hospitable. He smiled, recalling a night that turned into three days. Waking up with a samurai sword on the pillow beside him had been a bit weird, to be sure, but he realized they'd never see times like those again.

As he passed the soundboard, he wondered how Eddie, at the heart of the deception, would kill the hologram. At first, the realization of which way his old friend and engineer's divided loyalties had fallen had been stinging, but Uncle was used to the stab-or-be-stabbed nature of the business, and eventually it had simply hardened his resolve as to how this would turn out. He regretted denying camera access now, thinking it might be amusing to revisit this evening at a later date.

From his perch high above the stage, Roc peered down through the rigging to accustom himself to the distance. He'd practised his grip on the cable in the studio, but it was far from the reality just ahead. He'd only get one crack at this and hoped it wouldn't be to the sound of breaking bones. He almost felt nostalgic for his parachute as a wave of nausea rolled through his body. He leaned back, quickly righting himself, and realized that the queasiness probably had more to do with fear of people's reaction to his unexplained re-appearance than the gymnastic routine coming up. In the days leading up to this night, Roc had rolled over all concern for credibility once he'd realized that he had to be alive if he was going to have a life.

Marie, tucked behind a pillar in the rear of the theatre, followed Uncle's gleaming head around the room. She muttered another "*merde*" to herself as she adjusted herself awkwardly inside her billowy outfit, wondering how long the show would go on. Uncle had said the encore would be the likely moment, and it seemed a long way off, given how dragged-out these American rock shows were. Serge Gainsbourg and Jane Birkin would have been in the dressing room sipping Pol Roger and planning their evening in Montparnasse by now.

Fifty-Four

Riding the crest of the El Rey crowd's euphoria, The Cocktails reclaimed the power of their old music. Being onstage with the Molo Holo seemed not to diminish the intensity of the show at all, and whether the boys embraced their dance with technology or just forgot about it and played their instruments and sang their parts, no one could tell.

With one eye on the video screen in the VIP lounge, Uncle tried to extricate himself from an intense rant by his Strange Savage partner. In the balcony, Bobbie and Emma clutched arms, nervously looking down at the stage, knowing what was next.

While the applause for "Sky Train" was at its peak, Frankie stomped on his effects pedal, and the opening glissandos for "Swan Dive" rose in waves as intense shades of aquamarine and turquoise washed over the stage.

From his crow's nest above the rigging, Roc squinted down through the rolling fog obscuring the stage and the musicians. Working on his breath, he waited for Stick to count in the song, not realizing that the young drummer was on his hands and knees, crawling back to his kit after cutting the power for the holographic Roc. Knowing that his vocal cue was moments away, he decided to make his move. He grabbed the rope, yelled a fear-rejecting

"Haaaa" into the din and swung out above the rising cloud. As he lowered himself toward the invisible stage below, he heard the click of the drummer's sticks and on the downbeat was blasted by twin exploding flash pots and blinding white lights, accompanied by an avalanche of dry ice that enveloped the band and provided cover for his descent.

Clutching the rope with eyes squeezed shut, Roc endured a subsonic moan from Barry's bass that sent him reeling backwards as he touched down. As the lights shifted dramatically to a throbbing dawn amber, he could make out shapes on stage and spotted his acoustic guitar right where it should have been. Grabbing his instrument, he strode to centre stage and looked into the spotlights over the crowd, roaring and fist pumping. As the band hit the pause that led into verse one of "Swan Dive," Roc leaned into the microphone. "Thanks. It's good to be back."

The crowd shouted back in response, and Roc felt the blood rush through his body. He glanced to his right to see Barry stunned as the usual one-bar pause became two, three, then four bars. Behind his cymbals, obscured in fog, Stick grinned and held the time as the moment expanded. First Barry, then Frankie came to centre stage with awe-struck expressions before putting their arms over the now-real Roc's shoulders. Roc swung his guitar around and hit the opening chord.

> "Standing at the edge I leaned into the sky
> Held on to the air and closed my eyes ..."

At this point, Frankie and Barry raced back to their places, and the groove crashed in on cue with a rolling cymbal swell. The years offstage melted away as Roc dug into the song. He felt like he was looking down on the experience, a common theme in recent months, and maybe it was that sense of a cool remove that provided the clarity of the moment. During the solo, he walked upstage to Stick and mouthed something the drummer understood. Returning to centre stage, Roc took the final chorus up a notch in intensity.

> "This is my swan dive into you
> And freefall is all I can do."

Pulling the guitar off and holding it above his head, Roc leaned back on the waves of sound rolling off the stage. He handed the guitar to a surprised security kid down in front before singing the last line of the song.

> "This is my swan dive,"

Then added,

> "This is my swan song …"

Roc spread his arms and, silhouetted by another round of bright white flash pots going off, held the moment for that one breath, knowing he wanted to keep it with him forever. As Stick sent a tide of cymbal crashes surging over the crowd, Uncle realized that something unexpected was happening. He raced from the VIP section and spotted Eddie pushing through the tightening throng in an effort to reach the soundboard. Uncle trained his eyes on the stage and his old friend who seemed suspended above the roiling crowd.

Angling her body toward a pillar in the darkest part of the El Rey, Marie unbuttoned her dress, an act that would not normally go unnoticed, and pulled out the Mas 49-56 semi-automatic. Nonchalantly, she slid the telescopic sight into place and snapped the rifle to her shoulder like a veteran of the Algerian campaigns. Squinting and holding her breath, she focused calmly and squeezed the trigger as a raucous and rotund fan crashed into her from behind, sending the contents of a large plastic cup of Miller Genuine Draft airborne and Marie to the floor. The shot shattered the giant chandelier closest to the stage, and baubles rained down on the crowd. Roc dove, spread-eagled, too far into his motion to stop at the sound of the gunshot.

In the moments that preceded full chaos, the oblivious fan looked sadly at his empty cup then at a sprawled Marie. Sputtering an apology and reaching out to help her up, he noticed first the camouflage bra then the semi-automatic on the floor.

"Hey," he shouted, grinning stupidly, "it's Ooo lala!"

Eddie arrived at the soundboard just as the chandelier exploded, and he lunged for the mesmerized lighting director. He shouted in the man's ear, and in seconds the house lights were on. The doors to the club were flung open, and the crowd stampeded for the street. Bobbie looked down from the balcony on the melee in panic, hoping to spot Roc. As the lights came on, she witnessed a bewildering and frightening sight. Mixed into the crowd, she saw hundreds of Roc Molotov KROQ contest look-alikes swarming the exits and running into the night. Roc could have been any one of them.

Fifty-Five

Two Years Later

Roc's stomach landed hard a few minutes after the chopper that brought him from Monterey to Lompoc did, and it started acting up again as the taxi approached the prison entrance. He reread the visitor regulations:

Persons who are provocatively dressed may be denied the privilege of visiting.

Okay on that front.

Appropriate embracing, kissing, and handshaking by immediate family members within the bounds of good taste at the beginning and termination of visiting period only.

No problem with that one.

One handkerchief, a wedding band (no stones), eyeglasses. Clear plastic change purse or Ziploc bag.

Check.

A comb.

Not likely. At the entrance, he checked his refection in the no-doubt bulletproof glass and thought of how changed he would appear. His close-cropped greying hair and white-flecked beard effectively concealed the once-familiar face, but he wondered how it would look to someone who knew him well. Roc involuntarily clenched his jaw, and his body tightened into a knot going through the security procedures. He looked at the ultraviolet stamp on his hand as he was being escorted to the visiting area and realized that he had no idea what he was going to say to Karl Breit, California prisoner # 34721.

He found Uncle perched in the lotus position, apparently permitted, on a picnic bench under a eucalyptus tree in what seemed to Roc a surprisingly open, relaxed visitor area. Families gathered, laughter was heard, and the guards projected a relaxed scrutiny as Uncle spotted Roc and waved him over.

"Hey."

"Hey yourself. Thanks for coming." Before Roc could reply, Uncle gestured toward the far wall. "If you want a drink, you'll have to use the vending machines. Have you got change?" He got up to greet his friend. "How are you?"

Roc hesitated, not knowing if a handshake was allowed. "I'm fine. Good to see you. You look great."

"Thanks. You too. I dig the grey. Yeah, confinement suits me, I guess."

Roc nodded at the attempt at humour. "Looks like. Listen, I feel bad for not coming sooner, Uncle. I followed your legal woes in the *L.A. Times*. The days just seem to run together, you know...."

"No problem, man, I know what you mean," a serene Uncle smiled without irony. "Hey, I know congrats are in order, my brother, got a picture?"

"Of course," It was Roc's turn to grin. He reached into his Ziploc and pulled out his favourite shot of Bobbie and the baby.

Uncle nodded, smiling broadly. "Gorgeous." He paused and added, "Cute baby too. What's his name?"

Roc winced but ignored the Rodney Dangerfield moment. "Her name. Cassidy. We dress her in blue to confuse people." He marvelled at how nothing had changed except the location and the wardrobe.

"Did you see Danny's little guy?" Roc shook his head. "Oh yeah, I guess you wouldn't exactly be in touch. Looks like Junior Buddha in overalls."

"I'm happy for them. I'm not in touch with anyone, really, except Eddie; it's best that way."

Uncle shifted in his chair but maintained his guru posture, showing none of the old discomfort, Roc noticed.

"I've got a guy here who's a miracle worker." Uncle caught Roc's expression. "No, it's not like that; he's in for malpractice. Something about hypnosis and a Beverly Hills socialite who left his office thinking she was a flamingo, I don't know. Anyway, I've never felt better."

Roc wondered at Uncle's seemingly bottomless good cheer. "Frankie and Barry stepped in it, though." Uncle's voice took on a conspiratorial tone. "They were playing that big Chinese festival, Wallapalooza, back in March." He paused and cleared his throat. "Did you know I'm still managing them? Yeah, Candy's holding things down at the office until I get back. We've got a little hole-in-the-wall in Studio City, keeping costs down, you know. Anyway, The Cocktails thing ... so they're playing this historic festival, and bottom-line — great wall, shitty acoustics. The boys couldn't hear a thing, so they just kept turning up to ear-bleeding levels and thought that the crowd screaming in pain was just getting into it. You can imagine — power got cut, they got yanked, interrogated by the Chinese police, charged with 'inharmonious social activity,' and sent home, coach."

Trying to look sympathetic, Roc couldn't contain his smile as Uncle just kept rolling. "Hey, do you remember that little prick Chad Sparx from MTV?" He read Roc's face. "Yes, I guess you would. Well. He came to my office the day after the concert when all hell was breaking loose and ambushes me with his cameraman, accusing me of plotting to murder you in his stoner Geraldo style.

I wanted to tell him the truth, but in those days I'm not sure I knew how to. He had the registration from Marie's gun in my name, it was crazy." It was like Uncle was clearing the cobwebs from his memory. "I guess you haven't heard about Marie." Roc listened for a wistful note but couldn't find one. "No, why would you? Well, after the El Rey fiasco, for which I am eternally sorry for so many reasons, she and my old BFF Justin bolted for his old man's island, Bonaire, or some place that sounds like a vintage Chevrolet. I did help Sparx get Justin's label gig — that seemed to cool his tabloid ardour — who knew there was a wannabe corporate lackey under that tie-dyed t-shirt?"

Roc thought back to the El Rey show for the first time in a while, with the old mix of nostalgia and horror. The memory of finding himself on Wilshire Boulevard in a crowd of look-alikes was beyond disorienting. The fact that Eddie, along with Bobbie, was able to find him and take him back to the studio was a miracle. The depth of Uncle's deception in preventing Roc's comeback had been shocking at the time, but like everything else about the man, it could be explained, if not forgiven. Taking in Uncle's surroundings today, Roc knew he had let it all go; he'd had to in order to make this trip.

"So no surprise, following an attack of domestic boredom, Marie heads for Mustique, where her papa was shooting a Ski-Doo commercial, I think it was." Uncle sounded like he'd been saving up these stories for this particular audience. "Of course, he's delighted to see his little praline, and at a party that night he introduced her to Robbie Williams. Later on, they're snogging on the beach, Robbie and Marie that is, and she cold-cocks a local paparazzo, which lands them all in jail. Next day, they wrote a song about the whole thing, cut it at Robbie's villa, and now EMI wants to restart her career, have her open for some French Spice Girls act. I know all this because she called me when she lost her luggage at De Gaulle like nothing had happened with us. It never ends, eh?"

Roc was feeling disoriented and grounded himself by looking around at the visitor scene, couples holding hands on tabletops, not-so-subtle security cameras everywhere, and a warm breeze blowing through the eucalyptus trees. Uncle seemed to be winding down, and a silence arrived at last. "Look, I'm sorry."

"No, no," Uncle cut him off, hand raised. "I mean, I'm sorry too. Let's just let all that stuff ride, okay?"

"I mean about you being here. I gotta say this. Emma would never have pursued the financial stuff to this point. She was protective of me and wanted everything on the up and up ... and I know Tabby wouldn't have wanted this either. I think once the lawyers started down that road ..."

Uncle held his hands out and tilted his head in the "everything is under control" gesture that Roc knew too well. "Roc. Roc. No. It was tax evasion in the end. Strange Savage stuff. Justin evaporated, and I had to go down, simple as that. Look, I'm out in forty-three days."

"Really? That's great."

"And ... I've found this incredible Goth country band in here. I'm trying to arrange for them to record in the piggery — there's a farm here, right — before they get out. It'll be a better story."

"Amazing." Roc smiled, relieved.

"Listen, I don't know what your plans are, but I'd always be there to help you take things to the next level. Could be better than the old days."

Roc took a deep breath and looked across at a burly guy reading to a toddler. He wanted to formulate a kind but firm reply to his old friend, but Uncle read the pause and jumped in. "Ah, hey, there's time for that. Listen, it's great to see you. What are you doing? Writing? Changing diapers full-time?"

Roc considered telling him about his new gig but thought better of it. "Oh yeah, lots of both. Gardening." He saw Uncle's eyes widen. "Really. Bobbie and I like to dig in the dirt together, and we're watching the migration of the monarchs these days. They love Big Sur."

Uncle sat and listened calmly. Roc wondered if he was thinking about his lack of freedom. "We go whale watching this time of year, and Bobbie's very involved in pelican rescue. Don't laugh, but there's a big bird-watching festival at Morro Bay. I think I got interested when *I* was incarcerated at Eddie's in Toluca Lake."

Normally, a call or some random business concern would have cut into this conversation long ago. He saw Uncle looking down, blinking, and didn't know what to say. He had nothing to offer — no future rendezvous, no professional plans, no caustic remarks about Uncle's love life.

"Sorry," Uncle barely whispered. "I'm happy for you. I'm out of here soon enough, and I've had time to consider a few things, values, priorities." He paused, and his tone brightened. "My buddy Delray's been here every week." Roc tried to conceal his distaste for the 'cowboy dude.' "I know what you think, but he's been working on himself big time; he's got a new band, the Divinos. Anyway, I'm sure you don't want to hear about this."

Uncle got up abruptly, looking at the clock on the opposite wall. "Got to get to my gig; I'm teaching phone hacking." He lowered his voice. "Very useful around here. We make these things called 'cheese boxes' for looping calls. Keeps me out of trouble."

Unthinkingly, Roc embraced Uncle, but no one seemed concerned. "Good luck, man. I'm sure Ed will keep us in touch."

Uncle just nodded and signalled to the guard that the visit was over.

Fifty-Six

Bobbie and Roc crossed the majestic Bixby Bridge in Big Sur, listening to the sound of the surf roaring off the rock face and back toward the ocean. Roc glanced at Bobbie and wondered if tonight would endanger their peaceful life in Northern California.

Bobbie looked back and read his anxiety. "Rich will have everything all set up for you, won't he?"

"Uh-huh." Roc looked back and forth from the ocean below to the road ahead.

"You want me to drive, baby? You're lookin' a bit skittish."

"I'm fine, and besides, there's nowhere to pull over."

"Okay. Well, I'm excited about tonight. 'Course, all I have to do is sit there and look appreciative, right?" Bobbie rubbed Roc's shoulder gently but got no reply. "You reckon Emma's all right with Cassidy? She won't get all wired up to that laptop of hers and forget to feed her now?"

"Oh, I think Cassidy will find a way of letting Emma know what she wants."

"I suppose, as long as she doesn't let the milk get all blinky. I know she loves her little sister, I just don't see much evidence of the maternal instinct, is all."

"Honey, she only held the baby upside down once. She was

nervous." Now Roc smiled at Bobbie and patted her hand.

"Emma, nervous? You shoulda heard her negotiating with that label guy for Rich's band. She's like fire and ice, that girl."

"That's different. Hey, what a glorious sunset. We've got to drive up this way this time of night more often."

Bobbie smiled. "Well, we will be all this week for sure."

"*If* I survive tonight. I am seriously doubting the wisdom of this. I feel like my daughter, the *older* one, is running my life."

Bobbie leaned over and kissed Roc on the cheek. "You'll be brilliant, sugar plum. I can't wait."

"Hmm."

"So, how was it seeing that jailbird friend of yours?" Bobbie hoped a change of topic would distract Roc from the challenge of the night ahead. "You haven't said word one about the old vulture."

Roc paused and reflected. "It was good, actually. Totally bizarre circumstances, of course. It was way more relaxed than you would imagine, but still terrifying if you allow yourself to think about not being able to leave."

Bobbie snorted. "Well, I for one am happier with him there. That old goat got his own sorry ass in a sling."

"Delicately put, my love." Roc smiled indulgently. "I know how you feel, honey. It is pretty grim, but Uncle seems to be handling it. He was full of business talk; he's actually managing The Cocktails, to the extent that they're manageable, from jail. I don't know how; I didn't ask." Bobbie listened quietly as Roc went on. "He told me a very funny story about them getting essentially deported from China for playing too loud." She was shaking her head, eyebrows arched. "Oh, and Danny and Gwen's little guy is doing fine."

"That's nice."

"He had a moment. I almost saw Uncle cry for the first time."

"Jalapeños in his lunch?"

"No, really. I don't know if he's changed or ever will, but I had to go see him. I can't undo the past, and with him and me, there's a lot of it."

"I know," said Bobbie indulgently. "Did you tell him about your gig?"

"Almost, but no. Okay, here's our exit."

Bobbie pulled out the directions. "Right on Munras, right at Alvarado, just past Mucky Duck and Goomba's. And you make fun of the Piggly Wiggly."

"There it is. I'll pull in back." Roc let out a big breath.

"JJ's in Monterey," Bobbie read, sounding impressed. "It's cute, honey, looks like a little pueblo. Reminds me of Tia's Ice House in Farcry."

Eddie was having a smoke outside the back door and warmly welcomed them. "Hey, you two. Rich is inside. The system sounds great; he's got it totally tweaked." He put his arm on Roc's shoulder and grinned at Bobbie. "How do you feel, Rocco?"

Bobbie answered for him. "He's a little antsy is all, Ed, but I've heard him practising from the garden for weeks, and he's going to be great, aren't you sweetie?"

Inside, Roc peeked through the curtains as Eddie escorted Bobbie to a table in the rear of an upscale southwestern restaurant with just over half the candlelit tables filled with thirty- and forty-something couples. Roc retreated to the tiny dressing room, packed with tablecloths and stacked chairs, where Stick was waiting. "Hey," said Roc as they executed the usual man-hug.

"You psyched?" Stick twirled his drumsticks. "This is Raoul."

"Raoul ... Sergei." Low-key greetings were exchanged. "Raoul's got his parts down cold. Says he grew up with The Cocktails stuff in Lyon. We should probably follow the set list at least for tonight, if that's cool."

"Sure," Roc replied as they heard Eddie's disc jockey routine over the p.a.

"Good evening, ladies and gentlemen and welcome to JJ's in Monterey. Hang on to your chairs, it'll be a rockin' affair as JJ's presents the world premiere of 'Sky Train,' all this week in their amazing tribute to Roc Molotov and the Cocktails."

As the band hit the stage and Stick counted in the opening to "Underwater Smile," the audience applauded warmly, and Bobbie smiled at the excited couple at the next table. She felt a shiver as Roc sang the opening lines of the song, and the woman next to her whispered to her date, "Doesn't look much like him, but he's sure got the voice down."

Acknowledgements

Thanks to Robin, the perfect party girl.

Stephen Stohn for friendship and wisdom.

The lads: Nelson Smith, Marc Jordan, and Jon Reid, for the nourishment.

Alannah Myles for singing my song.

"Uncle" Tim Tickner, pal extraordinaire.

Bruce Pirrie, the voice of unreason.

Lech Kowalski for the first look.

Allister Thompson, rock n' roll editor supreme.

The brilliant Dundurn team: Karen McMullin, Margaret Bryant, Caitlyn Stewart, Synora van Drine, Diane Young, Beth Bruder, and Jesse Hooper.

My family for being the net when I walk the wire.

And all my songwriting comrades.

MORE FICTION FROM DUNDURN

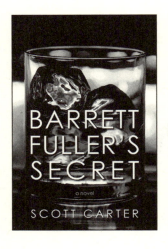

BARRETT FULLER'S SECRET
by Scott Carter
978-1459706934
$19.99

Barrett Fuller is a world-famous and very wealthy children's author who writes under a pseudonym because he's a self-absorbed womanizer and drug-user. His life changes when he receives an extortion letter, challenging him to live up to the morals he currently espouses in his books. He is presented with a series of tasks to complete or face having his identity revealed to the public, resulting in the ruin of his financial empire.

Richard Fuller, Barrett's nephew, has a secret too, and it's one no kid should bear. He knows why his father left the family and he's never told his mother.

When the extortionist challenges Barrett to spend time with his nephew, their respective secrets move towards a collision that will change their lives forever.

Visit us at
Dundurn.com | @dundurnpress
Facebook.com/dundurnpress | Pinterest.com/dundurnpress